A KILLING COAST

A KILLING COAST

A DI Horton Mystery

Pauline Rowson

This first world edition published 2012
in Great Britain and in the USA by
SEVERN HOUSE PUBLISHERS LTD of
9–15 High Street, Sutton, Surrey, England, SM1 1DF.

British Library Cataloguing in Publication Data

Rowson, Pauline.
  A killing coast. – (A Detective Inspector Horton mystery)
  1. Horton, Andy (Fictitious character) – Fiction.
  2. Police – England – Portsmouth – Fiction. 3. Detective
  and mystery stories.
  I. Title II. Series
  823.9'2-dc23

ISBN-13: 978-0-7278-8144-1 (cased)

All Severn House titles are printed on acid-free paper.

Severn House Publishers support The Forest Stewardship Council [FSC],
the leading international forest certification organisation. All our titles that
are printed on Greenpeace-approved FSC-certified paper carry the FSC logo.

MIX
Paper from
responsible sources
FSC
www.fsc.org FSC® C018575

Typeset by Palimpsest Book Production Ltd.,
Falkirk, Stirlingshire, Scotland.
Printed and bound in Great Britain by
MPG Books Ltd., Bodmin, Cornwall

For Linda Leader
For all the lovely walks and talks
and many more to come.

ACKNOWLEDGEMENTS

With grateful thanks to Ian Williams and his fascinating book *Diamond Coast: The Story of the Isle of Wight's Coast.*

ONE

Monday

'It's good of you to see me, sir, and so early.' Andy Horton followed the stooping silver-haired man through a small lobby into a bright and sunny lounge that overlooked the East Solent.

'Not at all, Inspector. And it's not early for me. Like many older people I don't sleep very well, and it makes a nice change to have company, whatever the hour. Oh, I know I've got all the company I need here,' Adrian Stanley tossed over his shoulder, as though reading Horton's mind. 'These retirement apartments are full of people like me, widowers, and widows, but sometimes it's nice to see a younger face. Coffee? Or would you prefer something stronger? You're off duty I take it,' he added, eyeing Horton's leather biker jacket. 'Not that that made much difference in my day. Policing was very different in the seventies and eighties before the politically correct brigade hijacked it.'

'Coffee, black, no sugar would be great,' Horton said smiling, thinking if Adrian Stanley drank alcohol at this time in the morning then he had a serious problem. There were no signs of the elderly man being an alcoholic though, quite the contrary; his lined face boasted a healthy complexion and his grey eyes were bright and keen for a man in his seventies. The small apartment smelt and looked clean.

Stanley stepped into the modern kitchen and flicked on the kettle. 'You can take your jacket off if you like. It is rather hot in here.'

'Thanks.' Horton eased off the Harley Davidson jacket taking a quick glance around the neat lounge with three easy armchairs, a coffee table in front of a fireplace, television, DVD, modern music system, and a range of family photographs on the mantelpiece of young children with their parents and grandfather. There were more of the same on a wall unit and here Horton saw a slender smiling woman beside Adrian Stanley in several photographs who, he assumed, was the late Mrs Stanley.

Horton draped his jacket over one of the two chairs beside a drop-leaf oak table noting the powerful binoculars on it, before turning towards the window. Stanley was correct; the room was hot despite the fact that the April sun had not yet gained full height or strength, but it was a bright morning and the apartment faced south. It was also on the top floor of the four storey modern building and the central heating was full on.

'You've certainly got a lovely view, sir,' Horton said gazing across the sparkling blue of the Solent at a handful of yachts heading into the harbour of Cowes on the Isle of Wight. He would like to have been out there himself, sailing his new yacht, *Mystery Lady*, but since buying it a fortnight ago he'd barely had the chance. And it was looking doubtful he'd get the opportunity to sail her this week. Not only was his stretched, under-resourced CID department experiencing a mini crime wave, but a new superyacht had moored up at Oyster Quays on Sunday, and that would act like a magnet to every toerag criminal for miles around. Horton had left a message for DC Walters to urgently check its security this morning. The last thing he needed was a high-profile robbery on his patch. He would have preferred to send Cantelli, but the sergeant would throw up the moment he got on the water and Horton didn't think the owner – a man called Russell Glenn, whom Horton had never heard of – would appreciate that on his nice shiny new yacht.

'It's one of the reasons I chose to live here,' Stanley called out from the kitchen, bringing Horton back to the matter in hand, which had nothing to do with his job. He was here on a personal matter, hence the early visit before officially being on duty. His heart beat a little faster at the thought that the former PC might have information that could help him trace his mother who had walked out of their council tower block one chilly November morning in 1978, consigning Horton to years of anguish and torment in a succession of children's homes. And on Friday morning he had an appointment with the social services department to view the case file that had been compiled on him while he'd been in care. He knew it would make grim reading and bring back painful memories, which was why he'd never requested access to it before. But events over recent months had forced him to confront the past, and now that he had embarked on this journey it appeared he was powerless to stop. His gut tightened at the thought that what he might eventually discover could be worse than he anticipated. But time to reflect on that later.

Stanley was saying, 'I told my son, Robin, that if I had to be cooped up in a flat then I wanted the illusion of space, which that view gives me. And there's always something to see.'

Hence the binoculars, thought Horton.

'You can look through them if you wish,' Stanley called out, again demonstrating that uncanny knack of reading Horton's mind. Horton wasn't sure he liked that but he guessed there were some things you never lost no matter how long out of the job.

He picked up the binoculars and quickly focused them in, surveying the Solent. It was, as usual, bustling with container ships, tankers, pleasure craft and fishing boats.

'With a view like this, sir, and your background on the force we could do with your help on Project Neptune,' Horton called over his shoulder.

'And what's that when it's at home? Diving for deep-sea treasure on sunken wrecks?'

'Not so dangerous and not so much fun,' Horton smiled. 'It's the brain child of our new Chief Constable, Paul Meredew. We've stepped up security because the American submarine, USS *Boise*, is due to visit Portsmouth in two months' time. We've been recruiting residents, fishermen, sailors and boat owners to report anything suspicious.' Horton zoomed in on a shapely dark-haired woman in her late twenties throwing a ball to a black mongrel dog on the beach below them, nice figure; the girl not the dog. She stopped to talk to a man in his forties carrying a dog lead.

'I read about that in the newspaper,' Stanley came up behind Horton.

Reluctantly Horton removed his gaze from the good-looking woman, who was ruffling the dog's fur in a way that made Horton very jealous of the mongrel, and swung the glasses on the man she'd been talking to who was now walking past someone launching a canoe from the public slipway. A jogger with his iPod plugged into his ears swerved around them. Finding nothing of interest in the parked cars on the promenade – two saloon cars and a muddy blue van – Horton lowered the binoculars on to the table and took the mug Stanley was holding out for him.

Stanley said, 'Nobody wants a repeat of what happened in Port Aden in 2000, and there's plenty of opportunity to launch an attack from a small vessel in the Solent or Portsmouth Harbour, similar to that attack on the USS *Cole*. It killed seventeen American sailors. Al-Qaeda, wasn't it?'

Horton nodded. 'Hence Project Neptune.' And Horton's boss, DCI Lorraine Bliss, had been appointed to lead the team overseeing it. It was Project Neptune that had rescued Horton from being shunted out of CID, as Bliss had threatened, and which had also reprieved DC Walters from being banished to the nether regions of the force. Bliss thought Walters idle and incompetent, and him a maverick cop because he didn't believe that you could solve cases by sitting behind a desk and shuffling endless bits of paper around as Bliss did. Thankfully, she had too much to occupy her time now to worry about breaking in a new detective inspector and detective constable. Working with top brass from the Ministry of Defence police, naval security, the Intelligence Directorate and private maritime intelligence company, Triton, Bliss saw Project Neptune as a step upwards and onwards. Horton sincerely hoped the latter would be sooner rather than later. She was also paranoid that something could go wrong, which meant a hundred missives a day cascading into his email, the latest of which was despatching him to the Isle of Wight on the police launch in about an hour's time to interview an elderly man who had reported seeing a mysterious light at sea. Normally Horton would have been delighted to be at sea but his desk was buckling under the weight of bureaucratic claptrap and unsolved crimes. Bliss was squawking for results and despite putting in extra unpaid overtime at the weekend he hadn't even made a small dent in it. Taking a trip to the Isle of Wight when a more junior officer on the Island could easily have dealt with it was time he could ill afford. But no doubt Bliss was making a point to those higher up. And time could be what he was wasting here, he thought, as Stanley gestured him into an easy chair in front of the modern electric fire.

'I'd be only too glad to help with Project Neptune,' Stanley said, settling himself opposite. 'It would give me a reason for peering through the binoculars without being accused of being a peeping Tom. The things people get up to you'd be surprised, or rather you would if you weren't a copper.' He put his coffee on a coaster strategically positioned on the table between them and eyed Horton curiously. 'But that's not why you're here. You said on the phone that you'd like to talk to me about a missing person case from 1978. You mean Jennifer Horton, don't you?'

Horton's heart jolted at the sound of his mother's name. He so seldom heard it spoken because only a handful of people knew about her and the fact she'd abandoned him when he was ten. Catherine, his estranged wife, was one, along with Sergeant Cantelli who was the closest friend he had in a lifetime spent shutting people out for fear of being hurt. Detective Superintendent Steve Uckfield, now head of the Major Crime Unit, and once a close friend was another. Their relationship had been tested over the last year when Uckfield had believed him capable of both rape and murder, the former of which had cost Horton his marriage despite him being exonerated and had wrecked his chances of raising his young daughter, Emma, who had now been banished to a boarding school by Catherine. Admittedly it was a good one and she'd wanted to go. He'd also agreed, but he couldn't help feeling anxious that she might be experiencing the same loneliness he had felt at his mother's desertion.

'You're the little boy she left behind,' Stanley said, his sharp grey eyes studying Horton carefully.

It hadn't been difficult for Stanley to put two and two together. Horton steeled himself. 'Do you remember the case, sir?' he asked evenly, pushing away the painful memories of his lonely and angry childhood, trying to sound as if he didn't care. He was also trying not to raise his hopes that Stanley might be able to tell him something that would help him discover what had happened to Jennifer. When Stanley remained silent, Horton prompted, 'You filed the missing person's report and spoke to Jennifer's neighbour, Mrs Cobden, at Jensen House. Jennifer was last seen leaving the flat at about one o'clock on the thirtieth of November 1978 wearing her best clothes and make-up, and was in good spirits. No one knows what happened to her next or where she was going, only that she didn't turn up for work that evening at the casino. I wondered if there was anything that stuck in your mind, anything different or unusual that might help me to trace her movements.'

Horton's mind flashed back. It hadn't been the first time he'd been left alone at night. Often he'd come home from school, open the letterbox and pull out a piece of string with the key attached on the end, get himself a drink from the fridge and a chunk of bread and jam, sit in front of the television and go to bed alone. But he'd always wake up to find his mother there. Except on the first of December she hadn't been. He felt the ache in the pit of his stomach as the memory haunted him.

'It was a long time ago,' Stanley said frowning.

But Horton wasn't going to accept that. 'Can you recall anything being mentioned about Jennifer's parents? Did anyone question them?' Horton knew the answer but he wanted to see just how much Stanley had forgotten.

'They were dead.'

Horton saw a slight narrowing of Stanley's eyes. The ex-copper knew Horton was testing him. Maybe Stanley could have gone higher in the ranks but perhaps, like Cantelli, he'd been happy to stay a sergeant. From what Horton had read about him, Stanley had also been brave and had earned himself the rare award of the Queen's Gallantry Medal in 1980 when he and another officer had gone in pursuit of armed robbers and had come under intense fire.

He said, 'Do you know how Jennifer's parents died and when?'

'No, but you can easily check that yourself, if you haven't already done so.'

Horton hadn't. He didn't have their death certificates but he could obtain copies. And he no longer had a copy of his mother's birth certificate, which, along with the only photograph he'd had of her, had gone up in flames when his previous yacht, *Nutmeg*, had been torched by a killer trying to scare him into dropping an investigation. It had only served to have the opposite effect. Since then he had run a check through the General Register Office but only for a record of Jennifer's death. He hadn't found it. That didn't mean that she wasn't dead though. Her body might never have been discovered; she might have died in another country. Equally she might have assumed another identity. Or her body could be lying in a mortuary somewhere unidentified, female unknown. If he allowed his DNA to be run through the database he'd have an answer to the last question but that would mean explaining why, and he wasn't prepared to do that, yet.

He said, 'Why weren't her friends questioned?'

'I spoke to the woman next door, and Jennifer's boss, George Warner. He owned a string of amusement arcades, nightclubs and the casino at Southsea where Jennifer worked. He said she was a bubbly, good-looking woman and had started working for him early in 1977.'

And that tied with what Horton already knew.

Stanley frowned in recollection of the case. 'There was another woman I seem to remember who said that Jennifer was seeing a man.'

'Irene Ebury. She's dead.' Horton had been called to an investigation in a nursing home in January and had discovered that Irene Ebury had been a resident there, and that her belongings had mysteriously gone missing. It had brought him into contact with Detective Chief Superintendent Sawyer, Head of the Intelligence Directorate, and the knowledge that Sawyer was interested in Jennifer's disappearance because he believed she could have been linked to a master criminal the Intelligence Directorate called Zeus. Was that the man Jennifer had run away with? Sawyer seemed to think so and he wanted to enlist Horton's help in finding him. But Horton had declined for fear of putting Emma's life in danger, though now that Emma was at Northover School Horton hoped she was safe from nutters and villains like this Zeus was reputed to be. By visiting Stanley, Horton knew he had publicly declared his interest in finding his mother and he wondered how long it would take for the lean, silver-haired chief superintendent to approach him. Not long was his guess.

He brought his mind back to George Warner and the casino where his mother had worked. The casino was now flats and George Warner and his empire long since gone. Trying to track down and speak to anyone who might have worked there and who would remember Jennifer, or know anything about this man she might have associated with, would take for ever and probably result in zilch. It was a dead end.

Stanley said, 'I'm sorry, Inspector, but there's not much I can tell you, and it's all on file. No one hinted at foul play.'

'Did you keep any of your notebooks where you might have jotted down something?'

'No.'

Horton wasn't sure if he believed him. It sounded like the truth and Stanley maintained eye contact, but then he had been a copper. 'What was the word on the street, the gossip about her and her disappearance? There must have been some.' Horton could hear the desperation in his voice and hated himself for it. When Stanley looked uncomfortable Horton wished he hadn't asked. He braced himself to hear what others had already told him over the years.

'There wasn't much. She probably got bored with being trapped inside a poky flat with a kid and wanted a good time, but that was only rumour.'

'What do *you* think happened to her?'

'It could have been true.'

Horton eyed the former policeman closely and saw only his concerned expression, and yet he felt there was something more. Perhaps Stanley was being economical with the truth to spare his feelings. Horton knew there had been two men in his mother's life in 1977 and that neither of them had been upstanding citizens, in fact, quite the opposite; villains to the core, and both were now dead. Jennifer's track record of choosing lovers wasn't exactly healthy, which made Horton consider briefly who his father was. But that was a road he certainly didn't want to travel down.

He said, 'Do you know what happened to her belongings?'

But Stanley shook his head.

'You went into the flat I take it?'

Horton thought Stanley looked uneasy. 'No. I spoke to the neighbour, to George Warner and a couple of his staff, and that was it.'

Horton wasn't convinced. Sensing this Stanley quickly added, 'I was a PC, told to talk to anyone who knew Jennifer Horton, and they were the only people I came up with. She didn't seem to have any friends outside work.'

There was something in Stanley's tone, in his manner and posture, that made Horton doubt this neatly wrapped excuse. He sensed there was more to it. Had Stanley or anyone really looked for Jennifer's friends? It seemed not to him. The more questions

Horton asked the more he seemed to generate and the fewer answers he got.

'Why weren't any fingerprints taken?' If they had been then they certainly weren't on the file.

Stanley shrugged. 'No idea. I'm sorry I can't be more helpful.'

Horton decided not to press him. For now. He rose and handed Stanley a business card. 'If you remember anything would you give me a call?'

Stanley took the card with a sense of relief, Horton thought. After a moment Stanley said, 'I hope you find out what happened to her.'

Part of Horton hoped so too, and another part of him hoped not, but he knew that not knowing would leave him with a permanent itch that would always need scratching.

He thanked Stanley and left with an uneasy feeling gnawing at him. As he negotiated the heavy morning traffic towards Gosport Marina he knew that Stanley had lied or rather he had held something back. Why? To spare his feelings? Possibly. But if so, what had Stanley uncovered about Jennifer's disappearance that was so awful he couldn't tell her son?

Horton shuddered. Perhaps he didn't want to know. But he was compelled to find out despite or perhaps because of it. Mentally he replayed the interview. Stanley had shown no curiosity about why and when Horton had become a police officer. He hadn't even been surprised. Why? The obvious answer was because he already knew, which meant either someone had told him, or Stanley had kept an eye on him over the years, and that seemed unlikely.

Secondly, Stanley hadn't asked him why he had chosen *now* to find his mother when he'd had years and the opportunity to do so before. Stanley hadn't so much as uttered the words, *I expected you sooner.* Either he was remarkably lacking in curiosity – which for an ex-copper was unusual – or he knew the reason why Horton was now raking up the past. Detective Chief Superintendent Sawyer must have interviewed Stanley and informed him that he might approach him. And perhaps Sawyer had left instructions with Stanley to say as little as possible and to contact him when Horton came calling. But why should he do that?

And another thing that bugged Horton, why wasn't Stanley curious about what he would do next in his search for Jennifer?

Stanley had simply said *I hope you find out what happened to her.* Did he not care or did he know that Horton would hit a brick wall? Or would someone keep Stanley informed? And there were only two people who could do that: Sawyer, or someone who knew the truth behind Jennifer's disappearance. Was that Zeus?

Horton felt a cold shiver prick his spine as he swung into Gosport Marina and made his way to the waiting police launch on the pontoon. The sight of the glistening superyacht across the narrow stretch of Portsmouth Harbour, moored up at Oyster Quays opposite, made him shelve his concerns about Stanley and Zeus and filled him with new worries. It was the size of a small cruise ship and would act like a ruddy great beacon for all the lowlife scum of Portsmouth, and those higher up the slime, including villains from London, who would take great pleasure stripping it of its spoils, and that was even without the added attraction of a high-profile VIP charity auction and reception being held on board on Friday night, before she sailed off to the Caribbean or wherever.

'It's a beauty,' Sergeant Dai Elkins said, following the direction of Horton's gaze.

'I prefer wind over motor,' Horton replied, discarding his leather jacket in favour of a sailing jacket and life vest.

'I wouldn't send it back if it was offered me.'

Horton let his gaze travel over the four-decked cruiser as PC Ripley throttled back the launch and eased it into the busy channel. The portholes on the lower deck were probably crew accommodation, while the first and second decks with the wide windows must be the living accommodation. There was a huge flybridge, a swimming platform at the aft of the first deck and a large RIB suspended on a davit from the rear. He hoped Russell Glenn had a good security system. DC Walters would report back on that, but Horton made a mental note to liaise with Inspector Warren, Head of Territorial Operations, to make sure that extra uniformed patrols were covering the boardwalk for the next five days, with additional officers on duty Friday evening for the reception. He could hear Inspector Warren's gripes: 'And just where the hell am I going to get them from?'

Horton phoned Cantelli.

'There's been another house burglary in the Drayton area,' Cantelli solemnly reported.

Horton cursed. That made four in the last week.

'They've all got the same MO: jewellery and cash taken, no mess, no fingerprints, no noise. Owners off the premises, back door panel neatly removed and matey climbing in by using it like a giant cat flap. Bliss is going ballistic. I don't think she appreciated it when I nicknamed him the cat burglar.'

'Bliss hasn't got a sense of humour,' Horton replied. But burglary was no joke.

'I'm reviewing all the case notes and checking criminal records to see if I can get a lead,' added Cantelli, 'but it looks as though this is a new one on the block.'

And something neither they nor the poor householders needed. Cantelli said that Walters had left for Russell Glenn's superyacht.

Horton rang off and as he did something in the marina caught his attention. 'Give me the glasses, Dai,' he commanded.

Elkins stretched them across and Horton quickly trained them on the marina.

'Something wrong?'

'Just thought I saw that blue van earlier this morning.' He'd seen *a* blue van outside Adrian Stanley's apartment block, but then there were thousands of blue vans in the country and hundreds in the area. He tried to read the registration number but couldn't. As the police launch headed further out into the harbour the van slipped out of his view. It couldn't have been the same van, or if it was then it was a coincidence. But Horton was suspicious of coincidences. *If* it was the same van, had it been following him? If so, why? Bloody Zeus was the answer. Shit, he was getting paranoid. Angrily he pushed all thoughts of Zeus, DCS Sawyer and Adrian Stanley aside. Enough of the past. He had a job to do and that was to interview an elderly man about seeing a mysterious light at sea, and the sooner he did it the sooner he could get back to some real work such as catching the scumbag criminal robbing houses on his patch in Portsmouth.

TWO

'On a good day, when the light is right, you can see France, Inspector,' Victor Hazleton declared, pointing at a telescope that Horton thought large enough to rival the one at Jodrell Bank. He wasn't surprised Hazleton had seen lights at sea; with that thing he could probably see the Eiffel Tower.

Horton eyed the dapperly dressed little man, with his blue and yellow spotted cravat, his beige cardigan over camel-coloured slacks and his walnut face and wiry grey hair, wondering if he was senile. Admittedly his view was coloured by what WPC Claire Skinner had told him and Sergeant Elkins in the patrol car on their way here after meeting them at the small harbour of Ventnor Haven. Apparently Hazleton had a reputation for seeing smugglers and illegal immigrants at every flicker of a sea light. Over the years he'd made a hobby out of reporting these to the local police who had long since learnt to ignore him, but this time, because of Project Neptune, Hazleton's report had landed on DCI Bliss's desk. Did she know about Hazleton's background? Surely the local police would have commented on it? But if she did know then why waste time and money by sending him here on a wild goose chase, thought Horton angrily. He calculated how quickly he could wrap this up and get back to CID.

'I said you can see France, but not with this,' Hazleton added, tapping the instrument he'd been peering through. 'Know anything about telescopes, Inspector?'

Horton silently groaned. Even if he had declared he was the world's greatest expert that wouldn't stop Hazleton from spouting forth on the subject. Elkins fidgeted beside him and Skinner stared stoically out to sea. Horton resisted the impulse to glance at his watch.

'This is a Meade sixteen-inch Lightbridge Deluxe.' Hazleton patted the large telescope beside him, 'It has an extremely high specification and makes target finding simplicity itself. From it I can view thousands of stars across the universe millions of light years away, the desolate terrain of the Moon and the surface detail of many planets. It's an astronomy telescope,' he said patronizingly, pausing to make sure his audience were hanging on his every word. Mistake. Horton didn't have time for this. He interjected.

'Which means you didn't see the lights out to sea through it.'

'No.' Hazleton scowled, clearly annoyed at being trumped and interrupted. 'For that I use this.'

He crossed to the right of the room and a range of low cupboards. Horton caught Elkins' raised eyebrows and Claire Skinner's apologetic glance before Hazleton swung round holding a slim wooden box. Carefully, and with tenderness, he opened it and extracted a sleek mahogany and brass antique telescope.

'This is a nineteenth-century day and night telescope by George Dolland. Yes, you may well screw up your face, Sergeant, in an attempt to recall the name,' he snapped at Elkins. 'Because you probably know Dolland as the firm of opticians on every high street. It has a relatively large objective lens, and the power is low, which means it's not really suitable for viewing the planets. But I can view galaxies and star-clusters, which is what I was doing on Wednesday night when I saw the light at sea.'

'What time was this, sir?' Horton asked. Hazleton flashed an irritated glance at the woman police officer, causing Horton to add, 'WPC Skinner has relayed what you reported but I'd like to hear it from you.'

'To check I'm not going gaga?'

Skinner's fair face flushed and she averted her gaze. But Horton was busy trying to interpret Hazleton's expression. He registered neither dislike nor disrespect for the young police woman. In fact he registered nothing; perhaps Skinner was of too low a rank to warrant any feelings in Hazleton, and the same went for Sergeant Elkins, because although Hazleton had shaken hands with Horton, he had made no attempt to proffer his hand to Elkins. Clearly, Hazleton was wealthy, if the size of the Victorian house and its location overlooking the English Channel was anything to judge by. Hazleton was also a snob.

'It was ten thirty-one p.m. or twenty-two thirty-one if you prefer. It was approximately a mile out to sea. There was only one light – white – flashing erratically for a few minutes. The sea state wasn't rough but it wasn't exactly calm either, moderate I'd say, so the light could have been dipping with the waves, as a craft made its way through it. I know it wasn't a regular shipping vessel because not only was it too close to the shore but the light was certainly wrong for it to be one of the ferries, cruise liners or container ships, which are usually lit up like a Christmas tree, and I would have seen them through the telescope. The same goes for a commercial fishing boat. In fact there wasn't another ship in sight. I scanned the area for several minutes.'

'What do you think it was?' asked Horton, curbing his impatience and trying not to think of all the paperwork that would be mounting up on his desk, which Bliss would be screaming for the moment he returned, conveniently forgetting she had ordered him here.

'A black or dark-coloured canoe,' Hazleton answered promptly. 'With a light on the for'ard and the canoeist dressed in black.'

This was beginning to sound more like a James Bond movie every minute, thought Horton, making sure to keep the irritation from his expression

Hazleton added, 'I called the coastguards; they found nothing but then they wouldn't. By the time they arrived it could easily have put in to any one of the coves along the coast or even reached Ventnor Haven.'

Horton swivelled his gaze to Skinner. She said, 'I went down to the shore but couldn't see anything and the houses are too spread out and the area too rural to make enquiries.'

And Horton guessed she had got a flea in her ear when she had suggested it. They simply didn't have the manpower.

Caustically, Hazleton said, 'If it's terrorists or smugglers they're hardly likely to broadcast what they were doing, or leave clues around for the police to find.'

'What do you think they were smuggling, Mr Hazleton?' asked Horton.

'Arms, booze, drugs, cigarettes, people? Could be anything.'

In a canoe, thought Horton? The drugs and cigarettes were a possibility, although they wouldn't have been able to stow much inside such a precarious vessel in the night in a moderate sea. But illegal immigrants were out of the question. And why would terrorists come ashore on the Isle of Wight in a canoe? Where would they have come from? Horton doubted they would have paddled all the way from France. Admittedly it was easier to gain access to Portsmouth via the Isle of Wight where they could slip across to the mainland on one of the ferries, which weren't checked or stopped. It was a possibility but a very remote one.

Stiffly, Hazleton said, 'I'm not senile, I know what I saw.'

'Have you seen it again?'

'I would have said if I had,' Hazleton replied tartly.

Elkins said, 'Have you seen any strangers about?'

Hazleton gave Elkins another of his withering looks. Horton thought he was rather good at them. 'It's April, Sergeant, and therefore officially the start of the holiday season. Of course there are strangers.'

It was time to end the interview. Horton stretched into the pocket of his sailing jacket and pulled out his second business card of the day. He wasn't sure if he was going to regret this, but if it was the only way to pacify the little man so be it. He said, 'If you see anything again, Mr Hazleton, call me.'

Hazleton took the card in his slim, liver-spotted hand with a smug smile and a glance at Skinner that said *someone believes me*.

They took their leave, earning a glare from Hazleton's middle-aged, surly cleaning lady, who Claire Skinner had told him was Vivien Walker. Her husband, Norman, was the handyman and gardener. And he did a good job, thought Horton, eyeing the beautifully tended landscaped garden with its exotic and tropical-looking plants, leading down to the cliff top. Skinner had said that the couple lived off the premises and had never seen any lights at sea while they'd been working at Hazleton's house, but claimed it didn't mean there wasn't one. 'They're very protective of the old man,' Skinner had explained.

And perhaps that was why Vivien Walker had appeared so hostile towards them. Clearly she trusted no one, which wasn't a bad thing when the elderly could be easy prey.

'Do you believe him?' Elkins asked, as they climbed into the police car, parked on the wide gravel driveway.

Reason told Horton that Hazleton's tales should be taken with a pinch of sea salt. But there was a small part of him that said what if it was true? What if this was a case of the boy who cried wolf and he ignored it? It would be his balls on the line, not Bliss's, if she had any, and he half suspected she did. She'd be sure to slope shoulders and see that he carried the can for anything that could be traced back to Hazleton, which was probably why she had sent him here, to cover her arse. But how could a small light at sea here, miles away from Portsmouth Harbour, be connected with the visit of the USS *Boise*? Surely the answer was it couldn't be. OK, so the American submarine would pass through this stretch of water but it would be miles out to sea and manned with its own armed guards before the Royal Navy escorted it in. Perhaps he should check the shore, though God alone knew what that would reveal except sand, stones and sea. Before he could give instructions to Skinner his phone rang. It was Cantelli.

'Andy, a woman's body's been recovered from the sea off Spit Bank Fort,' he relayed with a touch of weariness in his voice. Horton knew why, and it wasn't anything to do with being overworked, more the fact that someone was eventually going to have to break the bad news to relatives.

That decided it. No more investigating spurious lights at sea. He told Skinner to head back to the Haven. To Cantelli, he said, 'Any idea who she is?'

'No. There aren't any reports of a woman overboard. I've checked for missing women along the south coast over the last week, although I don't know how long the body's been in the sea, and there have been three women reported missing: two teenagers, aged sixteen and seventeen, both from Brighton, and one woman, aged forty, from Bognor Regis. They're bringing the body into the ferry port and I'm arranging for it to be taken to the mortuary. I'll also alert Dr Clayton.'

Horton glanced at his watch. 'I'll meet you at the secure compound at the ferry port quayside, Barney, in about forty minutes.'

That was pushing it but if PC Ripley throttled back they

might just make it. There was no point speculating who the woman was and how she had ended up in the sea but Horton wondered if they were looking at suicide or an accidental death. Elkins had heard nothing to give him any pointers either way.

As the sky darkened and the wind stiffened, Horton couldn't help wondering if the same fate had befallen his mother, only her body had never been washed up. He scanned the green-blue choppy sea as the Portsmouth skyline drew closer. Had someone lured Jennifer on to a boat and then killed her and thrown her body overboard? But why? Or perhaps she'd met a boyfriend on his boat and there'd been an accident. The boyfriend had been too scared to report it and had kept silent about it all these years. Horton was convinced that Jennifer could not have committed suicide; the reports of her being in good spirits when she'd left the flat scotched that. But then another thought slapped him in the face. Perhaps Jennifer had been stood up or thrown over by someone she thought had loved her and, distraught, she'd decided to end it all. *And leave him, alone?* No, surely not. But what was the alternative? That she'd run off leaving her child to the mercy of children's homes?

As the launch eased its way into the narrow entrance of Portsmouth Harbour, Horton was glad to put his mind back on the job. He caught sight of the round-shouldered, overweight and shambolic figure of DC Walters on the first deck of the superyacht. He was dwarfed by a man built like a brick outhouse, with a keen face and cropped fair hair. Russell Glenn, wondered Horton? If so, he looked more like a member of the Russian mafia than a successful businessman, though the two weren't mutually exclusive. Elkins couldn't enlighten him either. 'We haven't been introduced,' he said facetiously.

And neither was *he* likely to be. A fact that didn't worry Horton one bit, though he suspected others in the police hierarchy might be desperately trying to wrangle their way on board. He doubted though that someone like Glenn would handle his own security arrangements. Walters was probably talking to a member of the crew.

Horton felt the first lean spits of rain as the launch motored past the naval ships and eased its way towards the deserted quayside, not far from the gigantic berths of the commercial ferry port, where a continental ferry was belching out black smoke preparatory to sailing. The wiry dark-haired figure on the quayside looked up at the sound of the launch and a few minutes later Horton was replacing his sailing jacket for his leather one. He told Elkins that Cantelli would give him a lift back to Gosport Marina to collect his Harley and that they'd let him know what they discovered about the dead woman.

As Cantelli pointed the car in the direction of the hospital mortuary, he said solemnly, 'From what I saw of her, Andy, she looks as though she's been dead a few days.'

And Horton knew what that meant. He primed himself for the ordeal that lay ahead.

'There was something odd about her though,' Cantelli continued. 'It was her dress. Kind of old-fashioned I'd say: long-sleeved, high-neck and down to her ankles, and she was wearing trainers.'

That could possibly rule out suicide because most suicides removed their shoes before wading into the water to drown. 'Old or young?'

Cantelli pulled a face as he considered this then shook his head. 'Couldn't say.'

'That bad, eh?'

'Yep.' There was a moment's silence before Cantelli added, 'The clothes don't fit the descriptions of any of the three missing women but that doesn't mean it isn't one of them. They could have changed.'

'Does Bliss know about it?'

'I haven't told her.'

Then he would, and he also needed to report back on his interview with Victor Hazleton, which he swiftly told Cantelli about before trying Bliss's number. He got her voicemail. He didn't think there was any urgency to leave a message or call her on her mobile. He'd try again after they had the preliminary report from Dr Clayton, and by then they might have an identification.

Horton's stomach did its usual double somersault as the smell of the mortuary greeted them. Cantelli popped a fresh piece of gum in his mouth to try and distract him from it, but Horton knew nothing would, as he nodded at Tom, the mortuary attendant.

'Just finished taking photographs of her,' Tom said jerking his head at the fully clothed, filthy body on the slab. 'I'll fetch Dr Clayton.'

Horton took a breath and ran his eyes over the corpse. Cantelli was right, judging by the deterioration she'd clearly been dead for some time. There wasn't a great deal left of the soft tissue of the face; the eyelids, nose, lips and ears had all been chewed by the marine life. What remained was filthy, and what was left of the hair was matted with dirt, seaweed and sea life. The clothes were, as Cantelli had described, rather unusual. The dress was covered in multicoloured small flowers and had a ruffle at the neck, long voluminous sleeves with ruffles on the wrists and a high waistband that fell just under the breast. There were no pockets that he could see, but he hoped there might be some identification on her. What was left of the hands was dark bluish-pink and there were no rings.

The door from the anteroom swung open and Horton looked up to see the petite figure of Gaye Clayton advancing toward them with a smile of greeting on her freckled face. Despite the circumstances Horton found himself smiling back.

'Let's see what you've got for us this time,' she said cheerfully, running her practised eye over the corpse. 'Well, I can certainly certify death. As to the time, I'll be more precise when I conduct the autopsy, which I've scheduled for first thing tomorrow morning, but I'll give you an estimate once we've undressed her.'

Horton watched her ease down the ruffle around the neck and caught a glimpse of a slightly quizzical expression as she studied the head and neck.

'I can't see any obvious signs of cause of death, no bullet or stab wounds, and no visible marks of strangulation, although there is trauma to the skull, but that could have been caused by the body coming into contact with an obstruction in the sea.' She stepped back and nodded at Tom to begin undressing the body.

Horton tensed in anticipation and sensed Cantelli's heightened interest beside him as Tom eased off the sodden trainers.

'Size nine,' he announced, turning them over. 'Cheap, ordinary chain store make, marking too faint to read. Well worn, especially on the right foot, but size still visible on the sole.' He dropped them into one of the evidence bags on the nearby trolley.

Surprised, Horton said, 'Large feet for a woman. How tall would you say she was?'

'Five foot ten, maybe eleven,' answered Gaye. 'We'll measure the body, of course.'

Consulting his notebook, Cantelli said, 'Karen Jenkins, the missing forty-year-old, is five three, and the teenagers are five four and five six. So we can positively rule out all three.'

So who was she? Had anyone missed her? Perhaps she had lived alone. Horton watched Tom's big hands ease the dress up the purple, half-chewed flesh of the legs. He frowned in puzzlement as a pair of dark-coloured lightweight shorts came into view.

'Unusual underwear for a woman,' Cantelli said.

'But not completely unknown,' added Gaye.

Cantelli stopped chewing. 'She's wearing a T-shirt.'

'So am I, Sergeant, under this get-up,' Gaye replied, brightly, pointing at her mortuary garb.

'Yeah, but there are T-shirts and T-shirts, and that one looks more like a—'

'Vest,' furnished Horton, thoughtfully. It was loose, round-necked and short-sleeved, not the sort of garment to compliment the intricate and old-fashioned dress that Tom was now holding. And there was something else peculiar about the body, but before Horton could express it, Tom said, 'There's a label inside but with only faint markings on it. There's also a pocket in the side. It's zipped up. There's something in it.'

Horton's pulse quickened as Tom eased the small zip down, thrust his big hand inside it and retrieved a small object. It was a plastic key fob minus the keys and inside the small plastic case, shaped like a Christmas tree, was a perfectly preserved picture of a young woman in her late teens or early twenties, with dark curly hair and a broad smile.

Cantelli studied it, puzzled. 'Could that be a daughter or granddaughter who has died and, distraught, this woman took her own life?'

It was possible, Horton supposed, but it could also be a

photograph of the corpse itself taken when younger. Tom put
the key ring into a small evidence bag and handed it to Cantelli,
then he folded the dress carefully into another evidence bag.
Gaye stepped closer to the corpse.

'Anything wrong?' Horton asked as her brow furrowed.

'Plenty, but please go on, Tom.'

Horton saw a knowing glance pass between them. He
dashed a look at Cantelli and got raised eyebrows in return.
With his heart beating fast Horton watched as the mortuary
attendant eased the shorts carefully down the decaying legs.
Cantelli gave a low whistle and Horton drew in a sharp
breath. He could see exactly what was 'wrong' but it was
Gaye who expressed it.

'As I suspected, your she is a he,' she said brightly, pointing
to the genitals.

And a missing man wearing a dress certainly put a new
slant on things, thought Horton. It was an opinion Cantelli
ventured twenty minutes later as they headed towards Gosport
Marina to collect Horton's Harley. There were no further
surprises from the body and no indication either from Dr
Clayton of the cause of death. She estimated the man was
aged between thirty-five and sixty and that he'd been dead
four to five days, which took them back to last Wednesday or
Thursday. There was nothing to indicate, at this stage, it was
a suspicious death, and although Horton didn't much care for
the fact that the corpse had been wearing a dress there was
no law against it.

'A transvestite?' Cantelli posed.

The dress wasn't sexy but then Horton knew it didn't need
to be. 'Don't transvestites usually wear women's underwear?
Isn't that what gives them the buzz, wearing something feminine
and sexy close to the skin?'

'If you say so. Maybe he didn't have time to put it all on,
go the whole hog.'

'Possibly. But the dress, as you pointed out, Barney, *is*
old-fashioned.'

'Perhaps it was his mother's. Depressed over her death he
decided to end his life wearing her favourite dress. Or perhaps
he liked dressing up, got drunk, went cavorting around the

beach on a full moon and thought he'd seen Amphitrite beckon to him from the sea.'

'Who?' asked Horton, throwing Cantelli a surprised look.

'Greek goddess, Queen of the Sea. I thought being a seafaring type you would know that,' Cantelli grinned. 'Marie's got a thing about Greek mythology. Says it's helping her to write her first fantasy novel.'

Marie, at twelve, was the third of Cantelli's five children and had recently won a scholarship to a private school where she was blossoming. Horton hoped the same would apply to Emma.

Cantelli said, 'Or perhaps he was at a fancy dress party and always carried that picture with him, so he put it in the pocket, got pilled up, wandered off and fell into the sea from a cliff.'

In this job, thought Horton, they'd all seen ten incredible things before breakfast so anything was possible. Should there have been keys on the key ring though, he wondered, staring through the rain-soaked windscreen as Cantelli headed past the old town quay at Fareham down towards Gosport. And if so, where were they? Or had he simply carried the fob because of the picture?

'The girl's name might be on the reverse of that photograph,' Cantelli suggested, following Horton's train of thought.

'That *would* be nice.' Horton didn't think it would be that simple, though. 'Send it over to Joliffe and ask if someone in the forensic lab can open it without damaging it. Get a photograph of it first though.' He called Walters who took an age to answer. 'I was beginning to think Russell Glenn must have offered you a job as a security officer on his superyacht,' Horton grumbled.

'He's already got one, with muscles like Schwarzenegger.'

'A broad-shouldered man with cropped hair.'

'Yeah, how do you know that?'

'I know a lot of things, Walters, like you're eating your way through a packet of Hobnobs.'

Walters swallowed noisily. 'That boat's bloody huge, Guv. And it's got this state of the art security system that would make the scum cry.'

'I'm glad to hear it.'

'Infra sensors in every room—'

'Cabin,' corrected Horton.

'Yeah, and a GPS locator and notification system, which can raise the alarm by all means known to mankind. It's got an ignition immobilizer security alarm, as well as a marine security system alarm with a siren for every cabin, which is broadcast so loud that everyone will think the three minute warning's gone off, or so Schwarzenegger claims.'

'And his real name?'

'Lloyd.'

'First or surname?'

'Dunno. Just said he was called Lloyd.'

Horton sighed. How Walters had got to be a DC was a mystery to them all. 'Well let's hope he never has to put it to the test; on my patch at least,' Horton added, thinking that with the increase in pirate attacks on superyachts and commercial shipping in other less friendly waters Glenn probably needed all the security he could afford, and that was clearly a great deal.

Walters said that the press had been on asking for a statement about the body recovered from the sea. Cantelli could deal with it when he returned. He asked Walters to check for reports of missing men since Wednesday, then tried Bliss's line with the same result as before, getting her voicemail. He hung up without leaving a message. He'd be back at the station soon.

Cantelli dropped him outside the marina office where Horton asked the manager if he or any of the staff knew anything about the muddy blue van parked there that morning. No one claimed even to have seen it, but when the manager checked the CCTV footage on Horton's request there it was. It was difficult though to make out the registration number or any occupants, and no one alighted from it, which worried Horton. He headed back to the station with a copy of the footage after leaving instructions he was to be called if anyone saw the van in the marina. He wondered if the CCTV camera at the front of Adrian Stanley's apartments might have picked up a sighting of it, but then he remembered that the camera was only focused on the gated entrance and front door and not on the promenade.

Bliss's car was in its allotted spot and Horton hoped he'd be able to get to his office without her accosting him. He stopped off in the canteen realizing it had been some time since he'd last eaten and was paying for his sandwiches when Cantelli appeared.

'A young woman's just come in to report her father, Colin Yately, has been missing since Thursday. She heard about the body being found on the news, they didn't give out the gender, and she's concerned it could be him,' he said excitedly.

'And?' Horton asked knowing there was more by Cantelli's expression.

'She's the girl in the key fob.'

THREE

Hannah Yately looked up from her plastic cup of tea with a worried frown on her attractive dark features. Her chocolate-brown eyes swivelled between them and must have read something in their expression because her face paled and tears welled up. She was accompanied by a man in his early thirties and both were dressed in the black-suited uniform of the hotel across the road from the station. Even before the man introduced himself as Damien King, Horton saw it on his name badge.

'It's Dad, isn't it? That body in the sea,' she stammered. The man beside her squeezed her hand and turned an anxious expression on them.

This was the part of the job Horton hated the most, breaking the bad news to relatives, if indeed the man in the mortuary was this girl's father; just because her picture had been found on the dead man it didn't mean to say it was him. That could have been planted. But somehow he didn't think so. And how did you tell a daughter that her father had been found dead wearing a woman's dress? Simple answer: you didn't, not until you were sure it was him.

Horton began gently. 'Why do you think your father is missing, Miss Yately?'

Her troubled eyes flitted to Damien King. Horton guessed he was also her boyfriend as well as a work colleague. King gave an encouraging nod.

'Dad and I see one another once a fortnight, on a Thursday,' Hannah began. 'We go for a meal at Oyster Quays. Dad calls me the Wednesday before just to make sure it's OK and I haven't got to work. I said it was fine but he didn't show up, and he didn't call me either. I telephoned him but didn't get an answer. I thought he must have changed his mind. Dad doesn't have an answer machine and he refuses to have a mobile phone or a computer. So I couldn't contact him, and Damien and I were in London from Friday morning and all weekend. We stayed at one of the hotels in the chain we work for, just for a break.' Her face flushed deep red and Damien looked down at his hands. Horton guessed she felt guilty at having put her poor old dad completely out of her mind until this morning. 'I rang Dad this morning but there wasn't an answer. I thought he must have gone out. I tried him again at lunchtime, nothing, and then just after two o'clock when Damien heard on the local news that a body had been found in the Solent, I, well, we . . .' She fought to hold back the tears.

Horton wondered why she hadn't visited her father, but he'd save that question for later. He recalled Dr Clayton's estimate of time of death. Had Colin Yately set out to meet his daughter last Thursday and had an accident? But no; not in that dress. It didn't sound as though he'd killed himself, not if he'd spoken to his daughter on Wednesday and arranged to meet her, but they only had Hannah Yately's word on that. How could they be sure the conversation had gone as she said? Maybe they rowed and Yately, distraught, had decided to end his life. Horton wasn't sure where the dress came into it because he didn't think it was Hannah's, but who could tell? Time for speculation later. Facts first.

'What time did he call you on Wednesday?' he asked.

'Six o'clock.'

'On your mobile?'

'Yes.'

They might at least be able to check that *if* they needed to.

'How did he sound?'

'Happy,' she answered miserably.

'And you were looking forward to seeing him?'

'Of course,' she frowned, clearly bewildered by his questions. If they had rowed she wasn't going to mention it and there were no telltale flushes of guilt.

'Did he know you were going away together for the weekend?' Horton's eyes swivelled to Damien's and back to Hannah's.

'Yes.'

Horton noted that Damien hadn't been invited to the Thursday evening meal. He could have been working, Horton supposed. Or perhaps it was a father and daughter bonding thing. Yately might not approve of Damien. Or he might have held the opinion that no man would be good enough for his daughter.

Cantelli said, 'Did your father say what he was going to do on Thursday before meeting you? Was he working?'

'No. Dad's retired,' she replied. 'We were meeting in the pizza restaurant as usual at about seven thirty. He was coming over on the Fastcat from the Isle of Wight. He lives in a flat at Ventnor.'

That explained why Hannah hadn't visited her father to check if he was all right. But Colin Yately's address, Horton noted, was not far from where Victor Hazleton lived. Could there be a connection between Yately's death and Hazleton's light at sea? Surely not. For a start he didn't believe Hazleton and, secondly, they had no reason to believe Yately's death was suspicious. And they could certainly check whether Colin Yately had ever caught the Fastcat or any ferry on Thursday.

Cantelli again. 'Could you describe your father to us, Miss Yately.'

'I have a photograph.' She reached down into a handbag at her feet. Horton didn't like to tell her it probably wouldn't be much use in helping to identify their body.

Cantelli passed the photograph across to him. Standing beside Hannah Yately was an ordinary-looking sort of man in his mid fifties, slim-faced, with thinning brown hair, dressed in casual trousers and an open-necked checked shirt. The photograph had been taken in summer on the waterfront at Oyster Quays, with the Spinnaker Tower in the background.

Handing it back to Cantelli, Horton said, 'How tall is your father?'

'Five foot ten.'

About the height of their body.

'Inspector, is it Dad?' she asked, anxiously scrutinizing him.

Cantelli shifted beside him, sensing what he was about to say. There was no easy way to do this.

Gently he said, 'The description fits your father, and we found this.'

At a nod from Horton, Cantelli reached under the folder on the desk and pushed across the photograph of the key fob. Hannah Yately let out a cry and then gulped noisily before beginning to sob. Cantelli slipped out and moments later returned with a plastic cup of water which he handed to Damien.

'Drink this, Hannah,' her boyfriend urged quietly, ashen-faced.

Horton said nothing until she had drunk and composed herself. 'I understand this must be very upsetting for you, Miss Yately, and although that was found on the body it doesn't necessarily mean it is your father. But I'm not going to get your hopes up because it seems probable that it is him. If so, we need to find out what happened after you spoke to him on Wednesday. Do you think you could answer a few more questions for us?'

After a moment she nodded.

'Could you confirm that belongs to your father?'

'Yes. I bought it for Dad for Christmas about six years ago. He always carries it with him.'

'Does he keep his keys on it?'

'Yes. Weren't they with it?' she said, surprised.

They weren't but Horton wasn't going to mention that yet. 'Does your father have any distinguishing marks, tattoos, scars?'

She shook her head.

Cantelli said, 'Has he had any surgery?'

She swallowed hard and tried to pull herself together. Horton admired her for that. 'He broke his leg five years ago. He was knocked off his bike when working. He was a postman; he took early retirement three years ago. And he had surgery on his knee, cartilage problems, about ten years ago.'

'So your father doesn't work at all?' enquired Cantelli.

'No. He says he doesn't need much to live on especially since him and Mum got divorced.'

So that ruled out him wearing his wife's clothes, thought Horton, unless he secretly had a hankering for her and had taken some with him when they broke up, which was a bit weird but then he'd met some pretty weird people in this job.

Horton said, 'When did they get divorced?'

'They spilt up when Dad took retirement. The divorce came through about eighteen months after.'

'How did he take it?'

'He was relieved. My mum's not the easiest person in the world to live with,' she answered with an edge of defiance.

'And where is that?'

'Newport, on the Isle of Wight. My parents were married for twenty-three years, but when Dad retired from the post office Mum said it was bad enough suffering him at weekends and in the evenings, she couldn't stand being cooped up with him every day and night. I'd already left home and moved here to live with my boyfriend.' She looked as though she was going to cry again but Damien squeezed her shoulder and that seemed to give her the strength to continue. 'I work as a receptionist at the Ferry Port Hotel and Damien's assistant manager. Mum said she'd supported me through college and now she wanted a chance of real life, as she called it, and a bit of fun before she was too old. She seems to be having it too.'

Horton noted the bitterness in Hannah Yately's tone.

'I don't have much contact with my mother. Dad got over Mum throwing him out long ago. In fact, I think it was a relief. They hadn't much in common and Dad would never have left her, he's the faithful type. Till death do us part and all that . . .' She stalled, as she realized what she'd said, but instead of the tears came anger. '*If* it is him then he must have had an accident. Why else would he have been in the sea? Does my mother know?'

'We haven't spoken to her.' Horton added, 'Did your father own a boat, Miss Yately?'

Her surprised expression gave him the answer before she confirmed this with a shake of her dark curls.

'Did he know anyone with a boat, or ever go out sailing or fishing?'

'He never mentioned it. You think he might have fallen overboard?'

'It's a possibility.' Though Horton thought a remote one recalling how Yately had been dressed, unless he had been at a party on a boat, as Cantelli had posed. He said, 'We'll need to confirm identity.'

Her head came up, panic and alarm in her eyes. 'You mean you want me to—'

'No,' Horton quickly reassured her. 'We should be able to verify it is your father from fingerprints and DNA. Do you have a key to his flat? We need to check it out,' he added, hoping that neither she nor Damien King would ask why they didn't use the keys on the fob. Neither did. As she again reached down into her handbag, Horton wondered if they'd be able to check Colin Yately's flat tonight.

'Does your father own or rent the flat?' he asked.

'He rents it.'

So unless they could get hold of the landlord it would mean the local police making a forcible entry. Could it wait until tomorrow morning, by which time the keys could be sent over? A twelve hour delay probably wouldn't make any difference, he told himself, and yet there was a chance that Yately could be lying ill or dead inside the flat, that he was not the body in the mortuary.

Cantelli took the two keys she handed to him. 'One's to the front door, the other's to Dad's flat,' she said.

'We'll give you a receipt for it.' Cantelli asked if she knew the name of the landlord. She did, but not his address. She thought it was somewhere in Shanklin.

Horton said, 'What did your father do with his time?' She looked a little bewildered so Horton elaborated. 'He was retired so did he have any hobbies, interests?' But he might just as well have asked her how far the planet Mars was judging by her expression. Hannah Yately had the self-obsession of youth and he guessed her doting father had been there on those dining-out occasions solely to listen to her and not the other way round. Still, he and Cantelli would do the same with their children when they reached Hannah's age, and before that. Horton would give anything to spend a day listening to his daughter's bright chatter.

'He liked walking,' Hannah Yately said hesitatingly, as if unsure whether that constituted a hobby.

'Was there any particular place he liked walking, or did he have a favourite walk?'

'I don't know. He just walked.' She eyed him with an air of desperation.

'With anyone or alone?'

'Alone. I think. I don't know. He didn't have any girlfriends if that's what you mean, although he did seem happy. In fact, happier than I'd seen him in some time,' she added, somewhat surprised that she had managed to recall this. 'I asked him if he'd found himself a new woman; he laughed and said, better than that.'

'What did he mean?' asked Horton, interested in this new nugget of information and thinking of that dress.

'I've no idea,' she answered forlornly.

Cantelli said, 'What about male friends? Was there anyone he was particularly close to or that he talked about?'

She shook her head. 'Dad was very private. The so-called friends he did have were Mum's and they disappeared quickly after they split up. I don't know about his neighbours.'

Horton didn't need a psychologist to tell him that Hannah Yately took her father's side in the divorce. He again thought of his own daughter and hoped that he'd still be close to her when she was Hannah's age, despite Catherine's determination to keep him at a distance.

There didn't seem anything more Hannah Yately could tell them for the present. Cantelli got her father's date of birth and address, and the address of her mother in Newport on the Island. He asked if she wanted them to call her mother.

She looked tempted, then pulled herself up. 'No. I'll speak to her.'

Horton said they'd let her know as soon as they had further news on her father, and confirmation it was him, and watched her leave.

On the way back to CID, Cantelli said, 'I'll contact the ferry companies.'

Horton fetched a black coffee from the machine in the corridor outside CID, and took it to his office where he opened the sandwiches he'd bought earlier. As he ate Hannah Yately's comment jarred at him. *I asked him if he'd found himself a new woman; he laughed and said, better than that.* Had Yately found himself a new *man* and had something gone wrong between them, resulting in his body ending up in the sea? According to his daughter it was five days since he'd disappeared, but that didn't mean his death was suspicious. And there was no evidence to suggest it, so no need to alert Uckfield and the Major Crime Team. And no need, he thought, to seal off the flat, but he wouldn't mind taking a look at it, just to be sure they were dealing with Colin Yately's death. He could bring something of Yately's back for a match on DNA and fingerprints. And he could see if Colin Yately kept a stash of women's clothing there. The door burst open and Bliss stormed in with a face like it had supped on sour milk. Why didn't the bloody woman ever enter anywhere like normal people, Horton thought with a stifled groan.

'I was expecting a briefing, Inspector,' she barked.

'I've been interviewing the daughter of the man discovered in the sea. I believe it to be Colin—'

'I don't mean that,' she flapped her thin arm at him as though she was swatting away a particularly irritating wasp. 'I mean Victor Hazleton. I had to go into a meeting earlier this afternoon with Detective Chief Superintendent Sawyer and others involved in Project Neptune without the full facts of the matter. How do you think that made me feel?'

'Foolish and inadequate?' he replied brightly. *If the cap fits . . .*

'It's you who are inadequate, Inspector,' she raged, glaring at him. 'I take the matter of receiving information that could thwart a potential terrorist threat very seriously, and so should you. If you don't you shouldn't be in the job.'

Stiffly, he replied, 'Mr Hazleton's report of a light at sea poses no threat to shipping or the USS *Boise*'s visit. If it had I would have informed you immediately. It's unlikely there was any light. The elderly man has a reputation for exaggeration and fabrication.'

'Well I hope you're right.' She eyed him malevolently before continuing, 'We have a duty to protect visitors to the city and the community. DC Walters has sent me his report on the security arrangements on Russell Glenn's yacht; I expect to have yours on Victor Hazleton on my desk within the next two hours along

with your report on your team's performance targets for the next
month for my meeting with Superintendent Reine early tomorrow
morning. And I don't want a repeat of the fairy tale you spun
last month. Let me you remind you that our new Chief Constable's
mission is "lean and agile, delivering best value for the taxpayer".'

'Not sure we can do both,' Horton muttered, but unfortunately
Bliss had excellent hearing.

'Then you'd better start applying for another job. And I want
a full report on the arrangements you've made for the additional
security for Mr Glenn's superyacht for Friday night.'

He hadn't even started on that. He let out a sigh as she swept
out. If his CID department, already grossly undermanned, was
any leaner there'd be no one in it. He made a start on the reports
but with half his mind on Colin Yately. Bliss hadn't even been
interested in their body. Why? He didn't really need to ask himself
that question; with recruitment frozen and promotion severely
restricted because of government cut backs there was even less
chance of her shinning up the slippery pole, but she was going
to make damn sure that however slim her chances she'd get there
somehow, and that meant sucking up to the big brass. Project
Neptune was her chance to shine. And a cock-up on Glenn's
super-shiny new yacht would severely blot her copy book.

Cantelli knocked and entered. 'The Wightlink office wouldn't
give me the information over the phone. I told them they could
ring back and check I was who I claimed to be but they wanted
proof before they divulged the information.'

'Glad to see someone's on the ball.'

'I've made an appointment with them early tomorrow morning
and with Hovertravel in case Yately decided to come by hovercraft. I've traced the landlord to an address in Shanklin but haven't
contacted them. Do you want me to ask the local police to enter
the flat?'

'No, I'm going over as soon as I'm finished here.'

Cantelli rolled his eyes at him.

Quickly Horton added, 'I know I don't have to but I'm curious.'

'When aren't you? Need any help with that?' Cantelli gestured
at Horton's littered desk. 'And I heard what Bliss said.'

'No. Check if Walters has made any headway on those burglaries
and organize extra patrols for the area for the next couple of

nights, we might catch them at it. We'll also need additional officers at Oyster Quays for this charity bash on Friday.'

Horton knuckled down to finishing the reports and clearing his desk of some of the outstanding matters. He was surprised to find it was almost six o'clock when Cantelli knocked to say he was heading home and that Walters had already left. Horton rose and glanced out of his window. Bliss's car was still there. He'd intended catching the six thirty ferry and if he didn't leave now he'd miss it. By the time she saw or heard his Harley leave – and the witch had ears like a bat – then he'd be long gone. He emailed the reports Bliss had demanded and shut down his computer. Plucking his leather jacket from the coat stand, he was about to leave when his phone rang.

He cursed. It was bound to be either Bliss checking up on him or the front desk with a report of a crime he'd have to deal with. He should let it ring but with a weary sigh he lifted the receiver.

'Is that Andy Horton?' asked a female voice as far removed from Lorraine Bliss's harsh one as the equator was from the Antarctic.

'Speaking,' he answered cautiously, trying to recognize the voice and failing.

'It's Avril Glenn. Russell Glenn's wife, the owner of the yacht at Oyster Quays,' she added when he didn't answer.

Horton started, surprised. Why the hell was she phoning him? Then his heart sank, what had that lumbering detective Walters done now? This had to be a complaint. Then he registered her tone. It hadn't been angry, rather the opposite, quite friendly.

'You knew me better as Avril Bowyers,' she said with a smile in her voice before quickly adding more hesitantly, 'or perhaps you don't remember me. It was fifteen years ago.'

Avril Bowyers! My God! Their four month affair flashed before his eyes and stirred his loins. It had been before he'd met Catherine. His head reeled with memories of her shapely figure, those seemingly endless legs, her stunning blonde looks and that wicked smile that had matched her sense of humour, not to mention her passion. And now she was Mrs Russell Glenn and living on that ruddy great floating gin palace. What did he say? Haven't you done well? How are you? But he didn't need to say anything because she continued, 'Look, I know this is probably a shock and a cheek of me calling you out of the blue, but I wondered if you could meet me at Oyster Quays in the bar opposite the pontoon.'

'When?' he asked, his heart racing.

'Now, unless you're busy.'

He thought about that six thirty sailing to the Isle of Wight and Yately's apartment. He was convinced that Colin Yately was lying stone-cold dead in the mortuary. So did it matter if he delayed visiting the man's apartment for twelve hours?

He said, 'I'll be there in fifteen minutes.'

FOUR

Horton located her in the window seat overlooking the harbour. It had stopped raining and the wind had dropped, ushering in a calm, pleasant spring evening that had the strollers and shoppers out in force on the boardwalk. Looking at Avril Glenn, it wasn't difficult for Horton to rekindle those old feelings of lust and longing, not that they had needed much rekindling; his timber was so dry it could have been lit with half a matchstick, he thought, as she locked eyes with him and smiled. Heading towards her he knew that every male in the bar was thinking the same lustful thoughts as him. But she was married and that was enough to make a grown man cry.

'Hello, Andy.'

She smiled and it was all he could do not to grin back like some idiot schoolboy. The blood was pounding in his ears and his heart was racing as though he'd just run the London marathon, twice. The blue eyes were as beautiful and bright as he remembered and the mouth as enticing as ever. Her shoulder length blonde hair was more expertly styled and highlighted than he recalled, and her make-up more subtle. Her figure though was as shapely as he remembered, only now it was clad expensively in tight jeans and a long cashmere cardigan over a tight-fitting T-shirt, none of which had come from any department store. There were more lines around her eyes and mouth but who was counting?

'I don't remember the leathers,' she said in the flirtatious voice he recalled from the past. It had sent a thrill through him then, and it was no different now.

'I didn't have the Harley then.' Fifteen years ago he'd been a sergeant. That was no reason not to have a Harley, but he'd been in a rare car phase, which had lasted several years of his marriage to Catherine, until he'd seen the light and annoyed Catherine by selling his car and purchasing the Harley. Catherine had never liked motorbikes and had refused to go on it. She'd also forbidden him to take Emma on it. An order he hoped to disobey in the years ahead.

'You're looking good,' he said.

'Only good!'

'Great then.' He smiled and let his eyes travel to her left hand. The diamond of her engagement ring was big enough to attract a short-sighted thug from fifty yards. And her diamond and ruby encrusted watch would keep Portsmouth Council in funds for a year.

'It's OK, I've got protection,' she said, reading his thoughts.

Horton followed her glance to the adjoining table where he saw the man with broad shoulders he'd seen on the deck of the superyacht earlier, and whom Walters had nicknamed Schwarzenegger. How could he have missed those massive shoulders, matching muscles and close-cropped blond hair? Easy: he'd been ogling Avril Glenn. Wearing a black leather bomber jacket over a dark T-shirt and sipping mineral water, Lloyd looked as out of place as a miner at a lighting convention.

'Who's protecting your husband?'

'His security system.'

'Then I hope all his alarms go off at once.' She smiled as Horton added, 'Will your chaperone let me buy you a drink?'

'His name's Lloyd, that's his first name. Lloyd Durham, as in the city, but he's from Reading.'

'Not half so nice, though generally warmer.' And Horton was wishing Lloyd was at either place right now, or on that small cruise liner on the pontoon.

'Vodka and tonic, please. You don't have to buy Lloyd a drink.'

Good, because he wasn't offering. 'Won't Mr Glenn mind

you being here?' he asked. He was fishing and she knew he was.

'Russell is working.'

'Doing what?'

'Trying to buy Portsmouth Football Club.'

'You're kidding!'

'Yes, though I have been doing my best to persuade him. It might work yet.'

And with Avril doing the persuading, Horton wondered how Glenn could possibly refuse.

Horton went to the bar, nodding at Lloyd on his way and getting a nod in return. While he waited to be served he staved off his disappointment at not seeing Avril alone by wondering about Lloyd's background. Ex-job? Walters would have said if he were, though knowing Walters he probably hadn't asked. Ex-services perhaps, he looked fit enough for the marines or commandos. At least Glenn took protecting his wife seriously. Too seriously, he wondered briefly? No. Not if she went around wearing that kind of jewellery. And that made him even more concerned about Friday evening's reception. If Avril touted that stuff as everyday wear then what the devil would be on show on Friday night?

He returned with her vodka and tonic and a Diet Coke for himself. Taking the glass in her beautifully manicured hand, she managed to brush her fingers against his. His heart stalled and for a moment he wondered if it would restart.

'I heard DC Walters mention you to Lloyd this afternoon and I was curious to see if you remembered me.'

'How could I forget?' But he had.

'It was a long time ago. You haven't changed much.'

'Neither have you.'

'God, don't tell me I've wasted all this money on expensive beauty treatments.'

'Didn't need it and still don't,' Horton said gallantly, enjoying himself. He made sure to angle his body so that he couldn't see Lloyd.

She said, 'You know I'm married but how about you? Married, engaged, divorced?'

'About to be divorced and living on a boat, like you, but mine's a permanent home, and a row boat compared to your palace. It's in Southsea Marina. My marriage broke up last August. One child, Emma, nearly nine years old and beautiful.'

'Of course, with a dad like you. We don't have kids, never seemed to happen and I wasn't that fussed anyway.'

'There's still time.'

'No fear. Well, that's got that out of the way. What shall we talk about now?'

Horton wanted to know why she wanted to see him, but instead asked, 'How did you meet Russell?'

'He was staying in the hotel where I was working in the south of France. He asked me to work for him as his PA eight years ago and things progressed from there.'

Horton recalled that he'd met Avril when she'd been working as a receptionist in a local hotel, much like Hannah Yately he thought briefly, with a twinge of guilt that he'd postponed visiting her father's apartment. But one night wasn't going to make any difference when Yately was in the mortuary. *But what if he wasn't?* He should have checked or at least got the local police to check. He shifted and brought his mind back to when he and Avril had met. There had been a spate of thefts in the hotel where Avril was working. After a four month relationship Avril had called it quits by telling him she was going abroad to work.

'And you're happy?' he said.

'Who wouldn't be?' Her eyes slipped towards the boat.

It was an answer but not the right one, he thought. But then maybe for Avril it was, and she had got everything she'd ever needed and wanted. He recalled that she'd had it tough as a child, like him. But with her it had been a case of a drunken father who had pissed away most of his dole money for most of his life and had lived off his wife's earnings as a waitress. Avril had been left to her own devices as a child and hadn't received much education, but she'd worked hard, been bright, and, he recalled, ambitious and anxious to escape Portsmouth. Well, she'd certainly achieved that and now she'd returned in style. And perhaps that was the real reason why she wanted to see him, to demonstrate to someone who remembered her how well she'd done for herself, and how far she'd travelled from the poor working-class girl she'd been. But perhaps more importantly to show herself how far she'd come.

She eyed him steadily, twirling the glass in her slender hands. 'I suppose you think I'm showing off,' she said, reading his thoughts with uncanny accuracy that made him wonder if he was beginning to let his guard down too much. Adrian Stanley had seen through him this morning but then Stanley was ex-job, Horton reasoned. Maybe it applied to an ex-lover too.

'I guess I am in a way, but only to myself.' She gave a brief smile before the serious expression returned. 'I'm not here to rub anyone's noses in it because there's no one's nose left to rub. Dad died a year after I left to work abroad and Mum three years after that. There's no one I care to remember in Portsmouth, except you, and I don't need to show off to you. No, I'm here for several reasons and one is because the yacht was built in Southampton and launched from there last Friday, and we had to pick up three new crew members from the Superyacht Training Academy here in Portsmouth at the weekend.'

Horton hoped they'd been thoroughly vetted, along with the rest of the crew. There was always a possibility of a job being organized or coordinated from the inside.

'Do you know the academy?' she asked.

'Not much call for hiring superyacht crew on my little boat.'

She laughed. 'Pity you're a copper. You'd make a great skipper.'

'Wrong kind of boat, Avril. I like ones that have a bit of cloth on a pole.'

'Oh, the complicated, energetic kind,' she teased.

He nodded. Even if Glenn's boat was a sailing yacht, Horton knew that being so close to Avril and seeing her with Glenn would be enough to drive him nuts. He'd spoken the truth though when he'd said he didn't know the Superyacht Training Academy. He made a mental note to find out more about them, not because there might be anything suspicious, but because they were on his patch.

'And the other reason is this VIP charity reception,' he prompted.

'Yes. I can't say Russell's thrilled about it, he's a very private man and hates these kinds of flashy functions but I wanted to host it because I feel guilty.'

Horton raised his eyebrows. 'Because you're rich?'

'No, because I let my mum down.' Her expression clouded over and she sipped her vodka before continuing. 'Mum died of pancreatic cancer and I wasn't here to look after her or to say goodbye. She'd had a tough life with Dad being the shitbag he was. I didn't always see eye to eye with her, we rowed frequently, as you might remember. I thought her weak and pathetic for putting up with a drunk who treated her like a punchbag when he felt like it, and I couldn't get away from her, Dad and Portsmouth quick enough. But that was fifteen years ago, and I'd like to think I've grown up a bit since then. I know that Mum took the punches in order to protect me, and I left her to handle her cancer alone because I was shit-scared that I'd end up looking after her and become trapped. And I hate traps,' she added with feeling. 'Can you understand that?'

Horton nodded. He could.

'Mum never once asked me to come home, she never complained and I stayed away until it was too late. I returned for the funeral for one day and I was back on the plane as fast as my legs would carry me. The local hospice was marvellous to Mum so this is my way of assuaging my guilt, by thanking them and saying sorry to my mum.' She gave a sad smile before adding, 'All the great, good and famous from all around are paying for their tickets to come on board for caviar and champagne, including your new Chief Constable, Mr Meredew.'

That didn't surprise Horton. If Uckfield's father-in-law had still been the Chief Constable then no doubt Uckfield would have wangled himself an invitation. Horton doubted if mere Detective Superintendents were included.

Avril was saying, 'It's in aid of the hospice and we're holding an auction. I've got Oliver Vernon as auctioneer, he's an art historian and used to handling auctions so he knows how these things work. I've got jewellery, artworks, designer clothes all donated by some very famous people—'

'On board?' Horton asked, alarmed, wondering why the hell Walters hadn't told him this.

'No.' She smiled. 'We're showing the goods on screen in the on board cinema.'

'Of course,' Horton said airily, but he was relieved. Despite Lloyd's muscles and the state of the art security system, and extra patrols, Horton didn't think they'd be any match for an organized raid if it happened. His mind flitted to that blue van. Could it have been casing Glenn's superyacht? Not if it was the same one that had been outside Stanley's apartment some fifteen miles away.

'Oliver should be here in a moment,' Avril said, her eyes searching the busy boardwalk. 'And Dominic Keats. He's the Managing Director of the Superyacht Training Academy.' A glance at her watch had Horton quickly scanning the interior of the bar for loitering thieves. Even Lloyd looked jumpy. 'Ah, there's Dominic.'

Horton followed her gaze to a tall man in his early fifties with short dark hair, and an expensive sailing jacket worn over causal clothes. He halted at the top of the pontoons and stared around with a puzzled expression on his aquiline face, before stepping into the small marina office. Avril tossed back the remainder of her vodka and sprang up. Lloyd followed suit. Avril said, 'Come and meet him.'

Horton wasn't particularly keen to, but how could he refuse? Dominic Keats smiled as Avril greeted him warmly.

'This is an old friend of mine, Andy Horton; he's a police inspector so you'd better watch out,' she said, laughing.

Keats looked as though he'd just suffered a severe bout of indigestion but he took Horton's hand in a firm grip and smiled briefly and dismissively. Horton got the sense of an impatient, ambitious man who measured people in terms of their wealth and business potential, and as he clearly had neither, Keats wasn't going to waste time and energy on him.

'And here's Oliver.' Avril waved at a slim man, about mid forties, with fair hair and a close-cropped fair beard on a narrow but friendly face. He was casually dressed in jeans and jumper under a dark coat, carrying a canvas computer bag slung over his shoulder and trailing a small suitcase.

Oliver Vernon's grasp wasn't as firm as Keating's, but his light-blue eyes were intelligent and friendly.

'We've got some great pieces to auction,' Oliver Vernon said enthusiastically, after Avril had made the introductions. 'Thanks to Avril's persuasive skills.' Horton could well imagine. 'Some fine art, antique jewellery, exquisite antique porcelain as well as the usual, holiday for two on a millionaire's island paradise.'

'Not Russell's,' Avril added, smiling, 'but we're donating a four day cruise on the yacht. You could bid for it, Andy.' she teased. 'You are coming to the auction, aren't you? Please say you can make it.'

Horton quickly stifled his surprise and rapidly tried to think of an excuse to refuse. The obvious one was work but he found himself saying, 'Thanks. That would be nice.' *Nicer still if Glenn wasn't there.* Still, he was curious to meet the man who had made millions and won Avril's heart, or at least her devotion, even if she worshipped at the altar of wealth. But who was he to criticize? It was her life. He didn't know what the new Chief would make of his appearance on board though. Bliss would be sick with envy if she ever found out and so would Uckfield, he guessed. Horton hoped that neither they nor anyone else would. He'd come in for endless ribbing and snide comments.

'Great.' She sounded and looked genuinely pleased, but Horton still suspected he was being invited so that she could boast to at least one person who remembered her from her poverty stricken past. 'Eight thirty. Black tie. Now we'd better go, there's Russell waiting for us.'

Horton followed the direction of Avril's gaze and this time had to work hard not to betray his surprise, because Russell Glenn was not how he'd imagined. In fact he was the total opposite. Instead of being tall, good-looking, forceful and well dressed, he was of average height, scruffily dressed, wearing a checked shirt that seemed to be more out than tucked into his low-slung trousers. He had untidy grey hair, wore gold-framed spectacles and appeared to be in his early sixties. He looked anxious, understandably so, what with Avril sporting the crown jewels and a huge glittering superyacht on display in a city that had almost as many villains as it had pebbles on the beach.

Horton's eyes travelled back to Avril. He caught a shadow of unease on her face before she smiled her goodbye and entered the marina office with her guests. With Lloyd trailing behind them, Horton watched as they made their way towards the superyacht before bringing his eyes back on Glenn, only to find Glenn staring directly at him. He tried to read the expression on Glenn's face but it was difficult to interpret behind those spectacles and over the distance of several yards. One thing was clear though, Glenn was studying him intently. Perhaps he was jealous of anyone who knew his wife. But Horton didn't think it was that. It was as though . . .

'You can't afford it, Andy?'

Horton swung round to find a broad, tall man in his late forties behind him. Mike Danby, ex-Chief Inspector, had less hair than Horton remembered from eight years ago, but the penetrating green eyes that had terrified many a suspect in the interview room were as piercing as ever, only now they were smiling at Horton.

'You're looking prosperous, Mike,' Horton said, returning the smile while eyeing up the expensive leather jacket. 'Life outside the force obviously suits you.'

'It does, especially when you've got clients like Russell Glenn.'

Horton raised his eyebrows. 'You're providing extra security for this bash on Friday?'

'You know about it?' Mike Danby asked, surprised.

'We know everything in CID.'

'That's new then. When I was in CID we knew bugger all until after it happened.'

That was still occasionally true. 'How many men are you bringing in?'

'Not sure yet. Why? Are you interested in joining the party? I've got a few off duty cops on the payroll for Friday night.'

'I bet you have.' Horton could well imagine they were queuing up to earn some extra money.

'You should have joined me when you had the chance,' Danby added, smiling.

But Horton knew that life outside the force when it had been offered to him by Danby wasn't then a possibility. And it wasn't now. 'And miss all the bureaucracy and back biting in the station, never,' Horton said with irony. 'But I'm glad it's worked out for you. Have you worked for Glenn before?'

'No. Have you met him?'

Horton shook his head. *Only seen him.* Glenn had now vanished inside the superyacht along with Avril and her guests. 'How did he make his money?'

'Hotels, conferences, magazines, property, you name it he seems to have had the Midas touch. Buying up or taking over failing businesses and making them profitable before selling them off. Started with nothing, came from here too.'

'Portsmouth?' Horton asked, surprised. Avril hadn't mentioned that.

'Yes, but he left when he was a child. His father died in an accident when Russell was six and his mother moved to London.'

Horton again considered the expression he'd seen on Glenn's face. Perhaps Glenn had been marvelling at how much had changed in the city over the years. When Glenn had been six Oyster Quays hadn't existed and the entire area had been part of a thriving dockyard, employing thousands.

'Do you do much of this sort of thing?' Horton said, nodding at the superyacht.

'Specialize in it you might say, high-profile events around the country, sometimes abroad, pop stars at gigs, celebrities who need a little extra protection. I always need good men, if ever you're tempted . . .' Danby handed Horton his business card.

'I'll let you know,' Horton answered, pocketing it.

Danby glanced at his expensive watch.

'You'll be late for your meeting,' Horton said.

Danby eyed him shrewdly before reaching out his hand. 'Good to see you again, Andy.'

'And you.' Horton shook it. He watched Danby's progress down the pontoon, his mind returning to Russell Glenn. Just what had he seen on the man's face? Unease? Anxiety? Both? Maybe. But there had been something else. Defining what that may have been remained elusive so he abandoned it and consulted his cheap watch. It was almost seven. He hesitated.

So what was it to be, a late evening checking out Yately's apartment, or an evening on his yacht, alone? He often welcomed solitude but after the events of the day, which had brought the past back to him in more ways than he had expected, it felt an especially bleak place to be. He turned and struck out for the ferry.

FIVE

A n hour later he was pulling up outside a tall Victorian whitewashed house perched high above the small seaside town of Ventnor, nestling under the downs. On the staggered terraces beneath it, leading down into the small bay, Horton could see the lights of the houses in the gathering dusk and beyond them the great black expanse of the English Channel, with a faint light out to sea of a container ship. He climbed the steps to the front door wondering if Mr Hazleton had his eyes peeled to his giant telescope.

Extracting the key Hannah Yately had given them, Horton stepped into a spacious and clean hall with a broad twisting staircase facing him. There were two doors leading off the hall and one further down it past the staircase, but there was no sound from behind any of them and no sign of any of the occupants. His eyes travelled to his left to what looked like a stack of lockers in a sports centre, except these were numbered, up to seven, and each had a wide slit for a postman to slot the mail in. He wished he had Yately's key to it but it would either have to be forced open or they'd get the key from the landlord tomorrow.

Number seven was, as he had suspected, on the top floor. It was approached via the last flight of steps, much narrower than the others, but carpeted in the same green cord. It was the only flat on the floor and was evidently in the roof space. With a quickening heartbeat he registered there was no sign of a forced entry but then there didn't need to be if Yately was still inside it with his keys. And if that were so then who was in the mortuary and why had he been carrying Yately's key ring, minus the keys?

Horton stretched his hands into his latex gloves, and taking the second key he inserted it in the lock and pushed open the door. Silence greeted him and with relief he noted there was no smell of death. He found himself in a small lobby with two doors either side of it and a door directly ahead, which was the bathroom. In it he found a comb, which he dropped into an evidence bag for DNA and fingerprint comparison.

He wasn't here to search the flat, only to satisfy himself that Colin Yately wasn't inside it ill or dead, and a swift glance in the room to his left, which revealed a bedroom, and the room on the right, which led into the lounge with the kitchen off, confirmed to him that Yately wasn't here, and was therefore probably in the mortuary. He turned back into the lobby and re-entered the bedroom.

It was shaped like an inverted 'L' with a window on the far side facing him. The room wasn't very large, only about nine feet wide and about fifteen feet long. It was tidy with no evidence that it had been disturbed in any way. The single bed was made up with a navy-blue counterpane and opposite it was a low chest with several books on it, some about navy ships, others on local history. In front of the window was a telescope, but not like Victor Hazleton's antique one or his ultra modern white contraption; this one was mounted on a tripod and it was the kind of telescope that Horton was more familiar with.

Without touching it he bent down, and closing one eye, peered through it. It seemed to be pointing at the small marina of Ventnor Haven, which he'd come into earlier that morning on the police launch. Yately probably used it to watch the passing ships. If Horton combined that with the subject matter of some of the books on the chest of drawers did it point to some kind of subversive activity? Hardly, he thought, smiling to himself at his imagination, before another thought struck him: had Yately been recruited to Project Neptune? But if he had Bliss would have recognized his name. But then she hadn't stopped to ask him about the body, and he'd not had the chance to tell her. He thought it far more likely that while some people went in for trainspotting Yately had been into ship-spotting.

Straightening up, he supposed that Yately could have used the telescope for spying on people in the houses below. Perhaps Yately was a peeping Tom and that was the new hobby he'd hinted at to his daughter. But binoculars would have been more suitable for that activity and there didn't seem to be any here. The door under the eaves led into a wardrobe. Inside were Yately's clothes but no dresses. And rifling through the chest of drawers he found only male clothing.

Horton picked up the phone beside Yately's bed and keyed in 1471 to get the number of the last caller. The call was timed at three minutes past two that day, when Hannah said she had last tried her father before reporting him missing at the police station, and the number checked with that of Hannah Yately's mobile phone.

In the lounge, just as in the bedroom, there was restricted headroom because of the angle of the roof and Horton had to incline his head to avoid knocking it against the rafters as he crossed to the kitchenette to the right of an old, small wrought iron fireplace. The room was stuffy and felt claustrophobic. He wouldn't like to be up here in summer. Give him the boat and the open sea any day, he thought, opening the fridge. There was milk and cheese in it, which were beginning to go off. This must have been one of the servant's rooms years ago, he guessed, probably a large cupboard or perhaps another bedroom where the lowliest of servants had slept.

On the desk underneath the window in the lounge, Horton picked up a silver-framed photograph of Colin Yately with his daughter beside him. It was recent; taken about six months ago he'd say, on the promenade at Ventnor. Horton studied Yately's smiling features, but just as in the interview room when Hannah had handed him a photograph of her father, he couldn't equate it with what he'd seen on the slab in the mortuary. This time, though, he noted the receding light-brown hair, the lines around the mouth and the dark-brown eyes, which were like his daughter's. Yately looked a fairly innocuous sort of man. It was easy to imagine him in the uniform of a postman. But not in a woman's dress.

Slipping the photograph out of its frame, Horton placed it between the pages of his notebook. He didn't think Hannah would mind, and even though she'd already given them a photograph he thought this more recent one would be better for circulating to the media if they needed to trace Yately's last movements. He wondered if there were other photographs or an album about the place. Perhaps in the desk. On it was a large lined notepad with neat, thin handwriting. Horton popped the fountain pen beside it into another bag, again to compare fingerprints with the dead man's, before his eyes fell on the notes. Yately had written:

> In the early 1800s, Ventnor was a hamlet of thatched fishermen's cottages with an old mill, an inn and a couple of humble dwellings; by 1838 it had grown to three hundred and fifty inhabitants.

Horton flicked through the pages of writing, about fifty in total, and saw that Yately's interest was not only in local history but in the chines, creeks and coves on the east coast of the island. Perhaps this was what had given him the buzz which he had hinted at to his daughter. Could he have been on one of these cliffs when he'd fallen into the sea? But he was back to that damn dress again. And if Yately had gone out for a walk why not take his keys?

There was no sign of a suicide note anywhere. It was time to leave, but before he did he jotted down details of Yately's GP and dentist, and found three photograph albums in the desk. He didn't have time to study the pictures so he placed the albums into a bag. He wondered if he'd find a photograph of the former Mrs Yately or another female wearing that patterned dress. Locking up he got the impression of a solitary man, but not necessarily a lonely one.

Tomorrow they'd have the results of the autopsy and then make a decision on how the investigation should proceed if indeed there was an investigation. On the ferry he took the photograph albums up to the lounge with him. In a seat by the window, with a coffee and toasted bacon sandwich in front of him, he began to look through them but was distracted by

thoughts of all the photographs he'd taken of Catherine and
Emma. Catherine had probably lit a ruddy great bonfire of the
photographs of him when she'd kicked him out a year ago, but
there must be some left of him and Emma together and he'd
like to have them. All he had were two pictures of his daughter,
one of which he kept on his boat, the other on his desk.

His mind jumped back to his childhood. He couldn't
remember his mother taking photographs of him but surely she
must have done. So where were they? Had they been destroyed
when the flat had been cleared out? *Who* had cleared their flat?
His mind flicked to Adrian Stanley and what he wasn't telling
him about Jennifer. Checking his watch Horton thought it was
too late to telephone Stanley, but he would tomorrow.

He turned his mind back to the photographs in front of him.
There were many pictures of Hannah Yately through the ages and
of her proud and doting father. There were a few pictures of a
woman who must be Hannah's mother, wearing modern clothes
over the years, though to Horton they were slightly on the tarty
side, and she was either looking bored or posing into camera, but
there was no sign of the maxi-dress with the flowers on it. There
was an older woman who could have been Yately's mother and
Hannah's grandmother. Was she still alive, Horton wondered? If
so, perhaps she'd recognize the dress. But Hannah hadn't
mentioned her so he guessed she was dead. Still, they'd check.

As the ferry slid into port he eyed Glenn's superyacht lit up
like a giant advertisement in Piccadilly Circus. He recalled
Avril's jewellery, hoping it was safely locked away at night,
before his mind flitted to more pleasing thoughts of her shapely
figure and her smile. He speculated over her relationship with
her husband and the brief information Mike Danby had given
him, and decided to run a few checks on Russell Glenn before
meeting him on Friday night.

He headed straight for his boat, deciding that the items he'd
collected from Yately's flat could be sent to the Fingerprint
Bureau tomorrow. It was late, it had been a hectic day, and he
hoped that sleep would come easily. But it didn't. His head
was too full of Adrian Stanley, of Avril and Russell Glenn, and
of Jennifer Horton.

Tuesday

The seagulls were squealing in the harbour when he woke the next morning with a muggy head and with a determination to concentrate on getting to the bottom of Colin Yately's death. Dr Clayton would have the autopsy results today which might help to make things a little clearer.

By the time Cantelli returned from the ferry and hovercraft ticket offices Horton had telephoned Hannah Yately and told her what he'd found in her father's flat, which was nothing, and what he'd taken away. He said he'd let her know the moment they had positive confirmation and prayed she wouldn't ask him why he wanted the photograph albums. She didn't.

Cantelli plonked himself in the seat across Horton's desk. 'There's no record of Colin Yately travelling on either the Fastcat ferry, the car ferry or the Hovercraft but he could have paid by cash. However, no one I spoke to in the ticket office and none of the marshalling staff recognized him, so it's likely he never reached here.'

'Alive that is. He almost made it dead,' Horton said sombrely. 'I didn't find any evidence in his flat to suggest he was into cross dressing.'

'Perhaps he dressed up elsewhere because he was scared his daughter might find the clothes at his flat. He could have used a beach hut or been at a house near the sea or on a boat.'

'Alone or with someone?'

Cantelli shrugged. 'If he was with someone who shared his passion, he might be afraid or too ashamed to come forward. He could be married. Yately ended up accidentally in the sea leaving his keys and other identification in his trousers.'

'But why remove the keys from that fob?'

'Perhaps he'd put them on a new fob some time ago, only Hannah never noticed. He didn't want to discard the fob with the picture of his daughter in it because it was too precious to him, and that he always kept on him no matter what.'

Horton glanced at the photograph of Emma on his desk. Yes, he could understand that. Yately's daughter might be all that the poor man had had left and he'd needed the picture to remind himself he wasn't alone. Or was that how *he* felt, he thought gloomily? Only he didn't carry a picture of Emma. He'd learnt in the job a long time ago to have few personal effects on him in case they could be used against him, or destroyed or stolen.

He wondered how soon they'd get a preliminary report from Dr Clayton. He said, 'Ask Walters if he's managed to speak to Yately's dentist and his GP.' Horton had also detailed Walters to get Yately's comb and the fountain pen over to the Fingerprint Bureau. Thankfully, Walters had reported that there had been no further house burglaries overnight. Perhaps the extra patrols had deterred the robbers, but they couldn't keep them up. Horton called up all they had on the case on screen and began to trawl through it, looking for anything that Walters and Cantelli had missed and which could give them a hint of who it might be. He found nothing but sooner or later their burglar would slip up; unfortunately that meant another householder having to suffer the misery of being robbed.

He picked up the disc containing the CCTV footage of the blue van seen at the marina in Gosport and popped it into his computer. He saw that it covered the period from eight in the morning until when Horton had collected it just before one yesterday afternoon. A handful of cars arrived between eight o'clock and nine, and some of them belonged to the staff judging by the direction in which they headed after alighting. Two other cars entered: a top of the range BMW and a Range Rover, then Horton swung into the marina on his Harley at nine twenty-one. A few minutes later came the muddy blue van. Horton frowned. He didn't care for the closeness of the timing, or for the fact he could swear it was the same van that had been parked outside Stanley's apartment at Lee-on-the-Solent.

He reached for his phone. He wanted to know if Stanley had seen the van that morning or at any other time. But there was no answer. Horton watched the blue van pull away ten minutes later. He sat back concerned. Had it been following him? He hadn't seen it on his way to Stanley's flat or anywhere else since yesterday morning, and certainly not at his marina. And why should someone follow him? Unless they didn't want him talking to Stanley, and there was only one reason for that, but before he could reason any further the trilling of his phone sliced through his thoughts.

It was Dr Clayton. At last!

'It's a suspicious death, Inspector,' she announced grimly and peremptorily.

Horton's heart skipped a beat and he cursed silently. It was the last thing he wanted to hear. 'Tell me,' he urged.

'The presence of bleeding in the cranium suggests he was struck violently before entering the water. I found foam in the trachea and main bronchi and evidence of bruising in the neck and chest, which indicates he was alive when submersion occurred. Of course, further tests might confirm the presence of a drug or drink but I don't think it likely, because I found something else that shouldn't be there. There was evidence of marks on the wrists and ankles, and I found fragments of a fibre embedded in both, and in his mouth. At some point your body was bound and gagged.'

Horton swore to himself. His heart sank. 'But he wasn't bound when he was found,' he said, thinking aloud.

'He wasn't, and neither was he in the water long enough for any restrictions to have rotted. The ties could have become loose while he was in the sea but I'd be very surprised if they had, and even more surprised if the gag had worked its way off. He was only in the sea for about twelve hours, no more than eighteen hours certainly.'

'But you said—'

'That he'd been dead for four or five days. And he has. Decomposition was advanced, which is surprising at this time of the year when the sea temperature is still quite cold, barely reaching forty-seven Fahrenheit, and the colder the water the slower the decomposition. There was also no evidence of adipocere; that's the yellowish-white substance composed of fatty acids and soaps that forms after death on the fatty parts of the body like the abdomen wall and buttocks. It protects against decomposition.'

With dread, Horton said, 'You're saying that he was killed, his body left somewhere for a few days, then it was untied before being dumped at sea sometime between Sunday night and early Monday morning?'

'Worse.'

Shit. What could be worse, he groaned silently.

'The evidence points to the fact that the gag was removed but not the wrist and ankle restrictions. While he was bound he was submerged, hence the bruising in the neck and chest and the foam in the trachea as the poor man struggled to free himself. Then came exhaustion, followed by coughing and vomiting, loss of consciousness and death by drowning some minutes later.'

Horton drew in a deep breath. His gut tightened as Gaye continued.

'I think his captor knocked him out, tied him up and gagged him. When the victim regained consciousness his captor dropped him into the sea, removing the gag but not the wrist and ankle restraints. When the poor man eventually drowned, your killer hauled him out, untied him and left him somewhere on land, which is supported by the patterns of animal and bird life eating into the corpse. The body was then either washed out to sea or taken out to sea. The dress acted as a buoyancy aid allowing the body to float rather than sink as it would normally have done.'

Did the killer realize that or had he misjudged it, Horton wondered, his mind reeling from Dr Clayton's findings and seeing again that small ordinary flat and that average, ordinary man in the photograph. He'd seen nothing to indicate that Colin Yately should be bound and tossed into the sea to die. Should he have looked harder? Had he missed something? Clearly he must have done. To make sure that it was Colin Yately's body, he said, 'Can you confirm if he ever suffered a broken left leg?'

'Yes, and he'd had surgery on his right knee. He's about late fifties.'

That seemed to seal it but just for good measure, Dr Clayton added, 'Walters emailed me details of Colin Yately's dentist, it's why I've taken longer to get back to you. I wanted to check. I can confirm from examining the dental records on line that they match with the victim. It's Colin Yately all right.'

Horton thanked her and rang off. It was nasty and they were looking for a particularly callous and ruthless killer. But what the devil did Yately have that a killer wanted so desperately? Who could he have angered so much to warrant such a violent death?

He recalled Yately's daughter and the thought of what this news might do to her, as his mind raced with the implications of Dr Clayton's findings. They would need to return to Yately's apartment and take it apart. And although Horton doubted Yately had been taken captive at his flat it still needed to be treated as a crime scene, and with a sinking heart he thought that was what he should have done in the first place.

SIX

I t was a view shared by Detective Superintendent Uckfield who expressed it vehemently for the third time in an hour as Horton climbed the stairs behind him to the passenger lounge on the Wightlink car ferry. Horton said nothing. There was no point reiterating what he'd already said in Uckfield's office earlier about having no evidence to suggest that Yately's death was suspicious.

'He was wearing a dress, I call that highly bloody suspicious,' Uckfield had bellowed.

Horton didn't point out that it didn't necessarily follow that Yately had been killed. He'd told both Bliss and Uckfield that he hadn't had enough evidence to warrant posting a police officer outside the door to Yately's apartment and another outside the Victorian house for over twenty-four hours until they had the autopsy report, and that a piece of blue-and-white tape alone, saying 'Crime Scene Do Not Enter', was hardly going to deter anyone from entering the apartment if they wanted to.

Bliss didn't back him up. He hadn't expected her to. When he'd relayed Dr Clayton's findings to her, she'd accused him of gross incompetence, told him that he should have reported back to her as soon as the body had been found and that *she* should have made the decision. He didn't bother reminding her that he had mentioned the body, only she'd been too interested in Project

Neptune and his performance targets to listen. Even if she had listened he knew her decision wouldn't have been any different to his. She was covering her arse in case the investigation went tits up, and if it did then he knew who would carry the can. Him. So nothing new there. She finished her bollocking by telling him that his error of judgement could have seriously hindered the investigation. But Horton *was* irked that he'd made the wrong decision. Cantelli had told him that hindsight was a wonderful thing.

'That's no consolation to Hannah Yately if the delay means her father's killer goes free,' Horton had grumbled.

'Don't be so hard on yourself, Andy,' Cantelli had replied. 'I bet Bliss and Uckfield would have made the same decision.'

'Then I should have let them.' But that wasn't his way, and a few words of reprimand and threats weren't going to frighten him. What was done was done, but he wanted to be in on the investigation and discover who had tortured the poor man to death. It was also a matter of professional pride. He wasn't going to have this evil bastard of a killer laughing at him, because he'd cocked up, and he certainly wasn't going to have Uckfield's sidekick, DI Dennings, smirking at him when he returned from a course tomorrow. There was no love lost between him and Dennings, whom Dr Clayton had nicknamed Neanderthal man. He would wet his pants with glee at the thought Horton had made a balls-up.

Uckfield had insisted that he accompany him back to the Island and Yately's flat, because as Uckfield had said, 'You're the only bugger who's been in it and can tell us if anything's changed.' Horton wanted to look at it afresh in light of this macabre discovery. What had he missed last night? There had to be something that would provide some clue as to why someone had tortured and killed the former postman. He sincerely hoped the apartment was as he'd left it but he couldn't help having an uneasy feeling about those missing keys. And, as he had pointed out to Uckfield, he'd hardly searched Yately's flat, so wouldn't know for certain if something had been taken.

Bliss wasn't very happy about him being whisked away and neither was she pleased when Walters was pulled in to assist Sergeant Trueman in the major crime suite to dig up all the information they could on Colin Yately, while Cantelli and DC Marsden were detailed to break the news to Hannah Yately and to get further information on her father. They were also going to see if she recognized the dress. Horton didn't envy them having to tell Hannah that her father had been found wearing it. Cantelli was under strict instructions not to mention the restraints, as were they all. Uckfield had said, 'We keep that to ourselves. It's not to be released to the media and neither is the fact the victim was wearing a dress.'

As the ferry slipped out of dock, Horton bought coffee and sandwiches for himself and Uckfield, and found Uckfield at the far end of the ferry. Horton hadn't been surprised that Uckfield had wanted to view Yately's flat; he was hoping – just as Horton had been last night – that it might give him an insight into the man. Maybe in light of what Gaye Clayton had told him something new might spring to his mind, though he couldn't see what that could be.

SOCO had been despatched by an earlier ferry and Trueman had informed them that the local police had sealed off the flat and were starting a house-to-house with the photograph Horton had taken, and which Trueman had emailed to Sergeant Norris of the Isle of Wight CID who was leading the inquiry that end.

Biting into his sandwich, Uckfield said, 'Tell me again what you've got.'

For the third time Horton went through what had occurred. He knew that often on retelling people remembered something they'd overlooked the first and second time, but he wasn't people, he was a policeman, and nothing new had occurred to him.

Uckfield listened while eating and slurping his coffee, with a scowl on his careworn features. His mobile rang just as Horton had finished and clapping it to his ear Uckfield rose, with a 'Yes sir. On our way over now, sir,' before he stepped through the door on to the deck.

Horton rang SOCO. Taylor answered.

'We've only just entered the apartment, Inspector. It's too early to report anything,' Taylor replied slightly defensively in his usual nasal manner. But Horton heaved a silent sigh of relief that Taylor hadn't said it had been ransacked. Just to be sure, he asked if there were any signs of a disturbance. Taylor said not. That didn't mean the killer hadn't entered the flat using Yately's keys. And as Yately had been dead for at least five days then the killer had had ample time to go there before Horton had visited it last night. A point he'd made to Uckfield.

What kind of sadistic killer removed keys from a key fob and then neatly put the fob back in a pocket of the dress on a man he intended drowning, wondered Horton, drinking his coffee? The sick kind was the answer. But there had to be a reason.

Eager for action, he rang Sergeant Norris who also had nothing to report. Horton heard the unspoken 'give us a chance, we've only just started', and tried to curb both his irritation and impatience. He knew that Norris didn't like him and neither did the man's boss, DCI Birch, who was fortunately on leave. Horton had put Birch's nose out of joint a couple of times by resolving cases before the DCI. But Horton wasn't going to lose any sleep over it. He was rather glad though that the desiccated stick insect of a man was on leave. Uckfield was probably glad too because DCI Birch had nearly stitched Uckfield up on a recent case by threatening to tell the former chief constable, Uckfield's father-in-law, about an extramarital affair. Uckfield returned to his seat and judging by his scowling countenance his mood clearly hadn't improved.

'We're not getting any extra manpower. For Christ's sake, how am I supposed to run a murder investigation with three men and a dog?'

'Who's the dog?'

Uckfield glared at him. 'I told Wonder Boy this was a brutal, calculated murder and do you know what he said?'

Wonder Boy was the nickname given to Assistant Chief Constable Dean, who had been tipped for the post of chief constable only to find he'd been beaten by a late entrant and an outsider to boot. Horton was betting Dean was in seventh heaven because he could finally exert some power over a once favoured former chief constable's son-in-law who had previously ignored him. This was going to make for interesting times.

Horton dutifully took up the lead Uckfield had given him, 'What did he say?'

'"Do the best you can." Jesus, I'm not about to sit my ruddy A levels!'

'You told him that?'

Uckfield sniffed loudly. No, thought Horton, you simply said, 'yes, sir', not wanting to cock up your promotion chances.

Uckfield continued. 'I pointed out that it would be difficult to manage a major crime on the resources I have, but Dean said we've all got to pull together in the current climate with govern-ment cuts and straitened budgets. I'd like to put him in a sodding straitjacket. Dean's just echoing Meredew's corporate claptrap along with this useless government who think we can operate with a piece of string, a tin can and some cardboard cut-outs. Dean says he'll inform the chief and I'm to keep him fully briefed. Yeah, just so that he can ingratiate himself and claim all the credit, *if* we solve the case. Why should someone want to tie up and kill a former postman?' Uckfield said tearing into his sandwich.

It had been a question that had been reverberating around Horton's mind ever since Dr Clayton had broken the news to him. 'Absolutely no idea, unless he was heavily insured and hadn't changed his will, leaving everything to his ex-wife. She and a new boyfriend could have done it, although I'm not sure why they would torment the poor man first.'

'Because they're evil bastards.'

Horton had certainly met a few of them in his time.

With his mouth full, Uckfield said, 'Could it be the daughter and her boyfriend, hoping she'd inherit?'

'A poky, rented flat in the roof of a Victorian house? Hardly.' Horton said incredulously.

Uckfield sniffed. 'Perhaps he'd won the pools or lottery.'

'Then he would have *given* most of the money to his daughter.'

'You don't know that for certain.'

Horton narrowed his eyes.

'OK, so it's not the daughter,' Uckfield acquiesced, disgruntled, and gulped back his coffee. 'Why was he wearing a dress?'

'No idea, apart from the theories we've already discussed.' And Horton counted them off on his fingers. 'One: he could have been a cross-dresser and a lover killed him; two: he could have been at a party and someone took exception to his hobby of dressing up in women's clothes; three: the dress has some other significance, meaning it belonged to a woman Yately had at some time been involved with.'

'And hurt or even killed, and Yately's killer was set on revenge.'

Horton looked doubtful. 'Somehow I can't see Yately as a murderer.'

'We barely know the man,' Uckfield scoffed.

He was right.

Uckfield added, 'Let's hope the lab can get us something on the dress.'

'I think we'd have more success with a fashion expert.'

'Yeah, well you don't seem to have had much success so far.'

'I wasn't investigating a murder.'

'You should have been.'

He tensed. There was no need for Uckfield to keep rubbing his nose in it. 'Well, DI Dennings will be back tomorrow and no doubt he'll solve the case in five minutes flat,' Horton quipped.

Uckfield grunted and polished off his sandwiches. After a moment, Horton said, 'Are you still trying to get Dennings to transfer out of your team?' Uckfield had mentioned it in the past along with the suggestion that the job might be his.

'That's up to him,' Uckfield said, wiping his mouth with a large handkerchief.

'Is it?'

'Look, haven't I got enough to worry about with a major crime on my plate, a paranoid ACC and a beady-eyed DCI trying to waggle her slim arse on to my team and eventually take my place?'

It took a moment for Horton to realize Uckfield was referring to Bliss. 'You can't seriously believe Bliss is a threat?' he said, surprised. He'd also had no idea that Bliss had designs on the Major Crime Team. But there was still a DCI vacancy to fill, and maybe Bliss considered a Major Crime Team success would make her more visible in the promotion stakes.

'Dean likes her. And we all know why.' Uckfield sneered.

Horton raised his eyebrows in surprise. 'You think she's having an affair with him?'

'Wouldn't be surprised. She wouldn't be the first to drop her knickers to get to the top.'

That was a bit rich coming from a man who had slept around almost as many times as Rasputin. Horton didn't say so, though. That might be pushing his luck.

Uckfield added, 'She's probably already working out how she can get the new chief into bed.'

Maybe she wouldn't have to if Project Neptune was a success, thought Horton. But Bliss as DCI on the Major Crime Team was a terrifying prospect and meant he didn't want to be anywhere near it.

Uckfield fell into a moody silence that was punctuated by a telephone call from Trueman, who confirmed that Yately wasn't in debt and his GP said she hadn't seen him for five years, and then only because he'd had a touch of arthritis in his right foot. Yately had been a postman for twenty-two years, working out of Newport. He had an exemplary record, was rarely off sick and thoroughly reliable. A friendly man, but quiet, was the opinion of the manager. No scandal and no womanizing. Yately had taken early retirement three years ago aged fifty-five.

'And no mention that he liked to wear women's clothes,' added Uckfield grumpily.

As they were disembarking Horton's phone rang. It was Walters with the news that someone from Wrayton Lettings was on his way over to Yately's flat with a set of keys that would open the post box and a storage shed.

Walters added, 'Mr Wrayton asked why we wanted the keys and I had to tell him because he was blabbing on about warrants and all that crap. He wasn't best pleased.'

'About us not informing him?'

'No, about letting the flat to someone who managed to get himself killed. He said it lowers the tone of the area.'

Horton had been in the job long enough to believe that. Walters continued, 'Oh and he said could we officially confirm that Mr Yately *is* dead as soon as possible because he'd like to re-advertise the flat.'

'The caring type, then.'

'Yeah,' Walters sighed.

They made good time to Ventnor and Horton was relieved to see there was no sign of the press. There was also no sign of the stout Sergeant Norris, or his uniformed officers, except for one posted outside the front of the house, who told them the others were conducting their house-to-house enquiries and that WPC Skinner was waiting for them upstairs.

'Sounds promising,' Uckfield muttered.

Horton noted that the doors to the other apartments were closed, which surprised him. He'd have thought the nosy neigh- bour syndrome would have brought them out in their droves, or at least make them peek out, but then it was mid afternoon and they could all be at work, either that or Norris's officers were inside interviewing them.

They were about to head up the stairs when the officer outside hailed Horton. He found a spotty, slim young man of about twenty, dressed in a suit that looked about two sizes too big for him, with spiky gelled auburn hair, standing beside a small car emblazoned with the words, 'Wrayton's Lettings'.

'You the detective that wants the keys?' the young man said cheerfully.

Horton flashed his warrant card in response.

'Awesome. What's Mr Yately done? Drugs? Didn't seem the type.'

'Did you meet him?' Horton asked, finding he rather liked the youth.

'Yeah, showed him round the flat. Quiet type, shy, but then they're the ones you've got to watch. Dark secrets.'

'When did he move in?'

'Eighteen months ago. It was my first letting.'

'Has he ever been behind with his rent? Or complained about anything?'

'Never.'

Horton signed for the keys and returned to the hall to find an impatient Uckfield waiting by the post boxes. Horton opened Yately's to find the result disappointing.

'Junk mail,' said Uckfield with disgust, peering over Horton's shoulder.

There was nothing worth bagging up. Horton told Uckfield about the storage shed and they headed for it, at the rear of the building. Inside they found a bicycle with a padlock and chain, a pair of much used walking boots, a modern walking stick, an empty rucksack and some wet weather clothing. Horton recalled that the weather had been dry on Thursday so no need for Yately to wear his wet weather clothing if he'd gone walking, and the fact that his walking boots and rucksack were here indicated that he hadn't gone off hiking. They knew Yately didn't own a car so had he walked to meet his killer or taken public transport, or had his killer come here to collect him? He said as much to Uckfield as they climbed the stairs to Yately's flat.

'Let's hope the killer telephoned to make the appointment and we can get his number from the phone records,' Uckfield panted.

If only, thought Horton. 'One thing's for certain,' he said, 'Yately wouldn't have gone out wearing his shorts and vest. So wherever he went he undressed and put on that woman's dress, or his killer made him remove his clothes and put the dress on.'

'Yately could have been abducted from here during the night wearing his underwear.'

'If he was he went without a struggle.'

'How do you know that? The killer could have returned and tidied up the place. He has Yately's keys. For all we know this place could have been stashed to the rafters with gold bullion before you came here last night.'

Uckfield had a point, though Horton doubted the gold bullion bit. He smiled a greeting at Skinner, while Uckfield gave her the once over, and by the big man's leer it seemed he liked what he saw, which came as no surprise to Horton. Claire Skinner's pretty face flushed as Horton swept past her and he nodded a greeting at Beth Tremain, one of the SOCOs, who was in the bathroom. Then, following Uckfield into the small lounge, he found Taylor with his head up the chimney.

Uckfield said, 'Santa Claus isn't due for another eight months.'

'You'd be surprised what we find up chimneys,' Taylor rejoined, his voice muffled. Then, extracting himself, he said, 'You're right, nothing this time, not even a Christmas stocking. Plenty of prints in the room, though.'

'But not mine. I wore gloves.'

'Thoughtful of you,' muttered Uckfield.

Ignoring him, Horton scanned the room; his eyes fell on the narrow desk in front of the small window. Half a dozen steps took him swiftly to it. He registered the photograph frame minus the photograph of Yately and his daughter, which he'd removed, but stared down at the desk, puzzled; that wasn't the only thing that was missing.

To Taylor, he said, 'Where are the notes that were here?'

Taylor shook his head while Uckfield said, 'What notes?'

Horton tried to tell himself it was nothing. 'They were about the history of Ventnor.'

Uckfield looked bewildered. Horton didn't blame him. He was confused himself. Why would anyone be interested in them? And how could they have anything to do with the murder of Colin Yately? Simple answer: they couldn't.

'They were here last night,' he said.

'Can't see anyone killing a retired postman for that,' sniffed Uckfield, dismissively, echoing Horton's thoughts, but the notes *had* been there. He quickly tried to recall what he'd read, wishing now he'd paid more attention. There'd been something about Ventnor once being a hamlet of fishermen's cottages with an old mill. Why would someone take that?

Uckfield said, 'Anything else missing?'

Horton studied the desk and then surveyed the room. 'It doesn't look like it, not in here.'

He checked the kitchen. Everything was as he'd left it last night. He returned to the lobby and, with Uckfield and Taylor trailing him, made his way into the bedroom. Everything seemed the same as before: the bed, the chest with the books on it, the telescope. But something was different. Horton swiftly crossed to the telescope. Without touching it he peered into it.

'This is no time for stargazing,' Uckfield complained.

Straightening up, Horton said, 'It's been moved.'

'It wasn't me,' Taylor said quickly, 'or Beth.'

'Where was it facing when you looked through it before?'

Judging by Uckfield's tone Horton knew he didn't believe him.

'Ventnor Haven. The small harbour,' he added for the benefit of Taylor, who wasn't a sailor like him and Uckfield, although Uckfield owned a motor boat, not a sailing yacht. 'But I didn't focus it in.'

Uckfield said, 'You could have knocked it after looking through it.'

'I didn't touch it.'

'Maybe the cleaner did.'

Horton knew Uckfield was being facetious. He said, 'Whoever took the notes could also have adjusted the telescope and, as there is no sign of a forced entry, that suggests either the landlord's been in here with a master set of keys or he gave a set of keys to someone else, which I doubt, or Yately gave his keys to a friend, relative or neighbour, which would fit with why he removed them from the key ring; he didn't want to part with the picture of his daughter.'

'So you're saying the missing keys have nothing to do with Yately's murder.' Uckfield scratched his armpit.

'It's possible.'

'But why didn't this neighbour or friend collect the notes before today, when Yately's been dead since Thursday?'

It was a point that Horton had also been considering. And he had an answer. 'Perhaps whoever it is couldn't get here until late last night or this morning. They could have been away.'

'But—'

'Why did Yately give his keys to someone in the first place? He could have been planning to go on somewhere after meeting his daughter. Perhaps he intended being away for a few days.'

'With a lover?'

Horton shrugged. 'In between making these arrangements and meeting his daughter on Thursday, Yately met his killer.'

'Who was into bondage and women's clothes,' sniffed Uckfield. 'Sounds as though it could have been a sex game gone wrong or a jealous lover tied him up and drowned him.'

Perhaps, but Dr Clayton hadn't reported that Yately was homosexual.

Uckfield said, 'Could his daughter have come here after you?'

'No. She gave us her keys to her father's apartment and she didn't say she had two sets. Cantelli can check though.' Horton reached for his phone.

'Could have been the ex-wife,' Uckfield said.

'Why?'

'How the hell should I know? We'll ask her. Get her address from Cantelli.'

'We need to make sure the landlord hasn't lost a set of keys or given out a set to someone.'

Uckfield retrieved his phone from the pocket of his camel coat as he stomped out of the bedroom.

'How's Hannah Yately taking it?' Horton asked when Cantelli came on the line.

'She's upset and bewildered, as you'd expect, and she claims she's never seen the dress. I told her it was found *with* her father, not *on* him. I didn't have the heart to break that news to her. She'll find out soon enough. Her boyfriend is with her. I'm sure neither of them is involved with Yately's death.'

Horton briefed him about what they'd found in the flat. Cantelli said that neither Hannah nor her boyfriend, Damien, had gone out last night or this morning. They'd been anxiously awaiting any news. Horton said, 'Have you got Mrs Yately's address? Uckfield wants to interview her.'

Cantelli relayed it.

Uckfield was in the hall outside the flat on the phone when Horton returned to the small lounge. He asked Taylor if he'd found an address book. It might give them a list of Yately's friends, but Taylor shook his head. Horton searched but he didn't find one and neither did he find any scraps of paper with friends' names or telephone numbers scrawled on it. There were also no old Christmas or birthday cards stashed away. Along with the bank statements he'd seen yesterday he found some utility bills, paid, and the top copy of the last two telephone bills, but no record of the calls made. Trueman would request those. The paperwork would be bagged up and taken back to the major incident suite.

Horton then called Sergeant Norris and explained about the keys.

'No one's said anything about having keys to Yately's apartment but we'll check.'

Uckfield returned.

'Let's talk to the ex-wife and hope she's not the hysterical kind.'

From what Hannah Yately had said Horton very much doubted it.

SEVEN

'I know why you're here.' Margaret Yately gestured them into seats in the untidy cramped lounge of the narrow house in the narrow terraced street in Newport.

Horton pushed aside a blouse, skirt and a pile of cheap

magazines before easing himself into a chair that was so worn he thought he was going to end up sitting on the floor. The room stank of cigarette smoke, stale perfume, fried food and alcohol. Horton pulled his body to the edge of the seat, as Uckfield, ignoring the clothes, plonked himself squarely on top of them, stretched out his short legs and eyed Margaret Yately coldly. In front of them, high on the wall above a dusty and grimy fireplace, were the flickering images of repeats of a detective drama on a large plasma screen television that wouldn't have been out of place in a small cinema. The thought reminded Horton of Russell Glenn's superyacht and the forthcoming charity auction, which he might now be in danger of missing, *if* he was to continue working on the case and *if* it was still unresolved by Friday.

Margaret Yately reached for a packet of cigarettes from the mantelpiece with nicotine-stained fingers and long fingernails that looked painful rather than attractive. Horton swiftly took in the tall woman. She was in her mid fifties with scraggy bleached blonde hair, fashionably dressed in tight jeans, tucked into calf-high boots, with a low-cut off-the-shoulder T-shirt displaying black bra straps and a tattoo of a butterfly on one shoulder and a cat on the other. All this was squeezed on to a figure with rolls of fat around the hips and midriff. The sand had run out of this hourglass long ago.

'Hannah called me to tell me Colin was dead. She says he was murdered. I can't think why. He had no money.' Margaret Yately shook a cigarette from the packet and perched it on her pink-lipsticked mouth. Grabbing a cheap plastic lighter from the mantelpiece she flicked it on her cigarette and, still with it perched in her mouth, added, 'It *was* his body I suppose, the police do sometimes get it wrong.'

'When did you last see your husband, Mrs Yately?' Horton asked crisply. There didn't seem any point in wasting sympathy on her. He held her gaze.

'Ex-husband,' she said pointedly, jerking her head upwards to exhale. 'Last year, October. He was in town, shopping. He begged me to have him back. I said no way. I gave up my youth for him; I wasn't going to give up what I'd got left of my life.'

Horton didn't believe the bit about Colin begging her to take him back. That was just her vanity speaking. Admittedly his views were coloured by what Hannah Yately had told him but he was more inclined to believe daughter than mother. He wasn't sure he could believe her alleged last sighting of her husband either, though he couldn't see that she had any reason to lie about that. There was no evidence in this room of another man being on the scene, but that didn't mean there wasn't one. Or a few, come to that.

Uckfield said, 'Did you know where he was living?'

'Yes, why?'

'Did you visit him there?' asked Horton.

She widened her eyes, 'You must be kidding! Why should I want to do that?'

'Is this your marital home?' asked Uckfield.

'What's that got to do with Colin's death?' she said defensively, glaring at him, then a malicious glint crossed her face. 'Oh, I see, you think I've shacked up with a man and jealous of Colin he's gone out and killed the poor sod. Well you're wrong.' She picked some tobacco from her yellow teeth. 'The house was sold when Colin and I split up and we shared the proceeds. Not that there was much, him only being a postman. I rent this house and live alone, and Colin rented his flat.'

And Horton reckoned she spent most of her money on clothes, booze, fags and a good time. Not that that was any of his business, but he wasn't going to pussyfoot around being gentle with her, because clearly she didn't need it.

'Did Colin have any life insurance?'

'No idea.'

'Did he have a will?'

'How should I know?'

'You *were* married to him.'

'*Were*, yes. The only life insurance he had then was to cover the mortgage if he snuffed it before it was paid up. And he didn't have a will then.'

'Do you work?' asked Uckfield.

Her head snapped round. She bristled. 'Why do you want to know that?' Neither Horton nor Uckfield answered, forcing her to add angrily, 'Instead of badgering me with pointless questions you should be out there looking for his killer.'

'We are,' Uckfield said evenly.

She snatched a drag at her cigarette and irritably puffed out the smoke before answering with a scowl. 'I work in a pub on the River Medina, waitressing and bar work. It gives me a social life. I could have done better but I had Hannah to bring up and working with a child is not always easy, especially when you've got no relatives to take care of it and no money to put it in a nursery. Colin used to finish work early, being a postman, unless he was doing overtime, so when he came home, I'd go to work; pub hours suited me. And I like the company. All right?' She glared at them.

Horton said, 'Can you give us the names of any of Colin's friends?'

'There weren't any.'

Horton raised his eyebrows, forcing her to add, 'He was always a loner. No conversation, quiet, dull, while I'm the opposite. We were never suited but we stuck together for Hannah, well you do when you've got kids.'

'What were his hobbies, interests?'

'He didn't have any, not unless you mean doing crosswords and reading books.' Which, by her tone, she clearly considered unworthy pastimes.

Horton recalled the books on the chest in Yately's flat on naval ships and local history, which fitted with the notes and the telescope.

She made an elaborate show of consulting her watch.

'Working tonight?' Horton asked, studying the clock on the mantelpiece. It was three forty-five.

'I phoned in, told them about Colin. They said not to come in.'

Horton could see she wished she had gone to work now. 'Do you have any photographs of your former husband?'

'Hannah says you've got one,' she replied sulkily.

'Yes, but it might be helpful to look through photograph albums.' Horton was wondering if it might show them the dress Colin had been found wearing.

She scowled, clearly irritated. 'Colin took most of them.'

'Then you do have some.'

'I don't know how that can help you.'

'Perhaps you could get them,' Uckfield insisted.

'I don't know where they are,' she exhaled in exasperation.

In dangerous silky tones Uckfield said, '*If* you could look them out and call us when you've found them that would be very helpful.' He handed across his card.

Her brow furrowed, then she shrugged as if to say please yourself and snatched the card from him. Horton didn't think they'd get any sight of her photograph albums. Uckfield's phone rang and he ducked out of the lounge to answer it. A few seconds later Horton heard the outside door open. Clearly Uckfield didn't want Margaret Yately earwigging the conversation. He said, 'Did Colin own a laptop computer when you lived together?' She eyed him as if he'd just asked if her ex-husband had indulged in naked limbo dancing.

'He wouldn't even have a mobile phone and I had to throw the television on the tip before he'd buy a new one.'

That confirmed what Hannah Yately had said. Now for the tricky bit. Rising, and extracting a photograph of the dress from his pocket, Horton said, 'Do you recognize this dress?'

She stared at it, puzzled, and then at Horton. 'No. Why?'

'It's not yours?'

'I wouldn't be seen dead in that,' she declared. 'It's very old-fashioned.'

'It might be something you wore years ago.'

'I don't think so,' she scoffed, stubbing out her cigarette with vigour as her lips curled in a sneer. 'What's it got to do with Colin's death?'

Horton was reluctant to tell her, not because he thought she'd be shocked or upset, but because he could already anticipate her ridicule and he thought she was the type to blab, maybe even tell the national media. He hoped the shame of once being married to someone found dead wearing a woman's dress might stop her but he doubted it. He could see her playing the role of poor deceived wife. But Cantelli had given him the lead. He said, 'We found it with your former husband.'

'What was he doing with that?'

'We wondered if you might tell us.'

'No bloody idea.'

'It wasn't his mother's dress?'

'She's been dead years and her stuff went to the charity shop.'

There was obviously nothing she could tell them about the dress. Recalling the notes on Yately's desk, he said, 'Did Colin ever express an interest in local history?'

'He liked watching that history channel on television.'

That wasn't the quite the same thing but it was a link never-theless, and when you had nothing to go with a link was grabbed like a lifebelt. 'What about an interest in Ventnor?' he asked as Uckfield returned. Then Horton remembered something else he read, 'Or the caves and chines on the Island.'

She eyed him as if he was two sheets to the wind. That was a 'no' then. He caught Uckfield's glance, which said this was a waste of time, and he agreed. Horton politely thanked her for her help, wondering if she'd sense his sarcasm, but all he saw was relief in her bloodshot eyes. At the door he asked her if she had keys to her husband's apartment.

'Why would I want them?' she answered, incredulous.

Horton expressed his sincere condolences at her loss despite the fact they were no longer married, which seemed to cause her no embarrassment. He told her that they'd liaise closely with her daughter.

'Then she can tell me *if* you ever catch who killed Colin.' And with that the door closed on them.

Horton climbed into the car, noticing a twitch of net curtain opposite.

Uckfield said, 'That was Trueman on the phone. The landlord says he's not been in Yately's apartment and the second set of keys hasn't left his office.'

So they could rule out the landlord and daughter.

Uckfield said, 'Yately was well shot of her. Think she killed him?'

'Why?'

'Maybe she got fed up with him pestering her to take him back.'

'*If* you believe that. It's not much of a motive though.'

'It could be enough for a new boyfriend.'

Horton considered that. 'I think she was telling the truth when she said she didn't have a key to his apartment but we should still check her out, chat to the staff at the pub where she works, and ask the neighbours if there's a new man on the horizon.'

'No need, looks as though he's just arrived.'

A saloon car passed them and pulled up outside her house. Horton watched a man in his mid forties climb out. He was wearing a dark overcoat but as he turned on the doorstep Horton noticed the smart suit beneath it and the slightly furtive expression on his round face before he stepped inside. Something nudged at Horton's memory, and with a shock he realized it was connected with his mother. What was it about the man he'd just seen that had triggered it? His size, his appearance? His manner? Or all three.

'Married,' declared Uckfield. 'God knows what he sees in her.'

Was that it, Horton thought, as Uckfield turned the car back towards Ventnor. Had married men come calling on his mother? Not in the flat they hadn't, except for one man, and Horton had discovered who he was, and he was now dead. But they'd lived in a little terraced house before they'd moved to the council flat and he remembered it clearly, sitting in a row of similar houses in a crowded area of Portsmouth. There *had* been men, and he now recalled raised voices on one occasion, and he'd been sent out to play. How old had he been? Seven or eight? Younger? He couldn't say. He needed to check where they had lived. The census information would give him that.

'I'll ring in the car registration number,' he said, reaching for his phone. Trueman would trace the owner and they'd ask him whether or not he knew Colin Yately and when he'd last seen him. He hadn't looked as though he'd kill Yately out of jealousy or for money, but who could tell?

After he hung up, he told Uckfield what Margaret Yately had said about the dress.

'Trueman's sending it over to the university as soon as the lab has finished with it, which should be tomorrow. What was that stuff about caves and chines I heard you ask her?'

'Just something I read in those notes.'

Uckfield's phone rang. Horton leant over and put the call on speaker. It was Sergeant Norris and he sounded excited. 'We've got a witness who saw a man entering and leaving Yately's flat early this morning at about nine thirty-five. We've got a good description of him, about five-eleven, slim, grey-haired, in his early sixties, and what's more we've got a name. The neighbour got the car registration and we've traced it to an Arthur Lisle. He lives in Bonchurch. He was carrying a briefcase.'

Uckfield bellowed, 'Do nothing. We'll be there in ten minutes.'

Ambitious, thought Horton, though by the way Uckfield was driving maybe not.

EIGHT

Norris dashed through the rain and slid his fat backside into the rear of Uckfield's BMW, his trousers squeaking on the leather upholstery, his balding round florid face glistening from the rain and exertion. They were parked in a winding, tree-lined road of elegant Victorian terraced houses. The heavy rain and trees made it prematurely dark prompting lights to shine from several of the rooms, allowing a glimpse inside of subdued suburban life, but there was no light at Lisle's house.

'He's clean, no previous,' panted Norris. 'He doesn't seem to be in and his car isn't here, although he could keep it in a garage somewhere. It's a 1961 Morris Minor convertible, burgundy with a cream hood and cream leather interior. The man who saw Lisle – Grant Millbeck – lives in flat six, he was just off to work when he saw this man entering—'

'With a key?' Horton interjected.

'Well he didn't ring the front doorbell so he must have had one,' Norris tossed caustically at Horton, before turning his attention back to Uckfield. 'Then Millbeck saw the same man leaving and he was carrying a briefcase.'

'Why did Millbeck hang around waiting for Lisle to come out?' asked Horton suspiciously.

'He didn't. He'd forgotten his lunch box and went back to his apartment to collect it. He was just locking up when Lisle came down the stairs from apartment seven. Millbeck claims that Lisle didn't seem or look nervous. He smiled and said "good morning". Millbeck's seen the Morris at the apartment block a couple of times, and admired it, and he remembered the registration number because

it was unusual, MOG 61, so he wasn't worried about Lisle being
there.'

Horton addressed Uckfield, 'Lisle could be the friend Yately
gave his keys to. He probably removed the notes from the apartment with Yately's prior permission. He doesn't sound like our
killer.'

'You never can tell,' Uckfield said optimistically, adding to
Norris, 'Call up the nearest patrol car.'

'Just arriving, sir.'

Horton swivelled in his seat to see the police vehicle pulling
in behind them. There were no blue lights or sirens but he fancied
more curtains would be twitched in Grove Way.

Climbing out, Uckfield said, 'We'll start by being polite and
knock.'

Horton obliged, rapping loudly on the front door and then
pressing and keeping his finger on the bell to the right of it, but
all was silent. He stooped down and peered through the letterbox.
'No signs of life,' he said straightening up. Addressing Norris
he asked, 'Is there a rear entrance?'

'No.'

That made things easier. Uckfield stepped back and nodded
at the uniformed officer with the ramrod. Looking at the rather
flimsy front door Horton didn't think it would take much to break
it in and he was right. A couple of minutes later he was stepping
inside the hall straining his ears for sound. Only the solemn
ticking of a clock coming from the room to his left greeted him.
Arthur Lisle clearly wasn't here or if he was he was dead or
unconscious, and there was no reason why he should be either
of the latter. But it was the excuse Uckfield would give for
entering the house without permission and without a search
warrant.

Swiftly Horton took in the worn pale-blue carpet that looked
as though it had once been of good quality, the wooden balus-
trade, picture rails and architrave ceiling, before turning to see
that a small audience was gathering at the front of the house in
the pouring rain. He instructed the uniformed officers to get what
information they could on Lisle and his movements, while
Uckfield crossed to a telephone on a walnut table under the stairs
and with latex-covered fingers lifted the receiver. 'No answer

machine,' he said, punching in the number to get the last call. 'Number withheld.' He nodded Norris upstairs. To Horton he said, 'I'll take the kitchen, you do the lounge.'

Horton stepped inside the room on his left. Everything looked in place. It was neat and tidy if a little outdated and worn. There was a television in the corner by the bay window and a hi-fi system opposite it, both several years old. On the mantelpiece was the clock, which Horton had heard on first entering the house, and alongside it several family photographs and a picture of Lisle beside the Morris Minor which Norris had described to them. It looked in good condition and wouldn't be difficult to spot; classic cars like it were few and far between these days.

Horton studied the photographs. Arthur Lisle looked to be a happily married family man, lean and tall with brown hair turning to grey as the photographs showed him through the passage of the years. In every one he was smiling. In some he was accompanied by young children and a pretty, dark-haired woman. And he was also with the same woman dressed in walking clothes against the backdrop of some mountains, which, to Horton, looked like the Brecon Beacons in Wales. Other photographs were of two couples in their thirties accompanied by babies and toddlers. The Lisle family through the ages, he guessed. Not only did Arthur Lisle not sound like their killer, he didn't look like one either, although Horton knew that was a very dangerous and foolish assumption for a police officer to make. Yately had seemed an ordinary man but had ended up being brutally murdered. Why?

He reconsidered the third theory he'd expressed to Uckfield, that the dress found on Yately could have belonged to a woman Yately had been involved with. Was that woman connected with Arthur Lisle, Horton wondered, studying the photograph of the dark-haired woman? Had Lisle entered Yately's flat and taken those notes because they contained a reference to it? But if Lisle had killed Yately and taken the keys off him, why leave the photograph of Hannah Yately behind and why wait until now to visit Yately's apartment when he could have done so any time since Thursday? And why chance being spotted and recognized? No, Lisle had to be a friend and his visit to Yately's flat innocent.

He wondered where the Lisle family were now, especially Mrs

Lisle. There was no evidence of her in this room, no female magazines, no sewing or knitting, but maybe Lisle liked it that way. Perhaps he was a tyrant, despite the photographs. Some of the vilest bullies Horton had known had looked and behaved to the outside world like pillars of virtue.

He stepped along the hall and into a middle room. He could hear Uckfield opening and closing doors and drawers in the kitchen and Norris's heavy footsteps overhead. No one had shouted out to say they'd found either Mrs Lisle or her husband, so where were they? wondered Horton, surveying the old-fashioned dining room, which looked as though its current use was as an office. Would they return horrified and angry to find the police in their house?

Uckfield joined him. 'There's food in the cupboards and fridge so he wasn't planning on leaving.'

Horton's eyes ran over the mahogany table and chairs in the centre of the room, the sideboard opposite the fireplace, the books scattered on the table and on the bookshelves either side of the hearth, before coming back to the table. 'Where's the computer?' He pointed to a cable and charger that led to an electric socket.

'Perhaps he's taken it to night classes or is with friends,' suggested Uckfield.

Horton crossed the room and picked up one of the books. It was on local history and some of the others were on ships, including naval, merchant and passenger. Clearly Lisle and Yately shared the same interests. He glanced out of the narrow window to his right. It was still raining heavily.

'There's a shed at the bottom of the garden,' he said as Norris entered.

'No sign that Lisle was intending to leave. His passport's here.' Norris handed it to Uckfield. Horton looked over the Super's shoulder. It was the same man as in the photographs on the mantelpiece. There were a few stamps in it to show that Lisle had travelled abroad but nothing for the last six years.

'Any women's clothing?' asked Horton.

'None, but there's a photograph of a dark-haired woman beside his bed.'

Not divorced then, thought Horton, because if Lisle had been, that, along with some of the photographs on the mantelpiece, would have been consigned to the bin. Widowed? Possibly.

Peering into the garden Uckfield said, 'Check the shed, Sergeant.'

Norris made no protest but Horton could tell by his expression he wasn't best pleased at being sent out in the rain. Uckfield made to reach for his phone when a woman's voice, raised in anger, reached them from the front of the house. Uckfield threw Horton a questioning glance as they stepped into the passageway.

'What the devil is going on?' she demanded, glaring at both of them in turn, her round face flushed, her dark eyes smouldering with fury. 'What gives you the right to barge in here like this? Where's my father?'

'That's what we'd like to know,' muttered Uckfield, before stepping forward, flashing his warrant card and introducing himself and Horton. 'And you are?'

'Rachel Salter,' she snapped.

Horton had already recognized her from the photographs on the mantelpiece.

'What's happened?' she again demanded, but this time more warily. Then her face paled. 'Dad's had an accident.'

'Shall we go inside, Mrs Salter.' Uckfield stood solidly in front of her, stretching an arm towards the lounge so that she had no option but to enter it.

She went under protest and Horton could see she was torn between anger and fear.

'I think you'd better sit down,' Uckfield began, but that only made her stand more squarely in the middle of the room.

'Tell me, what's happened? He's not—'

'We believe your father can help us with our inquiry into the death of Colin Yately,' Uckfield quickly interjected.

Horton could see that the name meant nothing to her. She stared at Uckfield with a mixture of bewilderment and subdued anger.

Uckfield continued. 'Colin Yately's body was found in the Solent yesterday morning and your father was seen entering his apartment this morning. Do you know if he and your father were acquainted?'

'Obviously they must have been,' she said tartly. 'What's this man's death got to do with my father? Where is he?' Her eyes scanned the room as though he might be hiding somewhere. It was an instinctive gesture, Horton knew.

He said, 'When did you last see your father?'

She swivelled hot angry eyes on him, but the fury was there to mask her concern.

'Last Tuesday, why?'

'Have you spoken to him since?'

'No.'

'He didn't call you to say he wouldn't be in?' It was a silly question but he had a reason for asking it

'Of course not. If he had I wouldn't be here, would I?'

She eyed him as though he was thick and with a slightly superior manner, but Horton thought it was the truth.

She added, 'I come here every Tuesday before my evening class and have a cup of tea and a chat with Dad. My husband, Paul, takes our two girls to Brownies, then picks them up again and puts them to bed. Look, this is ridiculous; Dad's probably just popped out somewhere.'

Uckfield said, 'On the only day of the week you visit him? Surely he'd wait in for his daughter.'

'Maybe he's run out of tea bags,' she snapped, eyeing Uckfield malevolently.

'He hasn't,' answered Uckfield.

'You've searched the house!' she cried indignantly. 'I hope you've got a warrant because you shouldn't be in here without one.'

Smoothly Horton said, 'We were concerned for your father and had to take the decision to enter.'

'Concerned? Why should you be concerned?' she said mystified.

Uckfield gave it to her bluntly. 'Colin Yately's death is suspicious. Your father could be in danger.'

She almost laughed. A smile played at the corners of a generous and petulant mouth, before her forehead creased in a worried frown. 'My father's a retired solicitor and a widower. He can't possibly be in danger. And I've never heard him speak about this man, Yately.'

Evenly, Horton said, 'How long has your father been widowed?'

'Eighteen months, why?'

He'd been right about that then. But if Yately had been involved with Mrs Lisle then it was some time ago, making it more unlikely that Lisle had sought revenge, unless of course he'd only just discovered the affair. He asked her if she knew what her father's hobbies were and got much the same reaction as when he'd asked the question of Hannah and Margaret Yately, a blank stare. Again he had to prompt. 'What does your father do in his spare time?'

'He does the *Telegraph* crossword, the housework, shopping, gardening, reads.'

'Nothing else?'

'He *is* retired,' she emphasized as though Horton was an idiot.

He felt like saying that doesn't mean he's practically dead, or living such a dreary life he might just as well be. Instead he said, 'That usually means time to take up new interests.'

She looked surprised, as though her father couldn't possibly want anything more than to wait in every Tuesday evening for his daughter to condescend to have a cup of tea with him. It probably wasn't really like that, but he felt as though it was. Lisle's daughter was older than Hannah Yately, by about ten years, but her attitude towards her father was similar to Hannah's.

'Dad nursed Mum for three years,' she said defensively. 'Since she died he's found it hard to adjust.'

Yeah, and I bet you haven't asked him about that. 'I'm sorry,' he said gently, sensing Uckfield's impatience beside him and willing him not to charge in. 'What was your mother's illness?'

'MS,' she replied tautly and with a finality that said the subject was not open to discussion. And that put any possible affair Yately might have had with Lisle's wife even further back in time. It was looking more unlikely as a possible motive for Yately's death with Lisle as the killer.

'Was your father away over the weekend?'

'Not that I know of,' she answered, surprised.

So if Lisle had been given Yately's keys then why had he waited until this morning to visit the flat and pick up the notes? But perhaps Lisle *had* been away and hadn't bothered telling his daughter.

Norris slipped back into the room with a slight shake of his head. *Nothing in the shed then.* Horton thought of how Yately's body had been found, in the sea, and said, 'Does your father have a boat?'

She looked startled by the question. 'Yes. But he hasn't been out on it for ages.'

Uckfield looked as if he was about to say, 'That's what you think,' when Horton quickly interjected. 'What kind of boat?'

'A Cornish Crabber.'

And Horton knew that was a small day sailing boat, and one that could easily have been used to dump Yately's body. 'Where does he keep it?'

'Down in the bay by the slipway. It's on a trailer . . .' Then her dark eyes widened and Horton thought she'd made the leap between his question and Yately being found in the sea. He expected outrage but instead he saw genuine fear for the first time since she'd entered the house. 'You don't think Dad's gone out on it? Not in this weather?'

Uckfield said, 'We'll check. What's the boat called?'

'*Abigail*. It was my mother's name.'

Horton saw her eyes flick to the photographs on the mantel-piece, as Uckfield nodded at Norris, who then slipped out of the lounge. He'd despatch someone to check, but Victor Hazleton's tales of a light at sea again flashed into Horton's mind. Could Arthur Lisle have been out on his small sailing boat on Wednesday night killing Colin Yately? But even if he had been he hadn't dumped the body in the Solent then. For now he pushed the thought to one side and said, 'Your father owns a computer; do you know what kind?'

'Isn't it in the dining room?' she answered distractedly. 'It's a laptop; Dad must have taken it with him.' She crossed to the fireplace and seemed to be studying the photographs before she spun round and with a defiant stare, exclaimed, 'This is silly. There must be a perfectly logical explanation for all this.'

And maybe there was, thought Horton. 'Would your father have sent you an email perhaps to say he'd gone away for a few days?' he asked.

'He didn't.'

Uckfield this time. 'Does he have a mobile phone?'

'Yes. Oh, I haven't called him.' Alarmed, she reached for her mobile but Uckfield forestalled her.

'Could you give us his number? We'll try.'

She looked as though she was about to refuse then stiffly relayed it. Uckfield stepped outside to call it.

Looking anxious, she addressed Horton, 'Dad doesn't text. He says he can't be bothered and he hardly ever uses his mobile. Paul, my husband, insisted on him having one just in case he broke down in that old car of his. Perhaps that's what's happened,' she added hopefully, eyeing Horton as though willing him to say it must be so.

It was possible but he wasn't going to commit himself. He wondered if Norris had put out a call for it. The sergeant hadn't mentioned it but that didn't mean to say he hadn't.

'What does your husband do for a living?' he asked, partly to distract her and partly because he was curious.

'He's a builder.' She glanced impatiently towards the door awaiting Uckfield's return.

'Have you any idea what your father uses the computer for?'

She looked bewildered. Clearly Arthur Lisle's life was as much a mystery to Rachel Salter as Colin Yately's was to Hannah. Perhaps the son-in-law, Paul, knew more about his father-in-law's life and interests, thought Horton.

Uckfield returned looking glum. 'There's no answer, Mrs Salter. We'll keep trying. Perhaps you'd call your husband and ask if he's heard from your father.'

Glad to be doing something she quickly rang him. Horton listened to her side of the conversation, which was terse. The answer was obviously no, but before she could ring off, Horton interjected, 'Ask him when he last spoke to your father either by telephone or face to face.'

She obliged. Then she said, 'I'll call you back later. No, I can't explain now.' And she rang off.

'Paul hasn't spoken to Dad for about two weeks, but last week he saw him walking into Ventnor and waved and called "hello" from the van. He could have had an accident in that old wreck of a car. He might be in the hospital or lying injured somewhere.'

'We'll check the hospital,' Horton answered. There was only one on the Island so that wouldn't take long, but perhaps Arthur Lisle wasn't lying injured; he could be visiting someone and

have simply forgotten all about his daughter's usual visit. He
could have got his days muddled up.

'Is your father in good health?'

'Yes, excellent, why?' she asked antagonistically. Then quickly
following his drift, added, 'You think he might be confused, well
I can tell you Dad's mind is as sharp as a razor, and he wasn't
depressed either.'

Horton didn't pursue it. He didn't think Lisle had committed
suicide; why should he? *Unless, he'd killed Colin Yately*. He said,
'Does your father keep his car in a garage?'

'Yes. He rents one. It's the middle one in a block of three
along the road just before the footpath that leads down to the
bay.'

She made no further comment, obviously assuming her father
had gone out in his car. Horton interpreted Uckfield's look to
keep silent.

'If he gets in touch, please let us know immediately.' Uckfield
handed her his card. 'Or call the local police. We'll make sure
the front door is secured and then repaired, and we'll put an
officer outside the house and call you the moment we have any
news. Meanwhile, if you, or your husband, remember anything
about where he might have gone, please let us know.'

She protested that they were making an unnecessary fuss.
Horton toyed with the idea that she might be right but he said
nothing and neither did Uckfield. At the door Horton asked if
her father liked hiking.

'He used to with Mum, but he hasn't been for years.'

Horton had the feeling she wouldn't have known if he had
taken it up again and perhaps with Colin Yately. He took down
her address which, after she'd left, Norris confirmed was only a
few streets away. Horton thought it a little unusual that although
she lived close by she seemed to visit her father rarely and know
so little about him. But perhaps Arthur Lisle liked it that way.
Perhaps it was all Rachel Salter could do to bring herself to visit
him once a week because she disliked her father or was afraid
of him. Horton hadn't got that impression but then Rachel Salter
could be putting on a good front. They hadn't asked her about
Lisle's personality, because there was no need to at this stage,
and they hadn't asked her about the dress found on Yately's body.

They watched her climb into a new Land Rover and drive away. He was glad she hadn't insisted on accompanying them to the garage.

Raising his collar against the rain, Uckfield said, 'Lisle's mobile's completely dead. It didn't ring as I told the daughter, she'll discover that soon enough, which means he's ditched it.'

'Or it's been damaged in an accident,' suggested Horton.

Norris was hurrying towards them. 'The boat's still in the bay. Do you want it taken away for forensic examination?'

Uckfield said, 'Put a tarpaulin over it for now.'

Norris nodded and added, 'The old lady opposite says Lisle has been at a loss since his wife died eighteen months ago, but that he seemed a lot brighter of late. She saw him leave the house this morning at about nine fifteen. She hasn't seen him return but then she has been out. An officer showed her Yately's photograph but she claims she hasn't seen him. She says that she doesn't think Lisle has had any visitors since his wife died, except his daughter who comes every Tuesday evening. There's a son who lives in Singapore.'

And Lisle hadn't left for Singapore because he would have needed his passport. Horton wondered why the Salters didn't bring their children to visit of a weekend or in the holidays. And why Rachel hadn't mentioned her brother. Perhaps they simply weren't a close-knit family.

To Uckfield, Horton said, 'There's no evidence to suggest Lisle has anything to do with Yately's death. His phone could be broken and he could have forgotten his daughter comes on Tuesday, or perhaps he emailed her and she simply hasn't read her messages.'

'Well *I'm* not taking any chances. He's slipped through our fingers once, he's not going to do so again.'

Horton took Uckfield's barbed comment in silence.

Uckfield addressed Norris. 'We need Lisle's movements from last Wednesday evening through to this morning. Check specifically if anyone saw him over the weekend. I'd like to know why he didn't collect Yately's notes before today.' Norris made to leave when Uckfield forestalled him. 'Before you do, let's take a look in this garage. Bring the bolt cutters.'

The garage was a short distance down the road. As they headed for it Horton silently speculated on what they might discover.

He saw no reason to suggest that Lisle could have taken his own life, unless he *had* killed Colin Yately and, filled with remorse, he'd decided he couldn't live with the guilt. If that were so then would Lisle be slumped in his car with a hose pipe running from the exhaust, clutching his laptop computer?

The padlock was secure and there was no sign or smell of exhaust fumes. So it was unlikely they would find Lisle inside, but Horton's heart quickened a little as the padlock snapped and he lifted the handle and pulled up the garage door. There was no car, and no sign of Lisle, just some old tools, ladders, a bicycle and nothing more.

Addressing Norris, Uckfield said, 'Check the hospital in case Lisle's had an accident. Seal off the house and keep a patrol car here tonight, Sergeant. If Lisle doesn't show up we'll put out an all-ports alert for him tomorrow morning. Circulate details of his car. Also check with the ferry companies that he hasn't left the Island. And you'd better check if he caught any of the ferries over the weekend. Call me the moment you get anything. If he hasn't shown by tomorrow morning, widen the area asking for any sightings of him and we'll get a team into Yately's neighbourhood, though God knows where I'm going to get the officers from,' Uckfield added under his breath, before moving off and turning to Horton. 'Sergeant Trueman will get a search warrant for the house and I'll send DI Dennings over with DC Marsden to supervise it and handle things this end. Meanwhile, Trueman continues digging on Yately's background and I'll see if Wonder Boy will condescend to give me more officers.'

On the ferry Horton called Taylor for an update while Uckfield went up on deck to make his calls. Taylor reported that nothing surprising had been discovered in Yately's flat: no blood, no bits of skin or bone. And his findings confirmed that Yately hadn't been killed there. Horton hoped the analysis of Yately's skin taken from the body by Dr Clayton might reveal something about where he had been killed, though he wasn't overly optimistic.

Uckfield threw himself in the seat opposite Horton. He didn't need to be a mind reader to know the results of the Super's call. He could see by Uckfield's dark countenance that his plea for more staff had again fallen on deaf ears.

'I work with what I've got, which doesn't include you and

CID,' Uckfield growled. 'Dean says you're needed to make sure Russell Glenn's visit here on his superyacht goes without a hitch. Who the bloody hell *is* he?'

'A billionaire.'

'Oh, well that's all right then, knocks poor old postie Colin Yately into a cocked hat,' Uckfield replied with bitter sarcasm.

Horton agreed with the big man's sentiments. Protecting property and the wealthy always got top priority, and when they were combined there was no contest.

Gruffly, Uckfield added that Trueman had confirmed that the man they'd seen visiting Margaret Yately was Phillip Gunville. No form.

'What's his occupation?' asked Horton.

'No idea. Does it matter?'

'Probably not.'

Horton stayed long enough at the station to check the messages on his desk for any that were urgent. None were, although others might disagree. He didn't bother to check his emails to see what Bliss might have sent him. Collecting his jacket and helmet he headed for Oyster Quays for something to eat, telling himself that he could have gone somewhere else for food or back to his boat, knowing he was half hoping to bump into or see Avril Glenn on the deck of her floating palace.

He parked in a side street near the Isle of Wight ferry terminal and walked through to Oyster Quays, heading in the direction of an Indian restaurant he knew well, while turning over in his mind the facts of Colin Yately's death, including the manner and timing of it, the dress he'd been wearing, and the significance of Lisle's visit to Yately's flat and his subsequent vanishing act. The rain had stopped, leaving behind a still, chilly evening. Would Lisle show up bewildered about the fuss over his dead friend or was he their brutal killer? Horton wondered, pausing to glance at the superyacht. It showed no signs of life. His eyes travelled beyond it across the water to the lights of Gosport before walking on towards the restaurant. Perhaps Neanderthal man would have a breakthrough tomorrow and claim a result. Horton didn't much care for Dennings crowing over him, but if it meant a callous killer was caught then he'd live with it.

He made to push open the door of the restaurant when he

caught sight of a couple in the far right-hand corner. Quickly he stepped back into the shadows where he could study them without being seen. Their heads were bent low across the table but Horton recognized them instantly. There was no reason why Mike Danby shouldn't be enjoying an Indian meal but it was who he was with that surprised Horton. He wondered if the raven-haired Chinese detective, DCI Harriet Lee of the Intelligence Directorate, was there of her own accord, and simply enjoying a meal with a friend or lover, or was she on duty? If the latter, did it mean that the Intelligence Directorate suspected something was going to go down on Glenn's super-yacht, such as an armed robbery, hence Dean's reluctance to give Uckfield more staff? God, he hoped not. And if Sawyer believed that then why hadn't CID and the Major Crime Team been informed? Dean had said nothing about that to Uckfield.

Horton turned away, mulling this over. There was another possibility, one that fitted more neatly in with the need for the Intelligence Directorate to keep their cards close to their chests, and that was Detective Chief Superintendent Sawyer was inter-ested in Russell Glenn. If so, it had to mean that Glenn was mixed up in something illegal with international implications. But if he was then why risk coming here? Had it been just to please Avril?

Glenn travelled the world and probably had some shady busi-ness dealings behind him, but that didn't mean he was a criminal. But perhaps Glenn himself was the target for an international criminal. Or perhaps Glenn was Zeus.

Horton drew up sharply, causing the person behind him to almost collide with him, earning a 'Watch where you're going mate!'

Was it possible? No, Horton scolded himself, walking on. He was becoming obsessed with the bloody man! Zeus wasn't the only master criminal in the world. But as he entered the pizza restaurant, he couldn't help recalling that expression he'd witnessed on Glenn's face. Why had Glenn studied him so intently, and why had he looked so uneasy? Glenn might not be Zeus but he was certain that Glenn had recognized him. And from where, when and why, Horton intended to discover on Friday night.

NINE

Wednesday

Horton pressed his finger on Adrian Stanley's buzzer for the second time and waited in the heavy morning rain but there was still no answer. Where was the man, he thought with irritation? Stanley hadn't mentioned he'd be on holiday or away. But why should he? It was none of Horton's business what Stanley did with his life, and Stanley thought he'd told Horton everything about his mother's disappearance or rather everything he wanted to tell him, and that was a different matter altogether.

He climbed on his Harley, gazing around. There was no one in sight, not even the dog walkers had braved the weather on the wet April morning. The Isle of Wight had vanished in the grey mist of sea and sky. There was also no sign of a muddy blue van and no one had been following him. His sighting of it twice on Monday must have been a coincidence, or perhaps the van that had pulled into Gosport Marina some minutes after him had been a different one to that parked along this promenade earlier that same morning. He hadn't sent the tape over to the Scientific Services department and yesterday he had wondered if it was worth it, but with the memory of Danby and Lee's heads locked across that restaurant table, and thoughts of a possible raid on Glenn's superyacht, he reckoned he should do so and soon. One balls-up was enough for one week, he thought wryly, wondering how DI Dennings was relishing his mistake.

He found Walters in the CID operations room munching his way through a packet of Jaffa Cakes, but there was no sign of Cantelli.

'No idea where he is,' Walters said, with his mouth full, in answer to Horton's enquiry. Walters reported that there had again been no further house burglaries, which was a relief, but a two day respite didn't mean they'd ceased permanently or that the burglars had moved off their patch. He entered his office and flicked on his computer. Soon he was trawling the Internet to find out all he could on Russell Glenn, which was precious little for a man who had amassed such wealth, but what there was bore out what Mike Danby had told him on Monday. Glenn clearly had a flair for building up businesses and selling them at the right time. According to one of the articles Horton found on him Glenn had several properties around the world, namely in Monaco, Switzerland, Hong Kong and America. He no longer lived or owned property in England; probably, Horton thought, to avoid paying taxes. There was little about his childhood or his youth, except that his father had been killed in a dockside accident in Portsmouth, where his mother had been a seamstress, when Glenn was six and they'd left shortly after to live in London. Glenn had left school at seventeen and joined the Merchant Navy. He was reputed to be something of an art collector, hence his contact with Oliver Vernon, thought Horton. He called Walters in.

'Did you talk to Russell Glenn when you were reviewing the security arrangements for his yacht?'

'No, just Lloyd and the second mate, Martin Lawrence. I saw Glenn though in his study. The door was open but I didn't go in.'

'I want you to find out all you can about him, but we keep it between ourselves. I'll tell Cantelli but you're to say nothing to Bliss. Also run a check on Lloyd Durham, Dominic Keats and his Superyacht Training Academy, and Oliver Vernon, he's acting as auctioneer at the charity reception.'

Walters didn't ask why. Horton hadn't really expected him to and this time he found Walter's lack of curiosity a blessing rather than a curse. He plucked Mike Danby's business card from his wallet and dialled his mobile number.

'Having second thoughts about joining me, Andy?' Danby said after Horton had introduced himself.

'Just checking everything's OK with Glenn's yacht and for Friday night.'

'Fine.'

'No intelligence that something might be coming off?' Now was the time for Danby to tell him about his liaison with Lee the previous night.

'Not as far as I know, unless you know different. You're a bit of a dark horse. I didn't know you and Avril Glenn were old chums.'

Avril must have mentioned it. And no doubt Danby had told DCI Lee. He wondered if Sawyer already knew. Well he did now.

'How much do you know about Lloyd?' Horton asked, ignoring the fact that Danby was fishing.

'Why? Nothing wrong with him is there?' Danby replied warily.

'Shouldn't think so but I'd like to check him out and the crew members, thought you might help by giving me a list of them. Can't rule out an inside job.'

There was a moment's pause while Danby considered this and Horton got the impression he didn't much care for the idea. 'I've already checked them,' he replied a little stiffly.

'But not as thoroughly as we can, Mike.' He heard Danby sniff.

'OK, I'll email you the details.' It was said slightly grudgingly, before Danby added more brightly, 'Always willing to help an overworked CID department.'

'Thanks.'

Now let's see what happens. Would Danby report back to Lee, who no doubt had already carried out a thorough check on the crew, which had probably been passed to Danby? But Danby couldn't tell him that. Time to put that aside and get on with some work. He wondered if Uckfield had any more news on the whereabouts of Arthur Lisle or whether they had a lead on the Yately killing. He'd ask Trueman in a moment, he thought, punching the key on his phone to listen to his voicemail, and was surprised to hear Victor Hazleton's haughty tone.

'I've seen it again, Inspector Horton, the light at sea and it's exactly the same as before. Call me back and I will give you my precise report.'

Horton stifled a groan wishing he hadn't given the old man his phone number. He could see this being a regular occurrence. But then, he reprimanded himself, the call could be genuine, just as that first call might have been. Perhaps Hazleton had seen Yately's killer last Wednesday night and that might have been Arthur Lisle in his boat. If so, that meant Yately had been

killed somewhere along that coastline. He thought of Yately's
notes on the chines, caves and coves.

Hazleton had telephoned at twenty-one thirty-five. There had
been no further call from him and he hadn't left a message on
Horton's mobile phone, despite the number being on the card
he'd given him, which was surprising. Horton dialled Hazleton's
number but there was no answer. He left a message asking
Hazleton to ring him on his mobile number, which he relayed
again. Hanging up he wondered why Hazleton hadn't been on
the line several times since his original call, unless he'd gone
higher up, which from his knowledge of Hazleton was possible.
He'd probably complained to Bliss, and if he had then she'd
be bursting into his office any moment. He swivelled to look out
of his window. Her car wasn't there though, which meant she
might be attending a Project Neptune meeting. Hopefully that
would keep her occupied for the morning. Uckfield and Dennings'
cars were both in the car park.

There was a brief knock on his door and a flustered-looking
Cantelli entered. 'Sorry I'm late,' Cantelli quickly apologized.
'Molly's been sick all night and Charlotte's dead on her feet
having been up with the poor little mite. I had to get the kids
off to school. You'd have thought Ellen would have helped but
she's going through a "it's not cool to be seen with your siblings"
phase. Marie and Sophie got themselves off but Joe was playing
me up.'

'It's OK.' Horton briefed Cantelli about the call from Hazleton.
'Although I think he's fabricating these lights there's a small part
of me that wonders if his first sighting could have something to
do with Colin Yately's death. I've been thinking about what you
said, Barney, about the Greek goddess, Queen of the Sea.'

Cantelli raised his eyebrows. 'Amphitrite.'

'Yeah, and that's what Uckfield would think of me if I told
him, that I'd cracked up. But Yately's notes mention the chines,
caves and coves of the Island. Could he have uncovered a smuggling operation where Hazleton saw that first light at sea and
been killed because if it?' Horton sat forward. 'You said that
perhaps Yately liked dressing up, we know he didn't indulge in
his flat because there weren't any women's clothes kept there,
so he could have kept a stash of them in a hiding place, which

he visited on his walks where he could indulge his passion in secret. He went there Wednesday night and surprised the smugglers.'

'Having been in this job for more years than I could shake a stick at nothing would surprise me.'

'I'm going to pay Hazleton a visit and see if I can find out exactly where he saw this light on Wednesday night and last night. And I want to look around the area from the sea. It's OK,' Horton added hastily at Cantelli's horrified look, 'I'll get the marine unit to take me over, you needn't come. Don't want both Molly and you throwing up.'

Cantelli looked relieved and smiled his gratitude.

'Call Elkins and ask him to meet me at the ferry port in ten minutes and ask him if they've had any reports of this light Hazleton claims to have seen last night.'

Horton hesitated over telling Cantelli about his thoughts on Russell Glenn and the meeting between Mike Danby and Harriet Lee. He would, but when they had more time to discuss it, because Cantelli was the only person he could confide in.

Horton reached for his phone and rang Trueman.

'There's still no sign of Arthur Lisle,' Trueman said in answer to Horton's enquiry. 'And he's not been in touch with his son or daughter. There's been no reported sighting of his car, but we're still waiting to check if he travelled to the mainland either by car ferry or as a foot passenger. We're treating him as a possible suspect, but we're not telling the press or his family that. The search warrant for the house should be with us later today, and I've applied for access to Lisle's landline and mobile phone calls. I'm still waiting for access to Yately's calls.'

Horton briefly contemplated telling Trueman his theory about Yately disturbing smugglers before deciding not to for now. He wanted to talk to Hazleton first. He said, 'Any sightings of Yately on Wednesday or Thursday?'

'No. As soon as the search warrant comes through, Dennings is going over and Lisle's boat will be removed for forensic examination and the team will also go into the garage. I'm hoping to get a report from the fashion expert on the dress later today. I'm also checking on Arthur Lisle's background. Do you want to know what I find?'

'I'm not on the case.'

'I'll let you know.'

Trueman rang off. Horton reached for his sailing jacket and crossed to Cantelli in the CID office.

'Elkins says they've no reports of anything suspicious at sea last night.'

'If Bliss asks where I am tell her I'm following up another enquiry of Hazleton's, which could have something to do with Project Neptune. That should keep her quiet for two minutes. Meanwhile, Barney, see what you can get on Victor Hazleton's background.'

The rain had stopped but the sky threatened more and the wind was stiffening. It wouldn't be the most pleasant of crossings but he'd been at sea in worse, and he hoped it would stay clear long enough for him to view the area where Hazleton had seen the light.

As he walked the short ten minute journey to the port he again considered his theory about Yately stumbling on smugglers who had killed him. Clearly Lisle and Yately were acquainted, so what if Lisle also indulged in the same interests as Yately – cross-dressing, although there was no evidence to support that. Perhaps he too kept a stash of his late wife's clothes, or any women's clothes, at the same place as Yately. For all Horton knew both men could attend cross-dressing conventions, and perhaps that was where Lisle had been all weekend. Lisle, with his computer and access to the Internet, could have discovered where a convention was being held. Or perhaps that was where Yately had been intending going on to after his dinner engagement with his daughter, leaving Lisle the keys to his flat. But that didn't explain why Lisle hadn't visited it until Tuesday.

He called Cantelli. 'See if you can find details of any cross-dressing conventions. Yeah, I know it sounds weird but indulge me.'

Horton turned into the subway that ran under the motorway, his mind racing with possibilities that didn't quite add up. Hannah Yately had said her father seemed happier than he had for a long time. If he was doing more than cross-dressing with Lisle, then had Lisle killed him, taken his keys, gone on to the convention and returned on Tuesday to check that nothing incriminating had been left in Yately's apartment? The notes might have given a reference to the location where both men indulged their shared passion, but he was back to where he'd started; there was nothing illegal about it. And why couldn't both men have done whatever they wanted to at Lisle's house where there was no one to disturb them?

Despite hitting a brick wall with his theories Horton wasn't going to give up on them yet, or the idea that Hazleton had seen something suspicious and that Yately could have stumbled on a smuggling operation.

The police launch was waiting for him on the quayside and soon they were passing the superyacht on their way out of the harbour. There was no sign of anyone on the decks. On the way across a rolling and bucking Solent that would have had poor Cantelli green and spewing up over the side, Horton asked Elkins for a chart and a map of the Island and went below with the sergeant to study it.

'This is where Victor Hazleton lives.' Horton pointed to an area just below St Lawrence to the left of Sir Richard's Cove, and beyond that Woody Bay. 'A small craft could have entered one of the bays as Hazleton himself said.' And was that where Yately had his hideaway? 'How far are they from Ventnor?'

'About three miles.'

Certainly not far then for a man who liked walking, but would Yately have walked there in the dark? And even if he had reached there before sunset, which was possible given that he'd telephoned his daughter at six o'clock on Wednesday evening, would he have planned to walk home in the dark? Perhaps he knew the route well and had a powerful torch so that it wasn't a problem for him. And perhaps the only time he felt safe to cross-dress was at night. But again, thought Horton, why not do so in his apartment? Yately had lived alone; he rarely had visitors, as far as they knew. His daughter didn't visit him, and even if she did, Yately could have hidden the women's clothes. So why not indulge his passion in the comfort of his own home? Because it wasn't enough to excite him. And the same could apply to Lisle. Perhaps they needed to be in the fresh air and risk being seen or discovered by someone.

Horton considered this but the more he thought about this

theory the more absurd it sounded, even though he knew that performing sex in public places excited some people, just as flashers got their jollies by doing it in places where they would risk being caught or seen. He was glad though he'd said nothing to Uckfield. Another thought also worried him, one he'd already expressed, if Yately had been a cross-dresser then why not go the whole hog and wear the underwear?

He brought his concentration back to the map and addressed Elkins. 'I'd like to know in which direction this light Hazleton claims to have seen was travelling. It might have been returning from an operation from further east along the coast of the Island.'

'You mean from around St Catherine's Point. That would take some skill in a canoe or small boat in the dark with only one little light to guide it. He'd have to be a very experienced sailor or a foolish one to have done it.'

'Or desperate,' ventured Horton.

'He'd still have to navigate around St Catherine's Point and many a ship has floundered on that. And it would be difficult to put in to a rocky cove even on high water at night, and without a full moon.'

'Smugglers have managed it before; they could do it again, especially if the rewards are great.'

Elkins acquiesced. 'Where did this small craft come from though?'

'A motor boat or fishing boat out to sea that Hazleton didn't spot,' suggested Horton.

'Nothing's shown up for that night?'

'What about last night any time from eight p.m. to midnight?'

'I've already checked and told Cantelli, but I'll check again to see if any new reports have come in.'

Elkins climbed back on deck as Horton peered at the map and then at the sea chart. All he could see marked on the latter was Puckaster Cove and Saint Catherine's Deep, a disused explosives dumping ground. He wondered if the small craft had come from the opposite direction out of Ventnor Haven. If he believed Hazleton's story about the light last night then checking the tide timetables he saw that high tide had been at fourteen fifty-five with low water at nineteen twenty-nine, and because the small yacht haven dried out at low tide no craft could have come out of there but it could have been launched from somewhere else on the nearby coast. But the word smuggler *had* featured in Yately's notes, he was sure he'd seen it. Yately had only been in the sea for a maximum of eighteen hours though, which was completely wrong for Hazleton's first sighting of the light at sea, but not if Yately had been kept somewhere bound and gagged, alive, as Dr Clayton had said, until his killer could dispose of him in the sea. And that somewhere could have been in a cave or chine or in one of the remote bays.

Horton heard the radio crackle into life as he considered this and Elkins hurried down looking flushed.

'Ripley's just picked up a message from a fishing boat. A car's been found in the sea at Chale Bay.'

'What kind?' Horton asked, as his head reeled with the news.

'An old Morris.'

Jesus! It was Lisle's car. 'Make for it.'

Horton called Uckfield.

'Yeah, we've just heard,' Uckfield said, sounding out of breath. 'I'm just boarding the ferry with Dennings. The warrant's come through for Lisle's house and I'm dropping Dennings off there to oversee the search. How the hell do you know about it?'

'I'm on the police launch for another investigation. We're heading for the car now.'

'Sergeant Norris is on his way. I've given instructions for it to be towed out and the area to be sealed off. No one's to touch it or go near it until I and SOCO get there.'

'I'll see to it.'

Horton called Cantelli.

'I haven't got much on Hazleton except he has no previous and he's not in debt. And he doesn't own a car.'

'I'm not sure I'll get time to interview him about his report now.' Horton quickly told Cantelli about the discovery of Lisle's car in the sea. 'Give Hazleton a call and see what information you can get out of him. He'll probably insist on talking to me. He's a snob, but I'm sure you'll be able to persuade him to open up. And, Barney, there should be an email from Mike Danby with a list of crew members on Glenn's superyacht. Walters is running a check on Russell Glenn, Dominic Keats and Oliver Vernon, give him a hand with that and the crew members, if you have time.'

'Anything I should know about?'

'I'll explain later.'

Cantelli didn't press him. Did the discovery of Lisle's car change his theory about smugglers and Yately stumbling on them, or about both men cross-dressing? It was too early to tell. But perhaps Lisle *had* killed Yately and then, unable to live with the guilt, had driven his precious old car into the sea to kill himself. Horton quickly consulted the map spread out in front of him for Chale Bay.

Climbing on deck, Horton peered through the stinging rain at the colour-washed Victorian and Edwardian houses above the small seaside town of Ventnor as they swayed and rolled with the swell of an angry sea. He looked for Yately's apartment perched under the downs but couldn't see it because of the mist and rain. He thought about those notes on Yately's desk. Ventnor had once been a small fishing village. It still had a fishing industry, mainly shellfish, and the fishermen who had spotted the car might have come from here, or from the mainland. And sensibly they were heading back there now.

As the countryside opened up to his right Horton surveyed it with impatience. He was anxious to get to Lisle's car but this had been the stretch of coast he had wanted to view. Much of it was rocky but there were one or two small bays with open fields behind them. He turned to Elkins. 'Where's Hazleton's house in relation to those bays?'

'About there,' Elkins pointed to Horton's left.

He saw a densely wooded area before the trees thinned out and he caught a glimpse of Hazleton's observatory as the launch whipped past, swinging further out to sea and around St Catherine's Point with its white landmark lighthouse. He'd sailed around the point many times, but not usually in such a rough sea, and this time he fancied he could hear the cries of the five little girls who had perished along with eighteen other crew and passengers of the *Clarendon* in 1836. But maybe it was the large flock of white gulls he could hear. He looked up to see the black tip of their wings before they vanished in the heavy grey blanket of sky.

Soon he was staring at the wet sooty black cliffs of the crumbling Blackgang Chine. Cultivated fields stretched out beyond the sandy beaches and cliffs. A large gash in the cliff with sheer sides told him they'd reached Whale Chine.

'There it is,' Elkins pointed ahead at the same time as Horton saw it. The maroon and tan Morris was half submerged in an incoming tide. He wiped the rain and sea spray from the glass on his watch. It was ten eighteen. Low tide had been just before eight, but because the weather was bad no one had seen it from the shore. It was also a more remote part of the island, particularly out of the main holiday season, and the weather would have deterred the dog walkers. It was surprising the crew of the fishing boat had spotted it at all. Ripley headed as close as he dared without becoming stuck on the sand. Horton asked Elkins to find someone with a RIB to take him on to the shore, and then he waited impatiently for it to arrive, wondering if they would find Arthur Lisle dead inside his precious car.

TEN

Uckfield rammed his hands into the pockets of his big camel-haired coat and hunched his neck into his collar against what had now become a chill drizzling rain sweeping off a grey dismal sea. It seemed to Horton more invasive than the angry rain that had already soaked through his clothes and frozen his bones, despite the sailing waterproofs. A farmer had loaned his tractor and a driver, who was finally hauling the car on to the shore. While Horton had waited for Uckfield to arrive he'd taken a call from Cantelli who'd said there was no answer from Hazleton. Horton told him to keep trying.

A quick survey of the area had shown Horton that Lisle could have driven off the road along the farm track and down on to the beach and into the sea. But then why wasn't he in the driving seat, wondered Horton, studying the old Morris Minor, as Jim Clarke stepped forward and began photographing it. It was empty.

'Lisle must have done a runner,' growled Uckfield.

'And ditch his beloved car?' Horton replied, surprised. It

seemed out of character but then he didn't really know much about the man.

'Maybe it wasn't so beloved,' said Uckfield. 'And it contained evidence of Yately's murder, which Lisle was hoping the sea would cover up.'

'How did he get away from here after ditching it?'

'How the blazes do I know?' Uckfield snapped. 'Maybe he swam.'

Or maybe he had an accomplice who picked him up by car or boat, thought Horton, but didn't bother saying so with Uckfield in the mood he was. Horton suspected that Dean was breathing down his neck, pressing for results and still refusing to budge on providing more manpower.

'I suppose he could have ditched it and then walked out into the sea to take his own life,' suggested Horton.

Uckfield brightened at that. 'Feeling guilt ridden after killing Yately. And feeling he had nothing else left to live for with his wife dead, a wife who had deceived and betrayed him.'

'We don't know that for certain,' said Horton, adding to himself: and a son living the other side of the world and a daughter who barely saw him. It was possible. He held his breath as Clarke nodded that he'd finished and Taylor carefully eased open the driver's door, making sure to stay well clear of any water cascading out. Beth Tremain did the same with the passenger door.

'No one inside,' Taylor announced.

Horton exhaled, thinking Lisle *must* have killed himself. He watched as Taylor removed the keys from the ignition and placed them into a small evidence bag while Beth Tremain examined the small front compartment on the passenger side.

'The usual car documents by the look of it, sir,' she said addressing Uckfield. 'Though there's not much left of them except pulp.'

Horton stepped forward and surveyed the interior. 'No sign of a laptop computer.' It wouldn't be any use if there had been one. But Lisle would hardly walk into the sea carrying it. Horton guessed he could have smashed it up and dumped it elsewhere.

They moved around to the rear. Uckfield nodded at Taylor to join them. Extracting a key from the evidence bag, Taylor carefully inserted it into the boot. It opened just a fraction with a small click.

'Jesus!' exclaimed Uckfield, stepping back, holding a hand over his nose as an evil stench wafted out to them.

Horton shivered as the suspicion of what might be causing the smell came to him. Perhaps Lisle hadn't walked into the sea and drowned. Perhaps he hadn't been collected by an accomplice. Perhaps his body was in the boot of the car and if it was then he certainly wasn't their killer.

He steeled himself for what he might be about to see and, with his heart racing, he watched Taylor prise open the boot. The breath caught in his throat and his stomach heaved as he stared down at the filthy sodden body furled into the small boot. DC Marsden retched and staggered away and Horton heard him being sick. Taylor gulped and blinked hard several times while Clarke stepped forward and began clicking away with his camera as though taking holiday snaps. But then Clarke, like them all, had seen some repulsive and heart-wrenching sights and each dealt with it in his or her own way. The tractor driver hesitated, undecided whether to jump down from his cab and take a look, clearly torn between curiosity and fear, before Horton said, 'I wouldn't if I was you, sir.'

'Who the devil is that?' Uckfield exclaimed, taking a big white handkerchief from his trouser pocket and making a show of wiping his nose.

Horton forced himself to study the corpse, which was curled up in the foetal position. It certainly wasn't Lisle. The skin was purple and the sea life had managed to penetrate the ill-fitting boot of the car. They were crawling over the corpse, but from what Horton could see they hadn't feasted too much on the soft flesh of the face, which bore out what Horton had already surmised, and from what they knew about the last sighting of Lisle's car on Tuesday morning, this body hadn't been in the sea for long. He took in the beige trousers, the sodden cardigan and the slight figure. There was something very familiar about it, but the yellow-and-blue spotted cravat tied at the neck confirmed his worse suspicions.

His heart sank while his mind tried to make some sense of what he was seeing. Silently he cursed, before solemnly announcing, 'It's Victor Hazleton.'

'Who?' cried Uckfield, swivelling to glare at Horton.

'He's an elderly man who reported seeing a mysterious light at sea just off the coast of St Lawrence on Wednesday night and again last night.'

'And you didn't think to tell me that?' cried Uckfield, glaring at Horton.

Horton took a breath. 'I didn't consider it connected with the case.' But he had, at least twice, and he'd almost mentioned it except for the fact that he, like everyone else, had thought Hazleton had been attention seeking. Well, now the poor little man was centre stage and he wouldn't be making any more reports of smugglers and illegal immigrants.

Uckfield glowered at him. 'This is the second cock-up you've made, Inspector. A killer is walking around free because you failed to seal off the first victim's flat and now another man has lost his life.'

Horton's fists balled. His jaw tightened with anger but it was directed at himself and not Uckfield. He knew that even if he had told Uckfield about Victor Hazleton, Uckfield would have thought it irrelevant but that wasn't the point. He'd taken his eye off the ball. His mind was too far back in the past; a past that was rapidly becoming an obsession and that could never be changed, whereas his present and the future could be, and that was what he should have been damn well thinking about: the job, not some bloody ancient conspiracy theory.

'So what else haven't you told me?' Uckfield sneered.

Tersely Horton reported, 'Hazleton telephoned me at twenty-one thirty-five to report seeing a light off the coast and left a message on my voicemail. I came here to interview him and to see if I could establish where this light might have been heading.'

'So Hazleton must have seen Yately's killer last Wednesday,' Uckfield snapped. 'And last night, when he saw the light again he went to investigate and got himself killed as a result. And that killer is Lisle. He used his boat last Wednesday to either rendez-vous with Yately or to get away after leaving his body on the coast.'

'But he couldn't have used it last night because . . .' Horton stalled, before quickly adding, 'Was anyone watching Lisle's boat?' He saw immediately by Uckfield's expression that they hadn't been. 'Lisle could have removed the tarpaulin, taken the boat out and brought it back on the high tide.'

'Marsden,' Uckfield bellowed. Marsden returned looking shamefaced, but no one was going to admonish him for throwing up. 'Get someone to check if the tarpaulin on Lisle's boat's been tampered with.'

Horton felt like saying touché, but didn't. It was an oversight on Uckfield's part but the big man was never going to thank him for pointing it out. And it was a minor victory which didn't assuage his guilt over Hazleton's death. Even if Lisle had used his boat there were still several points that didn't add up. He said, 'If Lisle used his boat to rendezvous with Yately somewhere along the coast near Hazleton's house and then drove his car out here, how did he get back to his boat? It's a considerable distance to walk and there's no public transport at that time of night.'

'He got a lift and that means someone will remember seeing him,' Uckfield said brusquely.

'And the dress found on Yately?'

'Yately had an affair with Lisle's wife and Lisle wanted revenge, and he was sick enough to put one of his wife's dresses on the body. Hazleton saw Lisle kill Yately so he too had to die.'

'But why put Hazleton in the boot of the car? Why not take his body out to sea and dump it?' insisted Horton.

'To cover up the evidence,' Uckfield declared with immovable certainty.

Horton wasn't sure, but Uckfield's theory seemed far more probable than his of both men indulging in cross-dressing and being discovered by smugglers.

Uckfield was reaching for his mobile phone. Horton heard him tell Dennings to look for photographs of Abigail Lisle in the house. They might be able to match the dress worn by Yately. They'd have to show the photograph of the dress to Rachel Salter, and Horton didn't envy the person who had that task.

He took another look at Victor Hazleton. He hoped the poor man hadn't been alive when he'd been locked in the boot and left there to die with the sea seeping in to drown him, terrified and panic stricken. But if Hazleton's killer was the same person who had tormented and killed Colin Yately then he was very much afraid he might have been. And was that vindictive evil killer Arthur Lisle? Horton would want to know a great deal more about the man before he could answer that question.

Sergeant Norris crossed to Horton. 'The farmer claims he heard nothing out of the ordinary last night or this morning and the residents in the two nearest houses didn't hear or see anything unusual.' The sergeant's eyes strayed towards the boot of the car.

'Did you know Victor Hazleton, the victim?' Horton asked.

Norris shook his head. 'I don't recognize the name.'

Coming off the phone, Uckfield turned to Marsden and said crisply. 'I want you to set up a temporary incident room at Ventnor working closely with Sergeant Norris. Norris, I want Hazleton's house sealed off immediately. Also get hold of the police doctor and get him over here before the ghouls come out in force. Yeah, I know the poor bugger's dead but we still need the doctor to tell us the bleeding obvious.' Norris nodded and hurried to his car parked above the bay. To Marsden, Uckfield added, 'I want an all-ports alert put out for Arthur Lisle; liaise with Sergeant Trueman on that.' Marsden shot off to join Norris. To Horton, he said 'Does Hazleton have any relatives?'

'Not sure. He has a cleaner and gardener.'

'OK, we'll call at his house, and we need all the information we can get on him.' Uckfield again reached for his mobile phone, this time obviously to tell Trueman to start researching Victor Hazleton's background, when Horton forestalled him. 'Cantelli's already started on that.'

Uckfield said, 'Then he can carry on working on it with Trueman.'

Horton wasn't sure what Bliss would think of that but that was Uckfield's problem, not his. He wondered how much, if anything, Cantelli and Walters had managed to check out on Russell Glenn and his yacht crew, or whether Cantelli had had much joy researching cross-dressing conventions, something he still hadn't mentioned to Uckfield and wouldn't, not now. It didn't seem relevant. Horton wondered if he should drop his research on Glenn. They probably wouldn't have time for it anyway. And perhaps he should do the same with Adrian Stanley. He should let the past go.

With Uckfield on the phone, Horton turned his back on the

sea in an attempt to find some relief from the penetrating rain
and rang Cantelli, telling him why he couldn't get an answer
from Hazleton's phone and that Uckfield wanted him to work
closely with Trueman on Hazleton's background. Cantelli said
he'd found nothing on cross-dressing conventions. 'I could check
with Vice,' he added.

Horton told him to forget it. He then rang Bliss and swiftly
brought her up to date, expecting a similar bollocking to the one
Uckfield had given him, for slipping up, but Bliss was more
concerned whether Hazleton's death was connected with Project
Neptune.

'Superintendent Uckfield doesn't believe so,' he said, and he
told her Uckfield's theory.

'I'll have to report it to Detective Chief Superintendent Sawyer,'
Bliss said. 'Keep me fully briefed, Inspector.' She rang off.

Horton crossed to the Morris Minor and addressed Taylor. 'Is
there anything in his pockets?'

Tentatively, Taylor reached towards the body and eased his
slim hands inside the trouser pockets. He extracted a set of keys,
which he dropped into an evidence bag and handed to Horton.
There were five, two of them the large old-fashioned sort. Horton
then telephoned Dr Clayton. 'Anything more on Yately?' he
enquired.

'I'm still waiting for the results of the tests.'

He asked her whether Yately's body had revealed any homosexual tendencies and got a firm 'no'. He then told her about
Hazleton's death, adding, 'When can you come over and do the
autopsy?'

'Early tomorrow morning. I'll arrange it with the hospital
mortuary.'

'Thanks.' He told her that the police launch would bring her
over and a car would collect her from Cowes Marina and take
her to the mortuary in Newport. He called Elkins who was waiting
offshore in the police launch and briefed him about the discovery,
giving him instructions to return to the mainland. He'd go back
with Uckfield, and he asked Elkins to collect Dr Clayton from
the port in the morning.

The Island police doctor arrived twenty minutes later. He could
tell them little about how Hazleton had died, possibly a blow to

the head, and that he'd been dead for approximately thirteen hours, maybe less, maybe more, which meant that Hazleton must have been killed shortly after making that call to him at twenty-one thirty-five.

They stayed until the body was removed, watching it from the comfort and warmth of Uckfield's BMW, by which time Taylor and his team had left for Hazleton's house and a member of the press had arrived. Uckfield adroitly fended off questions from him with an 'it's too early to comment' remark. Horton had asked one of the local officers to organize the Morris Minor to be taken to the station garage in Newport for further forensic examination and to stay with it until it safely arrived. Then, giving directions to Uckfield, they headed back along the coast road to Hazleton's place. Uckfield relayed what Trueman had managed to get on Arthur Lisle.

'He worked in property conveyancing for a law firm called Wallingford and Chandler in Newport for thirty years. Retired three years ago.'

The same time as Yately, but that didn't mean much. 'And that's it?'

'Seems to be. There's no record of Lisle having left the Island by ferry or hovercraft any time after Thursday or returning, so unless he paid cash he was here, possibly at home, though we haven't got any neighbours yet who claim they saw him. I'll give a press conference asking for sightings of him. And there's nothing more on Victor Hazleton, yet.'

Horton thought of that impressive house filled with antique rugs and telescopes and an observatory to die for. To kill for? If he discounted Uckfield's theory then who would inherit? If they had killed him then why put the body in Lisle's car? And how did that connect with Lisle and Yately; one a solicitor, the other a postman? What had Hazleton done for a living? Had he made a will? Had Lisle drawn up that will and had Yately witnessed it and someone now wanted it never known because it would disinherit them? But no, there he went again, thinking like a bloody Agatha Christie novel and being too damn fanciful. But was his smuggling theory as outlandish?

And what about Yately's missing notes? He knew Uckfield's thoughts on that subject: that they hadn't solely been about the history of the island; Colin Yately had written something about his affair with the late Mrs Lisle, which was why Lisle had been keen to retrieve them. *But not so keen as to go straight there after Yately's disappearance.*

They found Taylor and his crew outside the house. Clarke was photographing the stone-covered driveway which Taylor and Tremain were examining. It had finally stopped raining and a weak sun was descending towards a watery late afternoon.

'No blood markings visible to the naked eye,' Taylor volunteered as Horton and Uckfield climbed into scene suits. Horton thought it more a precaution than a necessity because he didn't believe Hazleton had been killed in the house. Still they couldn't take any chances. And he wanted no more slip-ups.

There was no sign of a forced entry and extracting the keys Taylor had taken from the dead man's pockets, Horton inserted one in the lock. 'Whoever killed Hazleton didn't want anything from here; otherwise they'd have taken his house keys, or broken in.'

'Lisle's not a thief,' said Uckfield abruptly.

The house was still and silent. Everything was exactly as Horton remembered, the big oak staircase, the antique rugs on the polished parquet floor. It was chilly, but there was some heat emanating from an electric storage heater that looked out of place in the old house.

Taylor and Tremain started in the hall, while Horton slipped into the room on the right and Uckfield the one on the left. Horton found himself in what was clearly a dining room with a large oak table in the centre on a huge deep-red rug. There was some impressive orange-coloured glassware and china figures on top of a bowed glass-fronted cabinet against the wall, inside which was a selection of blue and mauve china cups, saucers and tea plates that clearly were not intended for use. There were also some impressive watercolours of country scenes hanging on the plain walls above a dado rail and panelling beneath. He peered at the signature on the paintings but the names meant nothing to him. He wouldn't mind getting an expert's opinion out of curiosity, rather than because of any connection with the case, because, clearly, as Uckfield said, robbery was not why Victor Hazleton had been killed and shoved in the boot of a car. And

there was no sign of a struggle in here. He thought of Oliver
Vernon on Russell Glenn's yacht. Perhaps he'd know a thing or
two about these antiques; he was supposed to be an expert.

He joined Uckfield in the lounge, where he was immediately
drawn to the French doors opposite. They gave on to the landscaped garden and a view of the English Channel that was
shrouded in the mist. There was nothing to see except a wide
expanse of grey sea, but on a fine day the view would be miles
and miles of sparkling blue ocean.

Nodding at the phone on a small table to the right of a sofa,
Uckfield said, 'The last call he made was to you and I can't find
any letters, or correspondence.'

Horton surveyed the spacious lounge with its old-fashioned
and rather faded furniture, before turning to study the porcelain
figures of dancers and clowns on the mantelpiece of a stone
fireplace spoilt by a modern electric fire. Along with them were
a vase and an unusual-looking clock. As Taylor entered, Horton
said, 'What's your opinion of these, Phil?'

'Valuable. Antique.'

Horton's view too. There were also more impressive paintings,
one a little abstract and striking. It was a sailing scene that could
have been anywhere along the coast but he fancied it was of
Cowes Week in August early last century. There were no family
photographs.

'Any idea what Hazleton did for a living?' Uckfield asked.

'Antique dealer?' suggested Horton. He wondered if WPC
Claire Skinner would know. She hadn't mentioned it when they
had been here before.

Uckfield said, 'Is there a study?'

'No, but there's an observatory.'

Taylor forestalled Uckfield as he headed for the door. 'It would
be better if you'd wait for us to finish, sir.'

Uckfield looked as though he was about to contradict him,
then he grunted. 'OK, let's talk to the cleaner, or rather we could
if we knew her address,' he added, glowering at Horton.

But Horton was saved from answering by Beth Tremain. 'This
might help, sir.' She handed Horton a piece of paper. 'It was
pinned on a notice board in the kitchen.' And clearly a reminder
to Hazleton of his staff's contact details. But had he needed it?

Horton wasn't so sure. He recalled Hazleton's dismissive attitude to WPC Skinner and Sergeant Elkins and thought he understood. The cleaner and gardener's details, as far as Hazleton was concerned, didn't merit the trouble of remembering.

As they headed for the Walker's residence, Horton wondered what Vivien Walker's reaction was going to be when she heard her boss had been brutally murdered.

ELEVEN

'It's those illegal immigrants, they killed him,' she snapped.

They'd found her in front of the television, with a box of chocolates and a cup of tea at her side, watching a TV game show that Horton had heard people talking about at the station but had never seen because he didn't have a television set on the boat.

'You've seen them?' asked Uckfield, surprised.

'No, but Mr Hazleton saw that light. It must have something to do with that. Who else could want to kill him?'

Norman Walker threw Horton an apologetic glance. Horton again got the feeling he'd had when first meeting Vivien Walker on Monday that she'd been involved with the police somewhere along the line. He noted that Norman looked more upset at Victor Hazleton's death than his wife. Perhaps she was just made that way.

'Do you know who Mr Hazleton's next of kin is?' he asked, perching his backside on the edge of a chair. Uckfield took the chair opposite. It was a stuffy little room crammed with knick-knacks and photographs that seemed to clash with the flock wallpaper and patterned carpet.

'There isn't anyone. Mr Hazleton wasn't married,' she answered warily.

'No nephews or nieces?'

'Not that I've heard of and no one ever visited him.'

'How long have you worked for him?'

'Fifteen years.'

'That's a long time.'

'So what if it is?'

Horton stifled a sigh. It was definitely one of *those* interviews. 'How about you, Mr Walker?'

His wife answered for him. 'Eight years.'

'And what are your duties?' Horton tried politeness, then wondered why he'd bothered; clearly it was wasted on this woman.

'I don't see that's any of your business.'

OK, *so that's how it is.* Leaning forward, he said harshly, 'It *is* my business when a man has been found brutally murdered. And I'm beginning to wonder exactly why you are so hostile. And why you haven't shown the slightest sign of distress at his death after being in his employment for fifteen years.'

The flush deepened. 'You think we had something to do with it?' she cried.

'Did you?' he asked coolly.

'No, we flaming well didn't and if you're going to talk like—' Mrs Walker sprang up indignantly.

'Sit down,' Horton said firmly and held her hostile stare. 'Sit down, Mrs Walker.'

After a moment she exhaled and sat down heavily. Horton said, 'Now shall we start again, and this time I'd appreciate a little more cooperation.' Horton shifted his gaze to Norman Walker who nodded sheepishly, while his wife pressed her lips together and eyed him through slits.

'What were your duties?'

She sniffed and said, 'I cleaned the house, did his shopping and cooked for him on Mondays, Thursdays and Saturdays. On Sundays I cook a roast dinner and do him up a plate and Norman takes it over.'

'Did you clean the observatory?'

'Only when he was in it and then he wouldn't let me touch his telescopes, afraid I'd damage them, though I've not so much as broken a cup or one of his fancy figurines since I worked there. He collects them and china. He was always coming back with something he'd picked up at some market or antique shop.'

'Have you ever seen any photographs of Mr Hazleton's family?'

She shook her head.

Uckfield spoke. 'When did you last see Mr Hazleton?'

'Monday, when *he* was there.' She nodded at Horton.

'What time did you leave?'

'Same time as always; two o'clock. Mr Hazleton was up in his observatory when I called out goodbye.'

Uckfield picked at his fingernails. 'On Monday did he say he was going to meet anyone on Tuesday?'

'No.'

'Did he have any telephone calls while you were there?'

'No.'

'How did he seem when you left him?'

'Annoyed with him,' she jerked her head at Horton, 'for not believing him. I suppose you do now it's too late.'

Horton held her accusatory stare. But he knew that even if he had believed Hazleton he wouldn't have prevented his death. To Norman Walker he said, 'What are your duties for Mr Hazleton?'

'He does—'

'I'd rather hear it from Mr Walker,' Horton interrupted firmly.

She pursed her lips together and gave him another hateful look but he'd had worse.

Norman Walker said, 'I do the gardening and anything that needs fixing in the house. I left with Vivien on Monday afternoon. She doesn't drive.'

Horton made no comment about Hazleton's house being within walking distance. He said, 'We'll need you to look over the house and tell us if you think anything is missing.' It seemed unlikely because there was no evidence of a break in, but Hazleton's killer could have used the keys and taken something from the house before putting the keys back in the dead man's pocket.

'Well we haven't stolen anything,' she snapped.

'No one said you had,' Horton replied somewhat wearily, before adding, 'Did Mr Hazleton talk about his past: his loves, life, job, experiences?'

She swivelled her hard eyes on him. 'He used to work for a firm of solicitors.'

Horton's ears pricked up at that. He resisted a glance at Uckfield but knew he was thinking the same. Lisle had worked for a legal firm, but then many other people did too. It was probably just coincidence. 'Doing what?' he asked before Uckfield could.

'He was a clerk,' Norman answered, drawing a scowl from his wife.

'Office manager,' she corrected.

'If you believe him; you know how Mr Hazleton liked to exaggerate.'

'But not about that. Mrs Jarvis confirmed it.'

'Jarvis?' Horton quickly interjected in what looked like becoming a sparring match between husband and wife, and they could do without that.

'She's an elderly lady I also clean for. Wallingford and Chandler drew up her will years ago and she told me Mr Hazleton was in charge of all those solicitors and the office.'

Horton sensed Uckfield's heightened interest at the name of the firm; it was the same one Arthur Lisle had worked for. Coincidence? He didn't think so. Hazleton must have recognized Arthur Lisle when he saw him killing Yately. He asked how long Hazleton had worked for Wallingford and Chandler.

Mrs Walker answered. 'Don't know but he told me he retired in 1986.'

Hazleton must have been quite young to retire, Horton calculated, in his mid fifties, and that was a long time before Arthur Lisle had retired.

Uckfield said, 'Do you know or have you ever heard Mr Hazleton mention a man called Arthur Lisle?' She shook her head. Her husband did the same. Horton stretched across a photograph of Lisle but they both stared blankly at it. He then tried one of Yately but again got a negative response.

'Did Mr Hazleton mention who was named in his will?' Having worked for a legal firm Horton felt sure he must have made one.

They shook their heads but Horton couldn't help noticing their sly glance. No doubt they were hoping the old man had been generous to them.

At a sign from Uckfield, Horton rose. 'We'll need you both to make a statement. And we'll arrange a time for you to go to the house. Meanwhile, if you could give me the keys.'

'We don't have any. He wouldn't give us one,' Vivien Walker announced. Horton studied her closely wondering if it was the truth. Maybe it was.

At the door, Norman said, 'How did he die?'

'We can't tell you that yet. There'll be a post-mortem.'

'Of course,' he nodded and made to close the door when Horton turned.

'Did Mr Hazleton own a mobile phone?'

'No. Said he had no need for one.'

'Can you tell me where you both were between seven and midnight last night?'

'You can't think we had anything to do with his death!'

Horton said nothing.

'We were in the pub from seven until eleven. It was quiz night, I'm in the team, and then we came home to bed.'

'Which pub?'

'The Bugle.'

'And at the weekend?'

'Here.'

'Do you own a boat?'

Horton might just as well have asked him if he owned a private jet; the answer was clearly no.

Uckfield already had the car door open when Horton said, 'Does Mr Hazleton own any other properties, or a boat?'

Norman shook his head. 'I never heard him mention anything.'

In the car, Uckfield said, 'What was all that about owning a boat?'

'I wondered if the Walkers could have killed both Lisle and Hazleton if Hazleton had left them something in a will.'

Uckfield snorted. 'We know who killed Hazleton: Arthur Lisle.'

Horton still thought he'd get Trueman to run the Walkers through criminal records.

Uckfield said, 'Hazleton could also have been shagging Abigail Lisle years ago and Lisle recently discovered it along with his missus's affair with Yately. Maybe he read his late wife's diaries.'

And that sounded highly plausible. Despite his vowed intentions to stop thinking about the past Horton's thoughts veered back to his mother. Had she kept a diary? If so, nobody had mentioned it and no diary had been passed on to him. Therefore it was unlikely, unless that diary had contained something incriminating or implicated someone in her disappearance, and that made him wonder if their council flat had been searched either by the police or by someone else who could possibly have had a key or forced an entrance. There was nothing on the missing person's file to indicate either. And Adrian Stanley, by his own admission, hadn't even entered the flat. But Horton had seen his discomfort when he'd asked the question.

'I need a drink.' Uckfield's voice crashed through his thoughts

'The Bugle?' Horton said, catching the Super's drift.

'Might as well kill two birds with one swallow and I'm bloody hungry.'

Over fish and chips, which Horton didn't feel much like eating after viewing the body of Victor Hazleton, the landlord and landlady of The Bugle confirmed the presence of the Walkers in the bar the previous night until just after eleven o'clock and denied knowing Arthur Lisle and Colin Yately. They claimed they had never seen either man when Horton showed them photographs and neither had they seen Lisle's Morris Minor.

Uckfield headed for Lisle's house, where Dennings, who had phoned as they were finishing their meal, said they'd completed the search without finding any love letters or diaries.

'There are some missing pictures in the albums though.' Dennings indicated the gaps and eyed Horton moodily, clearly put out by his presence.

'Where's the daughter?' Uckfield said, disappointed.

'In the kitchen with her husband. I haven't shown her the photograph of the dress Yately was wearing, but I told her about the car and Hazleton being found dead in it. She claims she's never heard of Victor Hazleton, and neither has her husband. She thinks her father's in the sea and wants to know if we're searching for him.'

Horton had already mooted that to Uckfield in the pub and had got a short answer: 'Have you any idea of how much a helicopter search would cost?'

A great deal, and then it was unlikely they'd find Lisle.

'No suicide note, I suppose,' Uckfield asked, hopefully.

Dennings shook his big shaven head. 'I've got all the paperwork bagged up. We can double-check it but I know there isn't one.'

Horton said, 'Perhaps he posted it and it'll arrive at his daughter's house tomorrow.'

Uckfield raised his eyebrows. OK, so Horton didn't believe

that either. It was just an idea. 'Not all suicides leave notes,' he added, before following Uckfield into the kitchen. Dennings' phone rang, forestalling him. With a scowl at Horton he answered it gruffly.

Rachel Salter sprang up from the table with hope and worry on her flushed face. 'You've found him?'

Gently, Uckfield said, 'There's every possibility that your father wasn't in the car.'

'Then how did it get into the sea?'

'He could have driven it there at low tide, abandoned it, and waded back to the shore.'

Paul Salter, a smallish muscular man in his early forties, said, 'Then where is he?'

'That's what we're trying to find out,' Uckfield said, trying without success to squeeze the exasperation from his voice.

Quickly, Horton asked, 'Have you any idea where he might have gone? To a friend's, a relative or somewhere that was special to him, or to him and your mother.'

Paul looked blank, while his wife answered, 'I've rung round all our relatives, not that we have many, only a couple of aunts on the Island, and none on the mainland, and they've not seen Dad since Mum's funeral, and he certainly hasn't gone to Singapore.'

'A friend's house, then?' Horton asked again, feeling Uckfield's impatience and wishing he'd leave and let him pursue his questioning in peace.

'Dad's a solitary man. Well, he hardly had time for friends with Mum being so ill for years,' she added defensively.

'That must have been very difficult for him, and for you,' Horton empathized.

She eyed him warily, looking for signs of insincerity. Horton got the impression of an embittered and maybe frustrated woman, as well as a rather self-centred one.

'It was,' she replied, tight-lipped.

'How long was your mother ill for?'

'Eleven years.'

Horton was surprised and showed it, prompting Rachel to add rather defensively, 'She wasn't too bad at first but it progressively got worse until Dad had to give up work and care for her. But I've already told you this.'

Horton thought that Rachel Salter had resented her mother's illness. Perhaps because her father had showered more devotion on his wife than he had on his daughter, and that reminded him of something Cantelli had once said about why Catherine was so hostile towards him and his demands for access to Emma: because she was jealous that he had loved his daughter more than his wife. He saw that it could be true of both his own circumstances and Rachel Salter's. He was no psychologist, just a policeman who had seen a great deal of human nature in all its guises, for better and worse.

He said, 'Your mother was an attractive woman from the photographs we've seen in the albums. You look as though you were a very happy family.' He wondered what Rachel's response to his probing was going to be. He heard Uckfield sniff.

'We were.' Her reply was crisp and hostile.

'But every marriage has its problems; were your parents happily married?'

'Of course they were. What are you saying?' She glared at him.

Uckfield made to speak but Horton broke in, 'Was there anywhere special for your parents?' Horton again asked, 'Somewhere they liked to go together?'

'No. And I know why you're asking. You think Dad might have gone there to . . . to kill himself. Well you're wrong. Yes, he was upset when Mum died but not enough to do that. I can't think what's happened to him. And I have no idea what that man was doing in the boot of Dad's car. Have you considered that my father's life could be in danger?' she demanded.

Horton ignored the question and her hostility. 'Did your father speak about his work or the people he used to work with?'

It took her a moment to answer and when she did she spoke grudgingly. 'Sometimes.'

'Who did he speak of?'

'For God's sake, I can't remember. You should be out there looking for him, not badgering me with all these questions and tearing the house apart.'

'Rachel, they're only doing their job,' her husband interjected.

'And not very well,' she snapped, glaring at him.

Horton saw Paul Salter flinch. 'And you're sure your father never mentioned Victor Hazleton.'

'Yes, I'm sure,' she almost shouted. Then her expression darkened. Horton could see her mind racing as she followed the conversation. 'My God, you actually think my father could have killed this man!' She ran a hand through her long hair. 'This can't be happening. It's ludicrous. Look, I'm telling you, Dad's had an accident, he staggered out of his car and someone stole it and put this . . . this other man inside. He could have been attacked.' Her faced paled as she realized that her father could also be dead.

While both scenarios were possible, Horton thought it unlikely. 'We've checked the hospital and your father hasn't been admitted.'

'Of course he hasn't,' she snapped, 'because he's lying in a ditch or he's fallen over a cliff. I want the search and rescue services out looking for him.'

Uckfield said, 'We're doing all we can to locate your father, Mrs Salter.'

She snorted her disbelief.

Uckfield's phone rang as Horton stretched into his pocket for a photograph of the dress that Yately had been wearing.

'Has either of you seen this dress before?' he asked, while Uckfield slipped out of the room.

Rachel glared at it then back at Horton. 'What has this to do with my father?'

'Do you recognize it?' pressed Horton gently.

'No.'

Paul shook his head. 'Me neither.'

'Do you know where your father was over the weekend?'

'Here,' Rachel said sharply.

'You saw him or spoke to him?'

'No. But he's always here.'

Just because she thought so didn't mean he was. There seemed nothing more they could get from the Salters. Horton tried to reassure them that they were doing everything they could to locate Arthur Lisle, but he wasn't convincing Rachel Salter.

He entered the dining room that Lisle had used as a study and gazed around it again, as though it might reveal something he'd overlooked the first time. Officers had been through the books and found nothing, and idly Horton opened one on the table that was about the history of British passenger ships. He turned to another about the history of the Isle of Wight coast. The last time he'd been in this room he had noted that Lisle and Yately had the same interests, which was in maritime matters and local history, the latter of which tied in with Yately's notes, but he still couldn't see where that got them.

He stepped outside, noting that Uckfield was in the living room in conversation with Dennings. It was a clear evening. Soon it would be dark. The streets were deserted, though there was movement behind the curtains and blinds in the neighbouring houses and those opposite. Horton stood and took in the air. He could taste the silence and smell the sea. He wasn't surprised the Victorians had celebrated the place as a health resort and a cure for tuberculosis with the air so clear, and with that came the memory of the notes on Yately's desk. Lisle had taken them and hadn't been afraid to be seen by a neighbour, so unless he was a callous murderer with nerves of steel, it had been an innocent gesture and one which indicated to Horton, along with the similarity in their reading matter, that the two men were working together on some kind of historical project, possibly to do with the sea and possibly, he thought, on something connected with the coast.

Then there was the connection between Hazleton and Lisle; they'd both worked for the same firm of solicitors and had done so at the same time. If Hazleton had met Abigail Lisle then and had an affair with her it was doubtful her daughter would have known about it. Maybe someone from Uckfield's team would find out more tomorrow when they visited Wallingford and Chandler. His phone rang. He thought it must be Cantelli, but he didn't recognize the number so answered it somewhat cautiously.

'Is that Inspector Horton?'

'Yes,' he replied, not recognizing the man's voice.

'I'm so glad I've got hold of you. I hope I'm not disturbing you. I'm Robin Stanley.'

Horton started at hearing the name. There was only one Stanley he knew.

'I think you know my father, Adrian.'

'I do.' Horton's mind raced. Why was the son calling him?

'I found your card in Dad's trouser pocket. He's had a stroke. He's in Queen Alexandra Hospital. He's been trying to talk and he's very agitated because he can't express himself clearly, but the nurse and I finally worked out what he was trying to say. We believe it's your name. I think he wants to see you.'

Horton's heart seemed to skip several beats.

'I might be completely wrong, Inspector, and I'd hate to waste your time,' Robin Stanley added hastily, 'but I wondered if you'd mind calling in to the hospital when you have a moment. I would really appreciate it. It might help him rest more easily. I know I shouldn't ask but—'

'I'll be there as soon as I can.' *So much for letting go of the past!* No wonder he hadn't got an answer to his call at Stanley's apartment this morning. He only hoped Stanley hadn't been lying ill inside. He didn't like to think that he might have been able to do something to help him.

It was bad timing for him that Stanley had had a stroke, he thought with a trace of bitterness, before reminding himself that the poor man hadn't invited one. Had Adrian Stanley really been asking to see him or were they mistaken in his feeble attempts to speak? And if he was struggling to speak then what more could Horton get from the sick man about the disappearance of his mother? Very little he reckoned.

He got the ward number from a grateful Robin Stanley and rang off. Uckfield's growl brought him up sharply.

'What are you standing out here for? Looking for a lost ship?'

No, thinking about a lost mother.

Uckfield zapped open his car. 'Let's see what Taylor's found at Hazleton's house.'

TWELVE

Nothing was the answer. They met Taylor outside who said there was no visible evidence that Hazleton had been killed there. The grounds hadn't been searched though and that would have to wait until the following day because it would soon be dark, and tomorrow the Walkers would also be brought here to tell them if anything was missing. Also tomorrow, Dr Clayton would tell them how Hazleton had been killed and hopefully give them some indication of what the murder weapon looked like.

Horton and Uckfield made a cursory search of the house. Only one bedroom was in use, with a view out to sea. It was cheaply furnished. There were no antiques here and the carpet was of the bulk standard chain store type, wearing thin in several places. Two of the other three bedrooms were furnished, with a modern divan bed in each and with heavy old-fashioned wardrobes and chests of drawers. The beds were covered with blankets or bedspreads of no particular note, the wardrobes were empty and the chests of drawers lined with brown paper and again empty. The storage heaters were turned off but the rooms had been dusted. The smallest box room was devoid of furniture.

Hazleton's bedroom yielded nothing much. His clothes, Horton could see by their labels, were expensive and of excellent quality and what jewellery there was looked to be valuable. The bathroom was dated and held all the usual medicines and toiletries, nothing to show that Hazleton suffered from any illness. In fact, by the lack of pills, Horton thought the elderly man must have been very healthy.

They climbed to the observatory. Taylor had given Horton the keys and indicated that one of the larger ones unlocked the door. As they stepped inside, Uckfield gave a low whistle of appreciation. 'Anything different? Telescope been moved?'

Horton ignored his sarcasm. 'No.' The large modern telescope was where Horton had last seen it two days ago on Monday and the antique one was resting in its box on the top of a low cupboard. Horton recalled Hazleton's lecture on its origins. No doubt it was valuable, like a lot of things in the house. It had been dusted for prints and as Horton picked up the box he thought that Hazleton would have had forty fits at the state of it. He opened it and gently lifted it out while Uckfield wrenched open the cupboard doors.

'That's what I like,' he said. 'A man with a method; makes our job a lot easier.'

Horton eyed the neatly stacked folders inside the cupboard before turning his attention back to the telescope. He put it to his eye and focused it in. There was a container ship in the distance. Then he pointed it in the direction of the shore.

'I could do with a hand here when you've finished stargazing,' Uckfield said grumpily.

There weren't any stars to look at but Horton didn't correct Uckfield. Replacing the telescope in its box, he took the two files Uckfield handed him: one was marked 'correspondence', the other 'personal information'. Inside the latter Horton found Hazleton's birth certificate and those of his parents, along with their death certificates. There were a few other personal items but no love letters, photographs, marriage certificate, and no will.

'According to his birth certificate he was born on the Isle of Wight in November 1932.'

'His bank balance is healthy,' said Uckfield, flicking through the statements.

After a cursory glance in the file marked 'House deeds', Horton read that the house had been purchased by Victor Hazleton in 1990.

Uckfield said, 'We'll take these with us and get a team in tomorrow in case there's anything else of use stashed away.'

Horton locked up the cupboard and the observatory. Uckfield gave instructions for a unit to remain until they were relieved by another. 'Don't want any more telescopes moving in the night or notes being pinched,' Uckfield added facetiously.

Horton said nothing. They returned to Ventnor and collected Dennings and Marsden. Heading towards the ferry, Uckfield said, 'Dennings, you'll head up the investigation over here from tomorrow with DC Marsden. Norris will book you into a bed and breakfast. Trueman will stay in the major incident suite and will be responsible for coordinating both ends of the investigation, which means you,' Uckfield tossed at Horton beside him, 'with Sergeant Cantelli, will interview the solicitors, Wallingford and Chandler, tomorrow morning.'

'What about DCI Bliss?'

'It's been agreed,' Uckfield said tersely. 'I want Lisle found.'

'That might be difficult if he's in the sea.'

'Then I want the evidence to confirm he killed two men and dressed one of them in his late wife's dress.'

Horton didn't think Cantelli was going to be very pleased about his seafaring trip to the Isle of Wight.

Uckfield added, 'Let's hope that Dr Clayton can give us something from the autopsy and this fashion expert can tell us something about the dress.'

By the way Uckfield said the word 'expert' Horton could tell that he didn't hold out much hope, but then the big man had an inbuilt distrust of so-called 'experts'. Horton wasn't quite so firm in his opinion but he understood Uckfield's scepticism; they'd heard too many 'experts' get criminals off the hook.

Uckfield continued. 'I'll give a press briefing tomorrow morning asking for sightings of all three men.'

Horton said, 'And Lisle's boat?'

Crisply, Dennings answered, 'There's no evidence to say it was used last night but it's being transported to the same garage where Lisle's car is and the forensic team will examine it there.'

So that seemed to be everything with the exception of one or two points. On the ferry, out of earshot of the others, Horton called Sergeant Elkins and asked him to liaise with Customs and the Border Agency for any intelligence on smuggling operations and to let Cantelli know if there was anything going on. Then he called Cantelli on his mobile. From the sound of the children's voices in the background Cantelli was at home. He asked if Walters had turned up anything on Glenn's crew.

'I checked with him before I left. There's nothing known on any of them or on Dominic Keats or Oliver Vernon. Hang on, I'll just get my notes.' There was a moment's pause then Cantelli continued. 'Keats is a former Royal Navy Commander, left six years ago to become a skipper on a private yacht and then set up the Superyacht Training Academy two years ago. Divorced with three children. His wife lives in Somerset and he has an apartment in Oyster Quays and a yacht on the Hamble. He's into yacht racing so there's quite a lot of information about him on the Internet. His business is booming, or so it seems from the latest company records. Oliver Vernon has a Masters Degree in Art History and worked for Landrams, the auctioneers, for three years before becoming a freelance valuer, researcher, lecturer and consultant six years ago. According to his tax record he also seems to be doing well for himself. His address is given as an apartment in London.'

'And Lloyd?'

'Ex-commando. Been working for Russell Glenn since he left the army eight years ago.'

That left Russell Glenn.

'There isn't much. He joined the Merchant Navy as a Deck Rating, Ordinary Seaman in 1968, working on tankers, and was promoted to Able Seaman in 1972. He then joined Carnival Cruises in 1978 until late 1981.'

'When in 1978?'

'December. He left them in October 1981. He was out of the UK until 1985 when he resurfaced as the owner of the Enderby hotel chain and started on his road to riches. Walters says he's left you some notes and some photographs he printed off the Internet on your desk. Do you want me to carry on looking into his background tomorrow?'

'No. Sorry, Barney, but you're coming with me to the Island to talk to Lisle and Hazleton's former employer. Uckfield's orders.'

Cantelli groaned. 'Knew I should have joined the Birmingham force.'

'The good news is the weather forecast says it's going to be a fine calm day.' Horton had no idea if it was but no need to tell Cantelli that.

'I've heard that before,' Cantelli said with justifiable scepticism. 'Think I'd better stock up on seasickness pills.'

Horton rang off and stayed on deck as the ferry slipped into the harbour. Lights blazed from the cabins of the superyacht. According to those dates it was possible that Glenn had known Jennifer before joining Carnival Cruises. Horton wondered where Glenn had been living until December 1978, and in addition which ports he'd sailed into while working on the tankers. It could have been Portsmouth if the tankers had been small; otherwise it was far more likely to have been Southampton or the oil refinery there. That didn't rule out the possibility that Glenn had met Jennifer; Southampton was only twenty-five miles away. Despite his earlier vows to concentrate on the present and the future, he knew he couldn't let go, particularly in light of the unexpected phone call he'd received from Robin Stanley. What could Adrian Stanley want to tell him? It was pointless speculating. He'd find out soon enough. The announcement came over the Tannoy for all car owners to return to their vehicles as the ship was about to dock.

Dropping Horton at the station, Uckfield told him and his team to be available for a briefing tomorrow morning, and half an hour later Horton was being shown into a small hospital room by a nurse. He apologized for the lateness of his visit. But the nurse wasn't put out by it. 'When you've only just come on duty this is early,' she said smiling down with concern on Stanley's recumbent figure. 'He's very troubled and restless, though you wouldn't think it now. And that's not helping his recovery. He's a little difficult to understand, he's been severely affected by the stroke, but if you listen hard enough and tune yourself in, you'll get the gist of what he's saying. If you sit beside him for a while I'm sure he'll soon realize you're here.'

Horton sat and stared at the sleeping man. His heart was pumping fast with anticipation of what Stanley might hopefully tell him. Was this the breakthrough he needed? he thought, with a mixture of dread and excitement. Or would it lead to yet another dead end? The sounds of the hospital intruded into the quiet room: the continually bleeping buzzer, a trolley clanging, people murmuring. How long would he have to wait?

His eyes scanned the room taking in a couple of get-well cards and someone, Robin Stanley, Horton assumed, had brought in a few photographs. He'd sounded a kind man on the phone, but voices as well as looks could be deceptive, as he knew only too well. Horton studied the photographs. Propped up on the bedside cabinet was one of a young man and woman with two fair-haired children. That must be Robin and his wife and kids, he thought, picking it up. Nice-looking family. It made him think of Emma, the only family he had left, and he hastily pushed away such thoughts before more nightmares of being isolated from her returned to haunt his waking hours.

Replacing the silver-framed photograph he turned to the one beside it of Adrian Stanley and his late wife. Stanley was in police uniform and his slim, elegant wife wore a mauve dress and jacket with some discreet but impressive jewellery – a necklace and brooch – a big mauve hat, gloves, handbag and shoes. But it was the medal that Stanley was holding that drew Horton's attention. It was the Queen's Gallantry Medal and the picture must have been taken at the Palace when Stanley had received it from the Queen. What a proud moment for him and his family.

He turned to study the lean grey-haired man lying in the bed and willed him to wake up. He looked much smaller and older than Horton remembered. Then, as though sensing his gaze, Stanley opened his eyes. Horton's heart quickened. Stanley seemed almost at once to register who was with him, and Horton thought he saw a hint of relief in the tormented eyes.

'You were asking for me,' Horton began gently, easing himself on to the chair beside the bed and praying no one would disturb them.

Stanley moved his head slightly.

'You wanted to tell me something about Jennifer?'

Again Stanley nodded. Horton's chest contracted and the sounds of the hospital faded into the far distance.

'You remembered something?'

Stanley closed his eyes. OK, it was the wrong question. Horton tried again. 'There was something you didn't tell me.'

Stanley opened his eyes and again gave that slight movement of his head.

Horton caught his breath. It was as he'd surmised. His body ached with impatience but harassing Stanley wasn't going to get him the information any faster.

'About *why* my mother disappeared?'

But Stanley's eyes remained shut. Horton thought he'd slipped back into sleep. Shit, this was torture.

He tried again. 'About *who* my mother went to meet that day?'

Still nothing. Horton took a breath. What the hell was Stanley trying to tell him? His brain scrambled to think. Stanley moved his head a little to his left but Horton could see it was an effort. His lips were trying to move but the sound was struggling to emerge. Horton tried to be patient.

'You discovered something and kept silent about it.'

Stanley's eyes opened. Horton thought he saw fear in them. 'You found my mother's diaries.'

Stanley closed his eyes.

'Photographs? A photograph?' Still the eyes remained closed. Frustration gnawed at Horton. He took a deep breath and willed patience. 'What did you discover, Adrian? Something dangerous? Dangerous to me and my mother?'

Stanley opened his eyes and his lips moved. Horton's heart quickened. This time some sound emerged from Stanley's frozen body and Horton desperately tried to tune himself in to it. It sounded like 'ouch'. But that didn't make sense. Puzzled, he said, 'I'd be hurt if you told what you knew?'

Again Stanley made a noise that sounded like 'ouch' and another word that sounded like 'dead'. Horton stiffened. 'Someone would be killed if you told what you knew or thought you knew?'

Stanley's body seemed to slump, although he never moved and his eyes closed. He looked greyer than when Horton had entered and his breathing was more laboured. Horton felt alarmed and anxious. He should call the nurse, but he didn't. He could see that the strain of trying to communicate through a petrified body had taken its toll on the elderly man.

Frustrated, Horton resigned himself to getting nothing more for now. He laid a hand on Stanley's arm. 'It's OK. I'll come back later when you're rested. Don't worry.'

Stanley opened eyes that were full of pain. Again he tried to move his head but only succeeded in moving his eyes to his left. Horton frowned as that same sound came feebly from Stanley's mouth: 'ooch'. Then he slumped, clearly exhausted.

Disappointed, Horton relayed to the nurse what had happened and left instructions for anything that Mr Stanley said to be written down, but he wasn't completely confident the message would be passed on to the other nurses who came on duty later. He telephoned Robin Stanley and after telling him what had happened he asked him to do the same thing if his father tried to speak again.

'Do you know why he is so anxious to communicate with you, Inspector?'

Horton wasn't going to tell him the truth, but he gave a version of it. 'I think he's trying to tell me something about an old case he was on. Did he ever talk about his cases?'

'Sometimes.'

Horton's pulse picked up a beat. 'Did he mention anything about a missing woman some time back in the late 1970s?'

'No. I don't recall that. He might have made some notes though. In fact, I teased him recently about writing his memoirs.'

'And are there notes?' Horton daren't hope.

'I'm not sure. I could look for you.'

'Thanks. I'd appreciate that. It might help.'

With his head spinning, Horton left the hospital and headed for home. Stanley definitely knew something about Jennifer's disappearance, which he had kept to himself for years. Had he been threatened? Had this master criminal Zeus got to him? But if that were so, surely Zeus wouldn't have let Stanley live. The Zeuses of this world covered their tracks. So what could Stanley know? And why keep silent? Had he known Jennifer Horton? That was a possibility. Had he been involved with her and kept silent because he'd been afraid for his job? Had he heard some snippet of news or rumour about her disappearance that implicated someone he knew, and kept silent to protect them?

Horton needed more than 'ooch', whatever that meant, and frustratingly for him and poor Adrian Stanley he didn't think he was going to get it.

THIRTEEN

Thursday

Horton reached his office early after a restless night. He'd drunk countless cups of coffee throughout a troubled night, which had only served to keep him awake, maybe deliberately so, because while awake he could control his thoughts; once asleep the nightmares would return. At one time he'd taken his drink on deck and felt the crisp night air chill his bones, hoping it would cleanse his mind of those terrible years. He'd turned to recollections of when his mother had been there and tried to recall the men he'd seen her with. Russell Glenn unwittingly came to mind. Now in his sixties, he would have been twenty-seven then. But Horton couldn't recall him. Perhaps one of the photographs Walters had printed off the Internet might jog his memory.

The sound of a car driving past in the early hours of the morning had caught his attention, causing him to wonder where the driver was heading at that hour. The road went nowhere except to Langstone Harbour and the Hayling ferry, which didn't run through the night. He'd waited for the car to return but it didn't. It was high water and he had strained his ears for the sound of a boat going out, but had heard nothing. Growing cold he'd gone below and had lain on his bunk, letting the slapping of the water soothe his troubled mind. Eventually he'd slept but only for a couple of hours.

Sipping his coffee and pushing his weariness aside he logged on to his computer and searched the police files for events in 1978. What had so preoccupied the police in November 1978 that they had only sent PC Adrian Stanley to investigate the disappearance of his mother, and he hadn't done that very thoroughly. But the reports from that period hadn't been scanned, which meant he would need to check them manually. He cursed softly. That would have to wait. He tried the local newspaper archives but they didn't go that far back either. All he could find was that Portsmouth football team had been relegated to the Fourth Division; so a visit to the newspaper office or the library to check the archives was needed.

Horton then called up the national news events of that year just for background. The Home Secretary announced a pay increase for police officers of an average of forty per cent. Those were the days. They were lucky now if they got four per cent and only then if they promised to make cuts. Yearly inflation was at just over eight per cent and interest rates at twelve and a half per cent. Naomi James broke the solo round-the-world sailing record by two days, the first test-tube baby was born, and Labour faced a vote of confidence.

He sat back feeling restless and agitated. There was something nagging at the back of his mind, something he'd seen or heard, but it refused to come to light. He rummaged around on his desk and found three photographs of Glenn that Walters had printed off. Two of them had been taken in the last seven years and were clearly publicity shots taken on the sale of two of Glenn's businesses. He wore the same gold-rimmed spectacles and was casually dressed; his hair wasn't as grey or as untidy as when Horton had seen him on Monday evening, but there was the same slightly shambolic, uneasy air about the man who was clearly uncomfortable in front of a camera. The other picture was of a younger Russell Glenn at a black-tie function, unaware that the camera was on him. Horton studied it. Glenn must then have been in his early to mid forties. He was still wearing glasses but Horton thought he caught sight of a different Glenn, one more relaxed, more confident, sharper.

He folded all three photographs and thrust them in his pocket before swinging round to stare out of his window at the clear bright morning. Had Glenn changed over the years? Had he lost his confidence, or rather his edge? Hardly, if he could afford to buy a superyacht. So who was the real Russell Glenn, the dishevelled man who looked ill at ease or the other sharper one?

The door to the CID room opened. That must be Cantelli or Walters. He pushed thoughts of Stanley and his mother from his mind and turned round, starting in surprise as he stared up at the lean silver-haired figure in the immaculate grey suit on the other side of his desk. Detective Chief Superintendent Sawyer of the Intelligence Directorate closed Horton's door behind him.

'Sir.' Horton made to stand, but Sawyer waved him back into his seat and took the one the other side of Horton's desk, where he crossed his legs and eyed Horton with a serious and assessing air.

'DCI Bliss tells me that Victor Hazleton's death is not connected with Project Neptune.'

'We believe it's connected with the death of Colin Yately.'

'Whose body was pulled out of the Solent on Monday.'

'Yes, sir.'

'And neither of these deaths has any connection with a possible terrorist attack on the USS *Boise*?'

Horton studied the lean-featured man with eyes as cold as marble. 'Not unless you know something we don't.' Which was always possible. He thought of DCI Harriet Lee with Mike Danby in that restaurant.

'By "we" you mean Detective Superintendent Uckfield.'

'Yes, sir. It's his case.'

Sawyer nodded. After a moment he said, 'But Hazleton did report two incidents of lights at sea.'

'Yes, although there is no corroborating evidence. He could have seen Yately's killer the first time but we're not sure that applies to the second sighting.'

Sawyer seemed to consider this.

Horton said, 'Have you evidence to show that Hazleton could have witnessed something connected with a potential terrorist attack, sir?'

'No. But that doesn't mean to say that he didn't. What theories do you have for his death?'

Horton wanted to say, why ask me? Why not Uckfield? But that could be construed as being insubordinate. That aside, he didn't think he'd get a straight answer anyway. Instead, with his mind whirling with thoughts of why Sawyer was here, he swiftly brought him up to date with what they knew and the most likely theory: Lisle had killed Yately for having an affair with his wife, and had then killed Hazleton because he witnessed the murder, or because he'd also had an affair with his wife.

Sawyer listened without showing the slightest sign of emotion or interest. Finally, he said almost casually, 'But you've no evidence to support this.'

'Not yet, sir.'

'And you agree with this theory.' There was a slight question mark in Sawyer's tone and behind it a hint of surprise.

Horton should have answered immediately that he did, but a moment's brief hesitation gave Sawyer his answer. Horton silently cursed himself for betraying his thoughts. But why was a Chief Superintendent interested in a mere Detective Inspector's theories? And why was *this* Chief Superintendent particularly interested? There were two answers to that question and Horton wasn't quite sure yet which was the correct one.

He said, 'It's possible.'

'What other theories do *you* have, Inspector?'

'None at the moment, sir,' Horton replied. He could see that Sawyer didn't believe him, but if he explained his theory about Yately and Lisle cross-dressing in secret in one of the bays on the coast and being discovered by smugglers it would sound incredible, probably because it was.

He heard the outer door open and the voices of Cantelli and Walters. Sawyer rose. But Horton knew he hadn't finished yet. He hardened himself for what was coming, while taking great pains not to betray any outward tension.

Sawyer had reached the door before he turned. 'How is the search for your mother going?'

'It isn't, sir.' Horton held Sawyer's unblinking gaze. The lean man's lips twitched with the ghost of a smile. Horton's stomach twisted. The bastard knew he'd been to see Stanley in the hospital and that he'd visited him in his apartment. The blue van sprang to mind. Had Sawyer's officers been in that? Had they been following him or watching Stanley's apartment? Both, apparently.

Sawyer said, 'You can still reconsider your decision to help us find Zeus.'

Horton had refused to be used as a sacrificial lamb to lure this master criminal from his lair as Sawyer wanted.

'It might help you to find out what happened to Jennifer.'

'I'll think about it.'

Sawyer didn't reply. He opened Horton's office door a fraction, before turning back again. 'How do you know Russell Glenn?'

This time Horton didn't bother to hide his surprise. He couldn't if he had tried. 'I don't.'

Sawyer nodded slowly and then swept out, leaving Horton confused as to the real purpose of the man's visit. What the hell had that been about?

Before he could formulate any kind of answer his door swung open and Bliss swept in with a worried frown on her high forehead.

'Why was Detective Chief Superintendent Sawyer here? What did he want? Did he ask for me?' she demanded.

'He wanted an update on Hazleton's death,' Horton answered calmly, and watched her face pale. He could see the thoughts chasing around her mind, and among them were fears that Sawyer didn't trust her and had gone to her DI to get the real story.

'What did you tell him?' she asked, eyeing him warily.

'The same as I told you. We don't believe it has any

connection with a potential terrorist attack.' Horton rose. 'Superintendent Uckfield wants us for the briefing.'

He swept past her, catching her off guard. She seemed too preoccupied with her thoughts to order him back. She wasn't the only one. As he made his way to the second floor and the major incident suite, with Walters and Cantelli in tow, his head spun with the implications of Sawyer's question about Russell Glenn. It could only mean one thing. Russell Glenn must have been involved with his mother.

The incident room fell silent as Uckfield perched his large backside on the edge of one of the desks, which seemed to give a protesting creak, and asked for an update from Sergeant Trueman. Dennings and Marsden had already left for the Island. Horton fetched a drink from the water cooler. His eyes fell on the photographs on the crime board of Lisle's sodden car and the furled up body of Hazleton in the boot. It seemed inconceivable that four days ago he'd been interviewing him about a report he'd considered a figment of the old man's imagination. He brought his attention back to Trueman.

'Wrayton Lettings claim that no one has had a fourth set of keys cut to Yately's flat. There is the master, and a spare set, which the landlord's already told us hasn't left the office, and one set was given to Yately. We know that Yately had two keys cut from the set to give to his daughter, so he could have had more cut and given a set to someone else.'

Uckfield said, 'Can't see why he should. He doesn't seem to have had any close friends and no other relatives. Unless he gave a set to his wife.'

Unlikely, thought Horton, based on what they'd seen of her and Uckfield said the same, only putting it more coarsely. 'If he did he must be a real glutton for punishment.'

Trueman continued. 'An officer has spoken to Margaret Yately's employer, who you might be interested to know is Phillip Gunville, the owner of the car you saw outside her house on Tuesday evening.'

'Consoling her in her hour of sorrow,' muttered Horton.

'He's married with two school-age children. Claimed he was visiting her because he was concerned after hearing the news about her ex.'

'Yeah, and we know *how* concerned,' said Uckfield, working a toothpick round his mouth.

'Gunville says he was working in the bar last Wednesday evening and after clearing up went to bed at just after midnight. His wife confirms it and that Margaret Yately was working there until half past eleven when she got her taxi home. Neither of them claims to know Arthur Lisle. We haven't asked them about Victor Hazleton.'

Uckfield broke in. 'Marsden will deal with that. And show them photographs of Hazleton and the dress. Dennings will also get officers showing Lisle's photograph at the three Island ferry terminals. The main thrust of our investigation is to assume that Lisle is our killer and that revenge could be the motive, and that's what Inspector Horton and Sergeant Cantelli will be probing when they talk to the partners and staff at Wallingford and Chandler.' Uckfield turned to address Horton. 'Find out all you can about Arthur Lisle and Victor Hazleton, and see if there is any link between that firm of solicitors and Colin Yately.'

'There is,' piped up Trueman. 'Wallingford and Chandler handled the Yately divorce.'

Uckfield beamed. 'Now we're getting somewhere.'

It was a connection, thought Horton, but it was a long way from Lisle being a killer. For a start, as far as they knew, Lisle didn't handle divorce but property conveyancing, and the timing was wrong for Yately meeting Abigail Lisle through her husband's firm, because Yately split from his wife three years ago, the same time as Lisle gave up his job to nurse his sick wife, according to Rachel Salter. He refrained from saying so and denting Uckfield's enthusiasm.

Uckfield said, 'So what else have we got on these three men?'

Trueman answered. 'Lisle's GP has confirmed that Lisle wasn't suffering from depression, in fact the last time he saw his doctor was when his wife died. He's never mentioned anything related to having problems with his wife or family. The fingerprints Dr Clayton managed to get from Yately's body check with the comb and pen Inspector Horton brought back from Yately's apartment. There are other prints in the apartment which could match Lisle's; the fingerprint bureau are checking them. They're also checking if they match any prints found in Hazleton's house. We won't get anything from the forensic examination on Lisle's garage, his boat and car for a few days. Apart from that all we know is that none of the men has been convicted of anything criminal, and they've all paid their taxes like good boys. We'll start on bank and telephone records when we have them, which should be later today. I'll also chase up the fashion expert to see if she can tell us more about the dress found on Colin Yately, but it was only sent over to her late yesterday afternoon. There's very little forensic on it, except for evidence of sand and gravel, which is still being analysed; we might get more on that in the next couple of days.'

'Might's no bloody good,' Uckfield grumbled, 'and I want it today, not next Easter. Tell them it's urgent.'

Horton caught Trueman's eyes; there was nothing in his expression to betray his thoughts but Horton knew that the sergeant had already told them that, probably three times.

Swivelling to glare at Horton, Uckfield said, 'Trueman will call Wallingford and Chandler to tell them you're on your way.' He hauled himself up and glanced at his watch. 'Time for my press conference. Let's hope the great British public can help us. DCI Bliss, *if* you can spare DC Walters we might need his help to man the phones here, although I expect most of the calls will be to the incident room at Ventnor.'

Bliss still looked too preoccupied with trying to fathom out why Sawyer would pay a special visit to one of her subordinates to protest. She left the incident room before them, no doubt on a mission to find some pretext to contact Sawyer and try to get the truth out of him. Horton knew she didn't have a hope in hell. Dismissed, Horton, Cantelli and Walters headed back to CID where Horton asked Walters to press on with his investigation into Russell Glenn's background, with particular emphasis on finding out where he had been between 1972 and 1978 while in the Merchant Navy, and where he had lived.

'When I'm not answering the phone in the major incident suite,' grumbled Walters.

'And in CID,' added Horton. 'Cantelli and I are off to the Isle of Wight.'

'Some people have all the luck.'

Cantelli disagreed.

On the ferry, Horton told Cantelli about his visit to Adrian
Stanley's apartment and his subsequent visit to the hospital,
drawing a worried frown from the sergeant. He hoped it might
take Cantelli's mind off the fact he was at sea. And he knew he
could trust Cantelli.

'I can't think what Stanley was trying to tell you,' Cantelli
said, puzzled, 'but it sounds as though you're right and he knows
more about your mother's disappearance than he let on.'

Horton then mentioned that he had an appointment to see his
social services case files tomorrow morning.

Cantelli said, 'I won't ask you if you're doing the right thing,
because you've obviously asked yourself the same question a
thousand times. What do you think the records will tell you?'

'How difficult and disruptive I was.'

'Which wouldn't be surprising given the circumstances. Will
you be able to handle raking up the past, Andy? It's going to be
painful.'

It already was but that was no reason to abandon it. He shrugged
an answer, adding, 'You know that it's only recently I've even
been able to think about it, and the more I do the more questions
I have about Jennifer's disappearance. What happened to her
belongings – her jewellery and clothes? What became of the
furniture in the flat, and my toys? Some came with me, but there
must have been more than a handful of cars and a football.'

A jag of painful memory fighting to cling on to what little he
did have stabbed at him. Eventually everything had been stolen
or destroyed. He'd quickly learnt that possessions didn't mean
much in life. And perhaps that was why he had travelled light for
years, before he'd found a family and a home of his own, which
in turn had been snatched away. Now he was back to travelling,
or rather living, light and that was how he vowed it would stay;
the yacht and what he could get on it was enough for him.

He added, 'Then there are all the photographs of her and of
us together, those of me as a baby, surely she must have taken
some pictures.'

'Perhaps the furniture was sold to pay bills and the photographs
destroyed.'

'They shouldn't have been though, Barney. They belonged
to me.'

'You think the photographs might be in the files?'

Horton shrugged. 'I doubt it, but there might be a record of what happened to them.'

Concerned, Cantelli said, 'Don't build your hopes up too high, Andy. There wasn't as much information recorded in those days as there is now.'

Cantelli was right. Horton knew that, and he also knew that when he did get to speak to Adrian Stanley again, he might not be able to say any more than he had last night.

Horton then told Cantelli about Sawyer's visit, leaving out the bit to do with Sawyer knowing about Horton's visit to Stanley and without mentioning Zeus. The less Cantelli knew about that the better, he reckoned. 'I think the Intelligence Directorate is interested in Russell Glenn.'

'They're not the only ones.' Cantelli eyed him curiously.

'What do you mean?' Horton asked, surprised.

'Apart from getting Walters to dig up what he can on Glenn I hear you're on the guest list for this posh do tomorrow night.'

Danby must have told Cantelli, but when and why? wondered Horton, before Cantelli added, 'PC Johns told me. He's moonlighting for Danby.' Horton groaned. That meant it would be all over the station. Bliss hadn't picked up on it yet and neither had Uckfield and Dennings, but it would only be a matter of time before they did.

'I told Johns to keep his mouth shut,' Cantelli said, reading Horton's thoughts. 'Otherwise I warned him that he might find his lucrative little sideline suddenly drying up.'

Horton breathed a silent sigh of relief, but he knew that it wouldn't be long before the information leaked out. Johns wouldn't be the only moonlighting police officer. He owed Cantelli an explanation. 'I knew Avril Glenn years ago, before I met Catherine.'

'Ah. Walters said she's something of a looker and much younger than her husband.'

'It's OK, I'm not getting involved. She asked to meet me and then invited me to this charity reception and auction. I'm still not sure why, though I suspect it's to show me how well she's done for herself, but I *am* curious about Russell Glenn. I saw him on the deck and although it was at a distance he seemed to recognize me. I'm not imagining it, Barney,' Horton quickly added to counter Cantelli's dubious look. 'And Sawyer's visit makes me think I was right.'

Cantelli frowned. 'If Glenn is under surveillance by the Intelligence Directorate it might be wise to leave him alone.'

'I can't.'

'I know,' Cantelli sighed. 'But for heaven's sake be careful.'

Horton gazed out of the ferry window at a calm, pale-blue sea, then back at his closest friend. 'I will.'

Cantelli nodded solemnly before his dark-featured face broke into a grin. 'Good. I don't want to end up being left with Bliss bellowing in *my* ear every five seconds.'

'Perish the thought,' Horton said lightly, picking up on Cantelli's mood. 'Now let's see if we can find out why two men are dead and one is missing, and, despite what Uckfield believes, I think there might be something in my theory about smuggling, especially after what Sawyer said, or rather didn't say. Did Elkins get back to you with any news from the Customs and the Border Agency?'

'He said there's nothing major on, just the usual checks at sea: randomly stopping yachts and motor boats and boarding the occasional container and cargo ship. There's no organized smuggling operation and certainly nothing to link with Victor Hazleton's claims of smuggling.'

Horton considered this for a moment. 'Have they been on board Glenn's superyacht?'

'I doubt it.'

'Why not? Just because he's rich doesn't mean he's not crooked; on the contrary, he probably is.'

'You're just prejudiced,' Cantelli said, smiling.

'You bet I am, and bloody suspicious.'

'I'll ask Elkins to find out.'

'But tell him not to make a big deal of it,' Horton quickly cautioned. 'I don't want them charging in like he's a Cuban drug baron.'

Cantelli frowned. 'Do you really believe Glenn could be involved in bringing in drugs?'

'It would be risky, but perhaps that's what turns him on. The charity reception and auction could just be an excuse for putting in to port.' He thought of the photographs in his pocket; perhaps Glenn's mild manner had fooled Customs and many others down the years. 'When's PC Johns on duty?'

'Now. He's working on Glenn's yacht tonight.'

'Call him and ask him to do a bit of undercover work tonight; see if he can find out if the RIB's been launched, and, if so, when and who went on it, but he's to do it surreptitiously. Do you think he can handle that?'

Cantelli nodded.

'And ask him to get a guest list for tomorrow night; that should be easy enough if he's going to be working. Walters can check them out.' Horton was very curious to see who the guests were.

Cantelli nodded and reached for his mobile phone. Horton was pleased to see that the activity and concern over his safety was helping to keep Cantelli's seasickness at bay.

He stared out to sea, watching the Isle of Wight coastline draw closer. He now knew why Danby had met Lee; something was going down on Glenn's yacht tomorrow night. It could be an armed robbery, but that would simply be a cover for what was really happening, and Horton guessed it was drugs. Perhaps Glenn had been involved in smuggling drugs while in the Merchant Navy and while working on the cruise liners. By 1985, when he emerged as the buyer of a chain of hotels, he'd made enough money to start his legitimate business empire, which could have been used, and still might be used, for money laundering. And *if* Glenn was dealing in drugs and *if* Glenn had known Jennifer, then had she too been involved? Horton didn't want to think so, and he had no recollection of his mother being an addict, but if she had been mixed up in Glenn's operation then she was most certainly dead. Could Glenn have killed her because she had threatened to expose him or posed a risk?

Again he considered whether Glenn was Zeus. But he was jumping ahead. The question was, did Avril know about her husband's illegal activity? He wanted to think not, otherwise why invite him? But his cynical copper's brain said that that was precisely why he *had* been invited: to provide a very good witness to say that nothing illegal could possibly have happened. Well, if Avril and Russell Glenn thought they could use him then they could bloody well think again. He turned his mind to the forthcoming interview with Wallingford and Chandler.

FOURTEEN

'I wonder if his first name is Raymond,' Cantelli said, silencing the car and nodding in the direction of a sparkling brass plaque to the right of the sturdy royal-blue door of Wallingford and Chandler in Newport. Horton knew that Cantelli's love of Raymond Chandler sprang from the film adaptations of the author's legendary novels rather than the novels themselves.

'His initial's R. So it could be,' Horton replied, climbing out and eyeing the three storey colour-washed Georgian house in front of him. It was spread over three floors, with two windows on the first floor and another two on the third. It looked much like the other elegant period properties in the quiet and respectable broad street, a stone's throw from the quay. There was no blatant advertising here, not even a sniff of ambulance chasing. Wallingford and Chandler looked discreet, expensive and exclusive, which made him wonder why they'd handled Colin Yately's divorce. This legal firm looked as though they were more used to dealing with bankers and businessmen, rather than postmen.

Cantelli made the introductions and showed his warrant card to the pretty blonde receptionist with the upper-class accent, immaculate make-up and beautiful dental work. As she rang through to Mr Chandler, Horton surveyed the room. It boasted a glittering crystal chandelier that looked as though it had come out of some grand opera house, probably had, he thought. There were soothing pale colours on the walls, elegant classical furniture, which they didn't test out, interior design magazines of the expensive kind, and highly polished floorboards over which were spread rugs that hadn't come from any discount warehouse. It could have been mistaken for an expensive consultant's room. He wondered how it had looked in Victor Hazleton's days. The same? Had Hazleton stamped his taste for antiques here, which had lived on after his reign, or had he acquired his passion for antiquities while working here?

Cantelli's hushed voice interrupted Horton's speculations. 'So who do you think our Mr Chandler will look like: Alan Ladd, Humphrey Bogart or Dick Powell?'

Horton's eyes scanned the walls, which boasted some remarkably good paintings of local beauty spots: the Needles, St Catherine's Lighthouse, Whitecliff Bay, along with other spectacular coastal scenes, before alighting on the wall behind the pretty receptionist where there hung an array of tastefully framed photographs which seemed to document the history of the firm from the 1800s to the present day.

'None of them if that's him,' Horton said, indicating the most recent pictures, where a dark-haired man with a high forehead, angular face and strong nose featured prominently. In a couple of them he was receiving awards and in others he was with groups of clients either golfing, fishing in a sizeable motor boat or at a gala reception.

'Ray Milland,' announced Cantelli firmly, following the direction of Horton's gaze.

'That could be Wallingford.'

But it wasn't. Ray Milland, or rather his lookalike, Chandler, rose from behind a big antique desk situated in a spacious and elegantly furnished first floor room, tastefully decorated in the same soothing pale-yellow as the reception area, and with the same period features; even the floorboards had been stripped and varnished and overlaid with a beautiful red deep-pile antique rug, which again reminded Horton of Victor Hazleton's house. He made a mental note to suggest to Uckfield calling in Oliver Vernon to value the items in Hazleton's house, and at the same time he could pump him for more information about Glenn.

Chandler, smiling, stretched out a strong hand, which Horton took. He found it dry and warm, and, as Rodney Chandler introduced himself, Horton noted his eye contact was assured and friendly, and his dark suit of excellent quality. They'd been offered refreshments, which they had refused. Normally Cantelli would have sunk a mug of tea but Horton knew he was still wary to accept anything so soon after his forty minute sea voyage, which miraculously had been sick free, although Cantelli had begun to look a little green as they headed into the terminal at Fishbourne. Horton had taken coffee on the ferry. As they'd disembarked Trueman had rung to say that his checks on Norman and Vivien Walker had shown that Vivien Walker had been convicted of shoplifting twenty-eight years ago when she was twenty-four. First offence. Nothing since. Shoplifting was a long way from murder.

'How can I help you?' Chandler asked in a rich deep voice. He gestured them into the two antique leather library seats opposite.

Horton said, 'We understand that Arthur Lisle and Victor Hazleton worked here.'

Chandler gave a gentle lift of an eyebrow as a demonstration of his surprise at the statement. Trueman hadn't revealed that when he had called earlier to make the appointment.

'They did. Why the interest, Inspector?'

Horton told him that Arthur Lisle was missing and that Hazleton's body had been recovered from the sea in suspicious circumstances. Chandler made the obvious connection.

'You can't honestly suspect that Arthur has anything to do with Victor's death!' he declared, incredulous.

'We're concerned for Mr Lisle's safety,' Horton replied cagily.

Chandler continued to eye him with an air of astonishment. 'You think Arthur could be mentally ill, that he's had some kind of breakdown or brainstorm and killed Victor? No,' he said firmly, shaking his head, 'it's impossible. He's as sane as you and I. Surely there must be a mistake. How did Victor die?'

'We're waiting on the results of the autopsy.'

'And just because Arthur is missing and they worked together you've assumed a connection and the wrong one, Inspector. Arthur could be on holiday.'

'Not according to his daughter.' Horton weighed up whether to tell Chandler that Hazleton's body had been discovered in Lisle's car. It would soon be public knowledge anyway and he wasn't getting far with his enquiries here. He gave Chandler the details and watched his eyebrow go up and down in surprise and disbelief.

'This is incredible, but I see why you said you were worried for Arthur's safety. He too could be a victim. But of whom? Who could possibly want to kill either or both of them?'

Horton didn't answer the question. Clearly Chandler wasn't going to believe Lisle had killed Hazleton. He said, 'When did Arthur Lisle retire?'

'Three years ago. He took early retirement to care for Abigail, his wife. She had MS. Sadly she died eighteen months ago.'

That confirmed what the daughter had told them and what Trueman had unearthed.

'Were they happily married?'

Chandler looked surprised at the question, then frowned. 'Yes. Why do you want to know that?'

'No hint of either of them having affairs?'

'None. I can't see where your questioning is leading, Inspector.'

Horton wasn't going to elaborate. He said, 'What was Mrs Lisle like?'

Again the eyebrow shot up but Chandler answered in a neutral tone. 'A very pleasant, friendly woman. Quiet.'

'Not the kind to cause her husband any problems then?'

'No.'

'Have you seen Arthur Lisle since he retired?'

'No.'

'And Mr Hazleton?'

'No. Victor retired a year after I started working here as a junior lawyer in 1985.' He swivelled around in his leather chair and gestured up at one of the photographs behind him. 'Following in my father's footsteps and my grandfather's. He established the firm here in 1870.' He turned back to face them. 'And my son is carrying on the family tradition. He's with a client at the moment; otherwise you could have met him. Maybe you'll have time before you leave.'

Was that a hint for them to hurry up and go, wondered Horton. Perhaps Wallingford and Chandler wasn't the type of legal practice to handle criminal law and having the police on the premises was rather demeaning.

Cantelli looked up from his notebook. 'Did Arthur Lisle work here when you first joined the firm?

'Yes. He'd been here for a few years. He's older than me by about eight years. I don't remember the exact date Victor retired but if it's important I can ask my secretary, Linda, to look it up for you.'

'Please,' answered Horton.

Chandler lifted his phone, punched in an extension and gave instructions to his secretary. As he replaced the receiver, Cantelli said, 'Could either man have visited the practice when you weren't here?'

Horton knew what Cantelli was driving at; he was trying to establish a link between Hazleton and Lisle which was more recent than 1985.

'They might have done. You'd have to ask the staff.'

'If we can, with your permission, sir.'

Chandler looked a little nonplussed and then annoyed. Horton guessed it was because he'd allowed himself to play into their hands. 'They are rather busy. And I wouldn't want the clients disturbed.'

'We'll be as quick and discreet as we can.' At a sign from Horton, Cantelli folded away his notebook and slipped out of the room. Horton knew the sergeant would also take the opportunity to ask the staff for their views on Arthur Lisle and probe for any hint or gossip of possible affairs.

Horton said, 'What was Victor Hazleton like?'

'I didn't really know him but I remember him being a small, very smart, rather fussy man, very particular. He had very high standards about how the office should be kept and how people should dress and behave, which to me, then at the tender age of twenty-five, seemed a bit extreme, but I've come to see how right he was. He also had a very good eye for detail. My father, and his partner John Wallingford, both sadly no longer with us, were very fond of him.'

His evidence bore out what Horton and Uckfield had seen in Hazleton's house yesterday. Horton said, 'What was his position here?'

'Office manager when I joined.' Which confirmed what Vivien Walker had told Horton. He wondered if that was how Hazleton had met Vivien Walker. Perhaps this law firm had been appointed to represent Vivien Walker on her shoplifting charge. If so, Horton was surprised that Hazleton had admitted her into his house full of valuable antiques, although to be fair she'd never committed another offence, or had never been caught, added his sceptical mind. Perhaps Norman Walker had mended her wicked ways.

Chandler said, 'Victor started as a clerk but my father recognized a valuable employee when he saw one.'

'There was never anything against Hazleton?'

'Good God, no! He was a scrupulously honest man and very hard-working.'

'We've heard he liked to exaggerate, nothing harmful, just stretched the truth a little in telling a few tall stories.'

'Well, I never heard him tell any or heard a word said against him,' Chandler replied a little stiffly.

But on Chandler's own admission he hadn't seen Hazleton for years.

Horton could hear the traffic in the silence that followed this announcement. 'Is there anyone here from when Victor Hazleton was employed?' Horton knew Cantelli would establish that but it might be worth comparing notes afterwards.

Chandler shook his head. So, thought Horton, Arthur Lisle had been the last link here with Victor Hazleton, unless you counted the man sitting in front of him. Shame. Horton would have liked a few other opinions and a bit more background on the elderly man who had become an unexpected victim.

'Do you manage the practice single-handedly, sir?'

'At the moment, yes, until my son becomes a partner at the end of the year.'

'So there are no Wallingfords left?'

'No. We'll be changing the name to Chandlers on the first of January next year.' He smiled. 'A new era begins.'

Horton returned Chandler's smile. 'Tell me about Arthur Lisle,' he said.

Chandler didn't speak for several seconds and Horton didn't prompt or press him. The lawyer was obviously considering his response. There was no need to read anything sinister into that.

'Arthur was a quiet man and highly intelligent, but, as they say, lacking ambition. He specialized in property law and could have gone much further in a bigger practice, but he was content to stay in conveyancing and here. He didn't even want to become a partner.' Chandler spoke as if that was both incredible and sad.

Did he draw up wills?' Not that Horton thought that was relevant, but he recalled one of his theories that someone wanted to suppress a will made by Hazleton in order to inherit and so had dispensed with a witness and the lawyer.

'A few times when we were short-staffed but it wasn't a regular occurrence.'

'Did either Victor Hazleton or Arthur Lisle make a will with you?'

Chandler's eyebrow again lifted in surprise. Horton couldn't help wondering how many hours he stood in front of a mirror practising that. Had someone once told him he resembled Roger Moore? If so, they had grossly misled the man.

'Arthur did. I don't know about Victor; would you like me to check?'

'I expect my sergeant already is. If Mr Hazleton did make a will with you, sir, we'd like a copy of it.'

'Of course.'

Horton didn't ask to see Arthur Lisle's will because he knew that Chandler wouldn't let him see the will of someone still living. Dennings hadn't found a copy of it in Lisle's house yesterday. And Horton didn't think it was relevant anyway. He said, 'What did Lisle do in his spare time?'

'I don't think he had much with his wife so ill for many years. He was devoted to her and his family.'

But his daughter didn't seem so devoted to her father, only visiting him fleetingly, once a week, thought Horton. He got the impression from the way Chandler spoke that being a family man was something of a black mark against Lisle and wondered why before answering his own question. DCI Bliss and Uckfield were the same; family first in their eyes meant lack of commitment. With them, as it had once been with him, he thought with a twinge of guilt, it was job first and family second. Well, he'd paid the price. And what of Bliss and Uckfield? Bliss was single and Uckfield barely acknowledged his family. Cantelli was different though, thank goodness, and he was right to be.

He didn't think there was much more he could get from Chandler and what he had got was precious little. He showed him Yately's photograph and asked him if he knew or recognized him. He drew a blank.

'I believe your firm handled Colin Yately's divorce eighteen months ago.'

'Well, he doesn't look familiar but then I don't handle divorce, and neither did Arthur. You'll need to talk to Susan Elizabeth Hague, only she's on maternity leave at the moment. I deal with business law and disputes, intellectual property. But why do you want to know about this man?'

'Could we have Ms Hague's contact details?'

'Terry Bramley can give them to you, he's our office manager. But you haven't said why you're interested in Colin Yately.'

Horton told him that he'd been found dead in the Solent and that they'd established a connection between Yately and Arthur Lisle.

'I see,' Chandler nodded thoughtfully. 'I heard on the news about a body being found at sea. I'm afraid I can't tell you how Arthur and Mr Yately became friendly but I suppose it could have been through this firm. What did Mr Yately do for a living?'

'He was a postman.'

The eyebrow shot up again. There was a tap on the door and Linda entered. 'There's no record of a will for Victor Hazleton. Sergeant Cantelli also asked me.'

And, Horton recalled, there hadn't been one in Hazleton's personal file in his house, so where was it? Had Hazleton actually made a will? Surely being a tidy man he must have done. If it was in the house then they'd find it. He wondered if the Walkers were there now checking to see if anything was missing and whether Dennings was with them. Well he'd have nothing to report back to Dennings about this connection. It was clearly a disappointing dead end. It seemed Cantelli had risked seasickness for nothing.

Horton thanked Chandler for his time and said they'd notify him if and when they had news of Arthur Lisle. He left Chandler looking concerned and headed along the corridor, glancing into a couple of rooms on the way. He found Cantelli in the last room on the first floor talking to a bald, fresh-faced man in his late forties, who was sitting in front of a computer at a desk that was laden with more paperwork than Horton's. Immediately Horton could see Cantelli was on to something and his heart quickened.

Swiftly, Cantelli introduced Terry Bramley, the office manager. 'Mr Bramley says that Arthur Lisle was here two weeks ago.'

'He asked to see an archive file,' Bramley said. 'From October 1980. They're archived off site and he asked me to request it.'

Horton knew immediately this was significant, although he couldn't see how. He said, 'You obliged even though Lisle was no longer an employee.'

'I didn't see any harm in it, especially as he'd worked on the case,' Bramley said defensively.

'What case?'

Bramley flinched at the sharpness of Horton's question. He flushed, saying, 'I, er, don't know. He wasn't specific, just said he wanted to check something on an old case he'd worked on.'

Was Bramley lying? Horton didn't think so, but he could see Bramley was mentally calculating whether his desire to oblige Lisle was going to get him into trouble. 'It was manic in here. I didn't have time to question him about it. Arthur is completely trustworthy and discreet. I gave him the number of the storage company and he rang through and requested the file himself.'

'And when was it delivered?'

'That day. I don't know what time but Arthur said he'd come back after lunch and I told him he could use my office. I had a half day.'

That was unfortunate from their point of view. 'Was the file still here the next day?'

'No. Arthur left a note on my desk thanking me and said he'd got the storage company to collect it.'

Cantelli said, 'Why didn't Mr Chandler mention this?'

'Because he wasn't here. He was out fishing, with a client.'

Convenient, thought Horton. So Lisle had slipped in, accessed the file and slipped out again without anyone knowing what he'd been searching for. Of course it could have nothing to do with his disappearance or Hazleton's death, but what was it that Lisle was so keen to look up? They needed to know.

'Could you phone the storage company and tell them we have permission to access the file.'

'Now?'

Horton nodded.

As Bramley picked up the phone, he said, 'Does Mr Chandler need to know about this?'

'I suggest you tell him.' Horton didn't need to add, 'before we do'. He got the address and telephone number of Susan Elizabeth Hague before they left and on the way to the storage company that was just outside Newport, Cantelli rang her, while Horton drove. Coming off the line a few minutes later, Cantelli said, 'She remembers the case very well, and Colin Yately. It was a straightforward divorce, no complications.'

'Lucky them,' muttered Horton, thinking of his own marital split and divorce proceedings that seemed to be stretching on for ever. Then he recalled the filthy, sodden, half-chewed body in the woman's dress and suppressed a shudder; poor Colin Yately hadn't been so lucky after all.

'She said that she usually handles divorce at the top end of the market, and the staff I spoke to confirmed that Wallingford and Chandler are expensive and exclusive but get excellent results for their clients. She liked Colin and she knew him very well because he was the firm's postman. So she agreed to take it on.'

That explained that and confirmed Horton's views about the legal practice. 'Did you get to talk to Chandler junior?'

Cantelli shook his head. 'No, he was still with his client but he handles wealth management.' Cantelli quickly consulted his notebook and read, 'Which entails estate and tax planning, business succession, charitable giving, trusts and asset protection. Would be nice to have some wealth to manage,' he added snapping his notebook shut. 'The talk is that Wallingford and Chandler are doing very well, thank you. Chandler runs a Range Rover and lives in a large manor house near Kingston, and Chandler junior is single but has a girlfriend who works in London. Junior lives in an apartment at Cowes Marina. The staff I spoke to all liked Arthur Lisle; there wasn't a bad word said against him; quiet, kind, calm and brilliant at his job. None of them remembered Victor Hazleton.'

Which wasn't surprising given that he had retired so long ago. Horton turned into a track. The sign said 'Lane's Farm and Storage Company'.

'Let's hope we can find out what Arthur Lisle was so interested in two weeks ago.' But even if they did, Horton wondered if it had any connection with his disappearance and the murder of two men.

FIFTEEN

They were shown into a tiny office at the back of a large building by a dour-faced farmer, who told them he'd diversified into archive retrieval and storage and converted two of his large modern barns because the farming industry was buggered. He now employed four drivers and two office staff and made more in one month from storage and shredding than he did in six from farming. Horton wasn't sure whether he believed him but that didn't matter. What did was the contents of the large storage box dated October 1980 that had been placed in front of them.

When they were alone, Cantelli lifted the lid and pulled out a contents list which was also inscribed on the front of the box.

Horton peered at it and ran through the names. He didn't recognize any of them as being connected with the case. 'Shouldn't take you long to look through that lot.'

'What's this "you"?'

'Don't want me crowding your style. While you're checking through the contents I'm going to take a look around the area at Hazleton's house.'

'Dennings won't thank you for trampling on his ground.'

'I *know* Dennings. He's in charge, which means he'll be in the incident suite trying to look and sound impressive, and barking out directions to any of the poor plods who are unfortunate enough to enter it.'

'It would help if I knew what I was looking for.'

'I'm sure you'll spot it, *if* it's there.'

'Don't forget to come back for me. I don't fancy being roped in to milk the cows.'

'There aren't any on this farm.'

'Then make sure *I* don't get filed away.'

As Horton headed across the Island to the east coast and Hazleton's house, he wondered why Lisle had been interested in the file from October 1980. He could have been looking up the address of a former client who'd become a friend and who he'd lost contact with. Or perhaps he was trying to trace someone related to a former client. It probably had nothing to do with the deaths, or Lisle's disappearance, but there was a slim chance it could have and therefore it had to be followed up.

A patrol car and police van were parked on Hazleton's driveway and there was no sign of Marsden's car, so the coast was DI Dennings clear, unless the goon had come in the patrol car, which Horton doubted; it would be beneath him. He showed his ID to the officer on the door, who told him the Walkers and DC Marsden had been and gone. From what he had heard they hadn't said anything was missing.

Horton was logged in and he found a handful of officers bagging up anything that could be relevant to the inquiry. From the landing window, as he climbed the stairs to the observatory, he could see others combing the grounds in search of a possible murder weapon or any evidence that the murder had taken place there. He speculated on what Dr Clayton's post-mortem might discover before pushing open the door of the observatory. It was stifling hot and he was alone. The light-blue sea was rippling under a clear sky that seemed to stretch for ever. All he could see on the horizon was a lone yacht with white sails steadily making its way around the island. *Lucky thing*. He focused the telescope on it and on board saw a man and woman wrapped up against the crisp April air. Catherine had never liked sailing. She'd been more at home on Uckfield's motor boat, despite the fact her father sailed a large yacht. But he knew that Dr Clayton liked sailing. Maybe he should ask her if she'd like to go out with him on his yacht. Perhaps she already had a boyfriend she went sailing with. He knew little about her except she was divorced.

He swivelled the telescope round thinking that perhaps Dennings was with her in the mortuary. That wouldn't please her. But as he'd said to Cantelli, Dennings wouldn't want to leave the incident suite and miss out on anything. No, he'd probably wait for Gaye Clayton to report back to him, and if Horton wasn't very much mistaken Neanderthal man would soon be hassling her for the results, unless he had something else to occupy his small brain.

Horton turned his concentration closer to the shore but he

couldn't see into any of the bays in either direction because of the lie of the land. The small bays and coves were tucked in under the cliff, which meant that Hazleton wouldn't have seen anything actually entering any of them, but he could have seen a boat heading for one of them as he'd mentioned.

He returned to the ground floor and crossed the garden where he again showed his ID to the officer-in-charge of the search, who reported that nothing resembling a murder weapon had been found, but as they didn't yet know what that was they were bagging up anything that looked suspicious. It wasn't a great deal, just the occasional branch, but nothing with bloodstains on it.

Horton found a path at the edge of the garden and soon he was striking out down a steep narrow track bordered by hedgerows that was leading him down to the sea. Would Hazleton have been physically able to climb back up this path at his age, he wondered? The man had been wiry and had looked fit so it was possible, especially if he had used the path frequently and by doing so had enhanced his fitness.

After about half a mile Horton emerged from the trees and shrubs to find he was crossing a small field which came out at the edge of a low cliff. He looked over it on to a small shingle bay. It was about two hours away from high tide so impossible to walk in either direction around to the next small cove, but he noted there was another track, which led down the cliff on to the shore. At high water it would be possible to get a small boat in here but there were clearly no caves and no chines, and nowhere for Yately to stash his store of women's clothes.

He reached for his phone to call Cantelli but there was no signal. He headed north, skirting the shore as he picked his way along the field until he could see down into the next very small bay. Again there didn't seem to be any hiding place. He turned and surveyed the lie of the land. To the west, directly behind where he was standing, the field led up to a dense thicket. To the north, the field continued for a distance until it gave on to a hedge and then more trees bordering the low cliff top. To the south, and the way he'd come, there was the pathway up to Hazleton's house. Horton frowned as a thought occurred to him. Had Hazleton been involved in smuggling?

Making his way back up to the house he tried calling Cantelli again and only managed to get a signal when he was in Hazleton's garden.

'You're still alive then?' he said when Cantelli answered.

'Just, but I'm beginning to get claustrophobic and bleary-eyed. Not to mention faint from lack of food.'

'Found anything?'

'I'll tell you when you pick me up and bring me some food.'

Horton smiled. 'OK.'

Cantelli was waiting for him outside, and beside him was the large box file. 'I called Chandler and asked his permission to take it away. Bramley had told him about Lisle requesting the file. Chandler wasn't very pleased about it and said that none of the clients in the file was to be contacted without consulting him first. I gave him the list of names and he said he already had them on the computer file in the office. He said he'd let me know which of them were still clients. There's too much to go through here and it needs Trueman's expertise, not mine,' Cantelli added after putting the box in the boot of the car and grabbing the sandwiches Horton had bought.

Between mouthfuls he explained what he'd found. 'The box contains a probate for Harold Jenkins who lived in Ventnor—'

'Well he's no longer one of Chandler's clients.'

'And we won't be able to speak to him unless we engage a clairvoyant. A divorce for the Barrington-Clarkes of Newport and three property transactions: one at Fishbourne, one in Newport and the other at Brighstone, which were all handled by Arthur Lisle.'

'Any of the cases involve Victor Hazleton?'

'His initials are on some correspondence but they're more plentiful on the probate matter. I've cross-checked the files with the index, there's nothing missing, as far as I can tell, but, as I said, we'll need to do a more thorough trawl through the documents and get some legal advice to see if anything could have been extracted from one of the files.'

'How many people are mentioned, apart from those working for Wallingford and Chandler and those involved in the legal process?'

'Nine,' Cantelli answered, biting into his sandwich. 'Six

connected with the buying and selling of the properties; the two divorcees and Harold Jenkins, of Ventnor, the deceased probate.'

'Who inherited?'

'From my quick read, and it was only brief, it was a nephew called Trevor Markham.'

And where was he now? 'Should there have been more money?' wondered Horton aloud, heading for Ventnor.

'Perhaps this Markham found out he should have inherited more and killed both Hazleton and Lisle for revenge.'

'Why bother when he could simply have exposed the fraud?'

'Revenge? Or perhaps he's a psycho case. Hazleton could have been swindling the account for years and stashing the money away for his retirement. Perhaps something triggered Arthur Lisle's curiosity, he checked the file, and discovered the fraud. And tells Yately.'

'Why?'

'Perhaps Yately is related to this Trevor Markham or knew him. Angry that his friend or relative got duped, he confronts Hazleton and gets killed. Then Lisle does the same.'

'But that means Lisle should be dead and not Hazleton.'

'Something could have gone wrong. They struggled. Lisle accidentally kills Hazleton, tries to cover it up and then, filled with remorse, kills himself by driving his beloved old car into the sea and drowning. His body is swept away on the high tide.'

'Why wouldn't Yately or Lisle have reported the fraud to us, the police, instead of confronting Hazleton?'

'Not everyone does.'

'It doesn't account for Yately wearing a woman's dress though.'

Cantelli polished off the last of his sandwich and frowned. 'No.'

'And that's our sticking point on everything, Barney, except for Uckfield's favoured theory of Abigail Lisle having an affair with Colin Yately, for which we have no evidence, not even a hint of it.' Horton then told Cantelli about his walk to the shore and the thought that Hazleton could have been helping smugglers. 'There's a direct route up to his house and he could have been reporting all this suspicious lights stuff to the local police to make them consider him an idiot and stop investigating.'

'Like that poem about Matilda telling such dreadful lies that when she did tell the truth about the house being on fire no one believed her and she perished in the flames.'

'Something like that. But again we're back to that dress. What are we missing, Barney?' Horton said earnestly.

'A lot,' was Cantelli's swift reply as Horton pulled up outside the temporary incident room at Ventnor.

Dennings, jacketless and perspiring, glowered at them as they entered. He had a phone stuck to his ear, as did the other two officers in the room, and no sooner had one replaced the receiver than it rang again. Horton knew why – people were phoning in with reports of sightings of Yately and Lisle thanks to the Super's earlier press briefing.

Slamming down the receiver, Dennings said, 'So far Arthur Lisle's been seen climbing Tennyson Down, flying a helicopter at Bembridge Airport, sailing a boat out of Yarmouth, dossing in a doorway in Ryde and jet skiing across the Solent to Portsmouth; next he'll be swimming the bloody English Channel.'

Horton plonked the archive filing box on Dennings' desk, causing him to start backwards. 'Present for you, Tony.'

'What is it?'

Horton quickly brought him up to speed with the interview at the solicitor's office and what Cantelli had found in the files. He said nothing about his jaunt to Hazleton's house, and his reconnaissance of the coastline there.

'You don't mean we have to waste time sifting through that!' cried Dennings incredulously. 'Just because Lisle wanted to check up on some old paperwork.'

Horton shrugged. 'Please yourself. It's your investigation.' Horton turned to leave, prompting Dennings to say, 'Where are you going?'

'Back to Portsmouth.'

'There's work to be done here.'

'Not by me and Sergeant Cantelli, there isn't. We were asked to interview Wallingford and Chandler and we did, with that result.' Horton jerked his head at the box.

Dennings made to reply but his phone rang. He glared at it as though he could silence it by sheer willpower but it refused to obey him. As he grabbed it Marsden entered the room followed by two uniformed officers, one of whom was Claire

Skinner. Horton returned her smile as he heard Dennings' end of the conversation. 'Look, I can't get there now, I'm busy.' There was a moment's silence while the person at the other end replied. Then Dennings said, 'Tell me what you've got . . . I don't want a report; I want you to *tell me now* how Hazleton died . . . I know it's complex, it's a murder case,' Dennings sneered. Horton silently winced. It didn't need many guesses to know who the caller was. It had to be Dr Clayton, and Horton didn't think she was going to be very pleased with the DI's attitude. Dennings' mobile rang. He snatched it up from his desk and, seeing who it was, said abruptly into his landline, 'Email me the key points,' before he rang off and turned his attention to his mobile.

Horton slowly shook his head and made to leave as he heard Dennings say, 'No, Guv . . . Yes . . . It's been mad here . . . I . . . Yes, she says she's finished. I can't . . . Yes he's here. Horton,' Dennings called out, then into his mobile. 'OK . . . but . . . Yes, Guv.' To Horton he growled, 'You're to go to the mortuary. The Super's orders.'

'Hope he squares it with my boss, then.'

Horton didn't wait to hear Dennings' reply. He was secretly pleased with the way it had played out, but he wasn't going to admit that to Dennings. He noted that Cantelli had already beaten a hasty retreat. Horton knew why. Even the smell of the mortuary was better than being stuck in an overheated room with a bad-tempered DI, and a cacophony of phones that would need to be politely answered.

Outside, Cantelli said, 'I almost feel sorry for Dennings.'

Horton threw him the car keys and an astonished look.

'I said almost. I wouldn't have eaten those sandwiches if I'd known where we were going.'

'You could go back and volunteer to man the phones.'

'Think I'll risk throwing up.'

And Dr Clayton's bad temper, thought Horton. But hopefully she'd have recovered her good humour by the time they arrived.

SIXTEEN

'I'm glad it's you,' Gaye said, 'because I might not have been responsible for my actions if I'd come face to face with that oaf who's supposed to be a detective. Surgery with a sharp knife on some vital parts might have been called for. Want to see the victim?'

'Might as well, now we're here,' Horton answered, hoping the body would look better than when he'd last seen it. It didn't. In fact, it looked marginally worse, with great ugly stitches across its forehead and up its chest where the mortuary attendant had sewn it back together again after Dr Clayton's rummaging around inside. Horton tried to equate the body on the slab with the little man he'd seen in the observatory and couldn't.

The skin was white and smelt just as awful as when the boot of the car had been opened and the gruesome sight exposed, but he again noted that the sea life hadn't eaten much into the flesh, the result of being in the boot and not in the sea for long.

Dr Clayton said, 'If you've seen enough I suggest we discuss it in more comfortable surroundings, for you that is.'

With relief, Horton and Cantelli followed her into a room off the main mortuary, where Gaye nodded them towards an anti-bacterial hand wash, while she headed for a sink. 'Have you traced the next of kin?' she asked, wiping her wet hands on a paper towel before tossing it in a bin.

'There doesn't seem to be anyone,' Horton answered, eyeing her casually dressed slender figure and finding himself comparing it with Avril's more shapely and more expensively dressed one. Annoyed with letting lustful thoughts intrude amid two horrific murders, he followed Gaye Clayton into the cubbyhole of an office, where she took the seat behind the desk and gestured them into the two opposite. Sitting back she eyed them keenly and crossed her jean-clad legs.

'It's difficult to give you an accurate time of death but in my opinion he was killed late Tuesday night or possibly in the early hours of Wednesday morning. I'd say between eight p.m. and one a.m.'

Which tallied with Hazleton's call to him on Tuesday evening at twenty-one thirty-five. 'Was he alive when he was put in the car?' he asked.

'The initial evidence suggests not.'

'Thank God for that,' Horton replied with feeling.

Gaye added, 'There is evidence of silt and sea in his mouth, and I need to fully analyse the contents of the stomach to see if it contains large quantities of water and debris, but it's my belief he died from a severe trauma to the cranium. There's been heavy internal bleeding and he was struck more than once. In fact, three times, and violently, with something heavy and quite narrow, about two inches in diameter. I can't say what though. That, along with the fact it's doubtful he'd fall into the boot of the car, slam it shut and drive it into the sea makes it homicide.'

'There would have been blood then?'

'Yes, on the killer and in the location where he was struck.'

And no blood had been found in Hazleton's house or on the driveway. He could have been killed in the garden but the officer-in-charge of the search hadn't found any bloodstained weapon while Horton had been there, and if he had after Horton had left then Dennings would have known about it. It was possible that the killer had disposed of the weapon and the rain had washed away traces of blood. Either that or Hazleton could have been killed in one of the bays. Only it had to be a bay with access to a road for the body to have been placed in the car, and Horton hadn't seen any road leading back from the shore on his exploratory expedition. He hadn't seen any tyre tracks either. He supposed that Hazleton's body could have been transported to the Morris Minor, which was some distance away, in something such as a wheelbarrow, but lifting and pushing a lifeless form would take some strength.

'The forensic examination of the victim's clothes might help you,' Gaye said. 'You might be able to identify seeds, soil or gravel on them which match with the locale. Was there any forensic on the dress found on Yately that could give you an idea of where he might have been killed?'

'Some sand and gravel but it'll take at least a couple of

days before we get the full results of the analysis. And so far we've found no evidence to suggest the dress belonged to either the late Mrs Lisle or Yately's former wife.'

'It's of excellent quality, and the stitching and design indicate it wasn't bought from any chain store. I've had another look at the notes we made of it at the time Tom removed it. I'd say it belonged to a woman the equivalent of UK dress size fourteen, and judging by its length a woman who was about five feet six inches tall.'

And from what Horton remembered of the photographs he'd seen on the mantelpiece in the Lisle household, and the height given for Arthur Lisle, it didn't sound as though the dress belonged to Abigail Lisle. She was a good deal shorter than her husband, who'd been described as being five-eleven, and Lisle's GP had confirmed that. They'd check Abigail's height of course.

Gaye added, 'As you know there was a faded label on the dress and I managed to enhance a photograph of it. It's difficult to make it out completely but I did get some letters.'

Horton sat forward keenly, as Gaye handed him a photograph of the dress and one of the label enhanced. Cantelli peered over Horton's shoulder.

Gaye said, 'As you can see. It looks like the name Thea.'

Horton's eyes connected with Gaye's for a moment as they both remembered the case that had brought Horton into contact with Thea Carlsson, the first woman he'd got close to since his marriage had ended. But it had finished before it had even begun. Thea had returned to her home country of Sweden and had given him no indication that she'd ever come back. With regret he'd been forced to put her out of his mind, but it was Thea who had urged him to continue with the search for his mother and it was largely down to her that he'd made the request to see his social services case files and made contact with Adrian Stanley. Horton wondered if Stanley had managed to say anything more about Jennifer.

'What's that?' Cantelli asked, pointing to more lettering that had been enhanced. 'It looks like an "O" and an "R".'

'I think it's the name of the label or designer. I'm no fashion expert, you only have to look at me to see that,' she smiled, indicating her jeans and T-shirt, 'but the design reminded me of dresses I've seen in photographs of my mother. I'd say it dates from the 1970s and that whoever owned it had some money during that decade. They've also kept the dress somewhere relatively dry and dust free because it was in good condition.'

If the dress hadn't belonged to Abigail Lisle then could it have belonged to someone who had gone missing years ago, or who had been killed; a woman the killer had a connection with and so too did all three men: Lisle, Yately and Hazleton. Horton thought he'd check reports of missing women for the 1970s when he returned to the station. It wasn't something he wished to delegate for fear the background on his personal life would be exposed and he certainly didn't want DI bloody Dennings trampling all over his past.

Cantelli's voice broke through his thoughts. 'I think my sister, Isabella, wore clothes like this. Could I have photographs of the dress and I'll ask her expert opinion?'

'Of course; I've also emailed it and that photograph of the label to Sergeant Trueman. Hopefully your fashion expert will be able to give you more information.'

Horton hoped so too. He said, 'How does Hazleton's death compare to Yately's?'

'The method is similar. If you remember Yately was also struck on the back of the head, but the weapon used in his case was much larger, about seven inches in diameter, and he regained consciousness. A single blow to the head is rarely enough to kill someone unless the victim is unfortunate enough to have a thin skull, but several blows can. And it doesn't always render them unconscious either, but it can make them dazed and confused long enough to be tied up, submerged and finally left to drown, as in Yately's case. This latest victim was much older, and his cranium considerably thinner, so the same strength of blow could have rendered him unconscious, then your killer finished him off with a few more blows. There's not much more I can tell you except the victim was very fit and healthy for a man of his age. No signs of living a life of excesses, and no major surgery, scars or tattoos and the like.'

'Fit enough to climb a steep track?' Horton asked, thinking of the one that led up from the small bay below the house.

'Definitely. Sound heart muscles, no clogged arteries or lungs. I doubt he ever smoked and his liver was in good condition.'

Horton rose. He was about to thank her when she said, 'Are you heading back to Portsmouth? I could do with a lift. Sergeant Elkins has been called away to investigate a boat theft at the Hamble.'

Horton willingly agreed. 'If Cantelli feels sick on the ferry he'll have his own personal physician on board.'

'I might need one,' muttered Cantelli.

She asked them to wait for her outside while she gave instructions about the body. In the car Horton rang Trueman and asked about the dress.

'It went to the fashion expert, Dr Louise Adams, this morning.'

'Give me her number. I'll call her and see if she's got anything.'

'With pleasure. It'll be one thing off my desk.'

'That bad, eh?' Horton rarely heard Trueman complain.

'Worse. The ACC keeps popping in to ask how the investigation is going, and if I'm not mistaken there might be another murder very soon and very close to home.'

Horton winced. 'I expect Dean's trying to impress his new boss. Probably giving him half hourly updates. Have you got anything more on Hazleton's background?'

Horton nodded at Dr Clayton as she slipped into the back seat. Cantelli started up and headed for the ferry terminal.

'His father was a fisherman and his mother a housewife,' Trueman answered. 'Victor Hazleton was their only child and he went to the local school in Ventnor.'

So no inherited wealth. Perhaps he'd won the pools. But Trueman said not. 'His bank statements only go back a year but I've been given access to his account. He has the state pension but no private pension, and no pension from Wallingford and Chandler, but there have been several large sums of money going in over the years.'

'How large?'

'Ranging from a thousand pounds to forty thousand pounds.'

Horton gave a low whistle. 'Sounds like blackmail.'

'It would if the sums of money started off small and got larger but they don't. From what I can see, and we've still got some way to go analysing the accounts, they start off large, then the amounts fluctuate. And there's no corresponding payment going out of Lisle's or Yately's accounts. We've also got some interesting information on Hazleton's house. He purchased it in 1990 for one hundred and twenty thousand pounds, which was a lot of money then, when the average price for a house was about sixty thousand. And he paid cash for it.'

'That's a fair sum for an office manager to cough up.' So where did he get the money? The late Harold Jenkins' estate? Or had he been correct when he wondered if Hazleton had been involved in a high-level smuggling operation all these years?

Horton said, 'Who handled the conveyance on his house?' He doubted Hazleton would have used his old firm because if the money had been come by illegally Hazleton wouldn't have wanted them to know about it. Unless Lisle had done the conveyance and hadn't asked questions at the time but had since grown curious. Or could Lisle and Hazleton have been into something illegal together? But if they had then Lisle certainly hadn't lived the rich lifestyle.

Trueman said, 'A legal firm in Ryde, no longer in practice, and neither is the estate agent he bought the house from. The previous owner is deceased.'

'Not called Markham or Jenkins were they?' Horton asked, thinking of that probate file Cantelli had perused.

'No. Deacon. We're checking through the telephone records for Hazleton, Yately and Lisle. There's no record of either Yately or Lisle telephoning Hazleton or vice versa, but there are records of calls between Yately and Lisle, with the last call from Yately to Lisle made the Monday before he died. It was only a short call of two minutes' duration. Lisle's mobile phone is pay-as-you-go so we can't find out who he's called or who's called him. The phone is still dead and it hasn't got GPS so we can't trace it.'

Horton swiftly told Trueman about the archive box file they'd retrieved with Wallingford and Chandler's permission. 'You'd better tell the Super in case Dennings conveniently forgets. The names in the files will need to be checked, especially the late Harold Jenkins' estate. Was Hazleton ever married?'

'No, and there's no personal correspondence in the files we've got from his house.'

And there didn't seem to be anyone around who had really known Hazleton, especially when he'd been a young man.

'There are also no receipts or invoices for the antiques in his house.'

And Horton couldn't see why he should throw those away when they would add value to the items, unless Hazleton *had* come by them illegally.

'Is the Super there?'

'Yes.'

On the ferry, Horton finally managed to get hold of Uckfield. 'I'd like to bring in an expert to tell us something about the antiques and paintings in Hazleton's house,' he said as soon as Uckfield grunted a reply. 'I know someone we can ask. I'll arrange it for tomorrow and I'd like to come over to hear what he has to say.'

'Don't see how that can help,' Uckfield said tetchily, but when Horton remained silent he grudgingly agreed, adding, 'Dean's given authorization for you and Cantelli to continue working on the team until Saturday morning. He hopes by then we'll have found Lisle's body or at least evidence to confirm he murdered Yately and Hazleton.'

Horton wasn't convinced they'd be able to meet that deadline and by the sound of it Uckfield wasn't either. He relayed what Dr Clayton had told them about the dress. Uckfield said he'd get Marsden to check it out with Rachel Salter.

Horton rang off, leaving either Trueman or Dennings to tell Uckfield about the archive file. He then called Walters, who had nothing new to report on Russell Glenn. 'You're lucky you got me, Guv. I've been answering the phone all morning.'

'Anything I should know about?'

'PC Seaton's picked up a report of a white transit van seen close to the last house that was burgled which matches with one seen at another of the properties.'

'Sounds hopeful. Follow it up.' That also reminded Horton about the CCTV footage of the blue van. He gave instructions to Walters to retrieve the disc from his desk and send it across to the Scientific Services department, then asked for the telephone number of the superyacht. A couple of minutes later, Horton punched it in and asked to speak to Mrs Glenn, announcing himself with his rank.

'Hello Andy, don't tell me you can't make it tomorrow night.

I heard about the body found in the sea on the Isle of Wight,'
she said anxiously.

'No, everything should be fine for tomorrow.' Of course he wasn't
sure that it would be with regards to the murder investigation, but
he was determined to make that charity reception come hell or high
water. He had an unscheduled appointment with Russell Glenn.

'I was hoping you could give me Oliver Vernon's telephone
number. I'd like his help.'

'On the case?' she asked, surprised.

'I need an antiques expert.'

'Ah. He's staying on board. In fact he's with me now. I'll hand
you over. It's Inspector Horton,' he heard her say.

Horton swiftly explained what he needed.

'Delighted to help, Inspector.'

'Would eleven fifteen at the Hover terminal on the Isle of
Wight be all right with you, Mr Vernon?'

'Fine.'

'We'll send a car to collect you. You should be back on the
mainland in plenty of time for the charity reception and auction.
Can I take your mobile number in case I need to get hold of you
or change arrangements?'

Vernon relayed it before handing the phone back to Avril. She
said, 'Is Oliver allowed to tell me about it when he returns?'

'I'll let him know. It depends on what he finds.'

'Of course. Perhaps you'll be able to tell me all about it
tomorrow night, if the case has been solved.'

Horton hoped so but he wasn't overly optimistic. He toyed
with the idea of calling Bliss and updating her on Hazleton but
as his death didn't have any connection with a suspected terrorist
attack, and as he and Cantelli were now officially working on
the case, he decided not to. He stood for several moments
watching the Portsmouth horizon draw closer and the ships
making their way in and out of the old historic harbour. The day
had clouded over and the wind was picking up. It carried the
threat of rain. He was glad they'd made it back before the sea
had become too rough, for Cantelli's sake. As the ferry swung
alongside the ancient walls of Old Portsmouth, Horton called the
number Trueman had given him for the fashion expert and was
pleased when she answered.

'I was just about to call Sergeant Trueman,' a pleasant female voice declared.

'You have some information on the dress?' Horton asked eagerly.

'Yes. I wondered if you could call in at the university, Inspector. It might be easier to discuss this in person.'

Horton glanced at his watch. 'We'll be there in about forty minutes.'

SEVENTEEN

D r Louise Adams greeted them warmly and offered them refreshment, 'It's from a machine, I'm afraid.' They both refused. 'I don't blame you,' she said smiling, pushing a hand through her long dark hair and waving them into seats in her small office, which was covered with pictures of fashion models, drawings and material samples. 'The tea looks like bathwater and probably tastes like it too.' She sat forward allowing Horton a glimpse of cleavage above the tightly fitting red dress. She was an amply proportioned woman in her mid forties and very attractive to look at, Horton thought. Clearly Cantelli agreed. In fact, Horton thought she reminded him of Charlotte Cantelli.

'I'm so glad you asked me about the dress. It's a fascinating find.'

In more ways than she meant, thought Horton. She'd been told it had been found in the sea but not how. Horton wondered if she'd made the leap between that and the news of the body being recovered from the Solent on Monday. They'd dropped Dr Clayton off at the hospital much to her chagrin; she said she would love to have heard what Dr Adams had to say but she was due in a meeting. Horton promised he'd update her. Outside the rain was spitting at the window in fitful bursts and the afternoon was drawing in as Louise Adams continued.

'It's in extremely good condition.' Her lively eyes flashed with excitement as she smoothed her jewelled fingers over the evidence bag containing the dress. 'I'm very honoured and thrilled to have been given the opportunity to examine it, thank you. Her dresses are such rare gems.' Her dusky skin flushed with animation. 'Oh, I'm sorry, I haven't said who. It's a design by Thea Porter.'

Dr Clayton had got the first name correct. They both stared at Louise Adams blankly. She smiled. 'You've never heard of her. But then you wouldn't be expected to, but she was extremely well known in the 1960s and 1970s.'

Horton said, 'Tell us about her.'

'Gladly. She was such an amazing woman. Born in Jerusalem on December twenty-fourth, 1927, raised in Syria, studied at London University and Royal Holloway College, Egham, Surrey. She was small, with red hair, loyal, generous and some would say a little eccentric; others, including myself, would say she was extremely artistic, talented and inspirational. Her designs are wonderfully magical and mystical but she wasn't a very good businesswoman. Her business went into liquidation in 1981, but she started again a year later. She had so much energy, you couldn't keep her down.' Louise Adams beamed at them and both men found themselves smiling back. Her enthusiasm was infectious, thought Horton.

She leant further across her desk allowing Horton an even greater glimpse of cleavage of which she seemed totally unaware.

'Thea Porter started by importing kaftans to cut up and make into huge cushions, but quickly saw that in 1966 kaftans were fashionable so she began to make them to her own designs using furnishing fabrics and braid. She became very popular with the rich and famous. Her clothes were very sexy like she was. She designed dresses and blouses in chiffon and expensive soft fabrics.'

Horton interjected. 'So whoever once owned these dresses would have had money?'

'Oh, yes. Even to buy one now, second, third or fourth hand, would cost a small fortune, unless you were very lucky indeed to stumble across one in a charity shop or jumble sale. Her clothes are often auctioned by Christie's. They're very sought after, especially in America.'

Cantelli looked up from his notebook. 'Were her clothes on sale in America in the 1960s?'

'They were, in New York in 1968, and she had another shop in Paris from 1976 to 1979. She mixed with rich, famous and powerful people but she was never overawed by them. She was loved by her friends but she was too unique and individual to be loved by all the fashion press, though she had her fans.'

And was Abigail Lisle one of them? wondered Horton doubtfully. It didn't sound like it.

Dr Adams sat back and continued. 'As the sixties gave way to the seventies the mini-skirt, though still popular, gave way to a choice of other styles. Women could choose between mini- midi- or maxi-skirts and a multitude of styles and influences, very much like the fashions of today, I'm pleased to say. Back then there was the hippy style, nostalgia for the past, first for the twenties, then the thirties, forties and fifties and finally the Edwardian era, and that's what this dress reflects. During the 1970s Thea began to design high-waisted midi- and maxi-dresses with voluminous sleeves in luxurious brocades, which you can see in this dress in the rich gold, red and black silk cord. Thea's Edwardian look also featured vintage trimmings, and this dress has them on the high neck, and on the end of the sleeves as a ruffle.'

Horton said, 'So this is definitely a design from the 1970s.'

'Yes, about 1975 or 1976, I'd say. In 1994, Thea got a form of Alzheimer's and died on the twenty-fourth of July, 2000.'

'What sort of woman would have bought these clothes?' asked Horton.

'One who loved quality,' was Dr Adams' instant reply. 'A very feminine woman who wasn't afraid to show it. A confident woman; artistic, successful, wealthy, knowledgeable.'

And that didn't sound like Abigail Lisle from what he'd heard from Rodney Chandler at Wallingford and Chandler, and it didn't match with what Rachel Salter had said about her mother either. But perhaps Abigail Lisle had once been that woman, before her son and daughter had been born. How old had Abigail been in 1975? Twenty-five, twenty-six?

'A young woman?' asked Cantelli, following Horton's train of thought.

Dr Adams considered her reply for a moment. 'Older rather than younger, and by that I mean a woman between thirty and fifty, give or take a few years. A woman roughly a British size fourteen and five foot six, who could carry off these clothes.'

Dr Clayton's estimate was spot on then. The age range as well as the height and size sounded wrong for the dress to belong to Abigail Lisle, though Horton wasn't discounting it completely yet, not until he heard back from Trueman. If the dress hadn't belonged to Abigail, and it certainly wasn't Margaret Yately's, then what had happened to this woman after 1976? And why had Colin Yately, a former postman, been found wearing it? Had he known this woman? Had Victor Hazleton known her? Although he was a humble clerk in the seventies, had he dated a wealthy, free-spirited and artistic woman? And had that woman a connection with Harold Jenkins, deceased?

'How often would you say the dress has been worn?'

Horton knew that Trueman would have the full forensic report, which would hopefully give them that information and more about where the dress had been kept. Unless the submersion in the sea had destroyed the evidence, and that might have been exactly what the killer had intended.

'It's difficult to be certain,' Dr Adams answered, 'because the fabric is of such high quality and the stitching so superb. But there is no sign of wear, no fading, and the seams are as strong as if they'd just been sewn. I would say it's not been worn very much at all.'

And was that because the owner had died shortly after buying it?

'Can you tell us where it was bought?'

'Not precisely, and I couldn't swear on oath to it, but most probably in New York.'

'So a woman who lived abroad or travelled?'

'Or was there on holiday or business, either alone or with her husband. Unless it was purchased for her by someone and brought back to this country. But equally, Inspector, she could have bought it in London. I'm sorry to be so vague.'

'No, you've been a great help. Would records of Thea Porter's customers still exist?'

'Unlikely but you could try the Victoria and Albert Museum. They might be able to help you.'

Horton thanked her. On the way back to the station he chewed over what he'd learnt and where that took them. Reading his thoughts, Cantelli said, 'Just because she bought the dress in 1976 or thereabouts doesn't mean to say that's when she disappeared or died. She could have lived until this year. But if the dress belonged to the late Harold Jenkins and his estate, then surely it would have been sold or destroyed long ago.'

Horton agreed, and there was no connection they'd discovered yet between Yately and the late Harold Jenkins. There was nothing for it but solid background work, checks and double-checks. Horton said nothing of his idea about a missing woman, or one that had died in mysterious circumstances during the seventies. It didn't seem relevant now because, as Cantelli had indicated, the woman could have lived a lot longer than that. Nevertheless, the idea had taken root in his mind and Horton knew that he would have to check.

In the major incident suite Horton relayed to Trueman and Uckfield what Dr Louise Adams had told them.

Grouchily, Uckfield said, 'Marsden's just called in to confirm that Abigail Lisle was five foot four and slim, a size ten dress, according to her daughter, but that doesn't mean Lisle didn't kill Yately or Hazleton and then himself, or that Abigail hadn't had an affair with both men. The dress could still have belonged to her. It could have been her mother's or a friend's or a charity find, and she knew its value and treasured it. Lisle couldn't bear to part with it on his wife's death until he discovered her diaries, or maybe Yately's diaries, when he was in his flat one day, and made Yately wear it and drown in it as some kind of sick ritualistic killing.'

Horton could see that Uckfield was not going to give up on his theory. Trueman confirmed that forensics had also said the dress had been barely worn, but they could get little else from it except salt water, sand and grit. They were still analysing Hazleton's clothes. It was agreed that tomorrow Trueman would contact the V&A and Horton would accompany Oliver Vernon around Hazleton's house. Trueman would also continue the checks on Victor Hazleton and Colin Yately. And Dennings' team in the temporary incident suite at Ventnor would start checking Harold Jenkins and the other names in the archive file, though Uckfield left no doubt he thought it a waste of time. Horton could see the investigation was set to be a long haul and was clearly going to drag on beyond Saturday unless another body turned up, such as Arthur Lisle's.

Cantelli went home. Walters had already left and there was no sign of Bliss. A disgruntled Uckfield prowled the major incident suite like a dyspeptic lion and Horton slipped back to his office while Uckfield took a call from Dennings. There Horton settled in front of his computer ignoring his paperwork and called up missing persons files for 1976. He had no idea what he was looking for but he started with the local area, it seemed as good a place as any, and the victims were local so perhaps the woman had been too.

There were two missing women for 1976, neither fitting the profile, none for 1977 and one for 1978, Jennifer Horton. There were also two missing men. In 1979 and 1980 there were three missing teenage girls and two boys, one aged fourteen, the other nineteen. Horton continued into 1981 and 1982 but nobody matched the profile or background that Dr Louise Adams had given him. This line of enquiry was clearly a dead end but he found himself returning to 1978. This time he checked out the profile of the two men who had gone missing the same year as his mother. One was aged forty-three, married with three children, who had worked in a factory on the Dundas Lane estate. It was known that he'd been suffering from depression. He had left for work one day and never returned. Horton spared a thought for the man's wife and children who had lived with uncertainty for so long. The other man was single, aged thirty-one. He was a local accountant whose mother had reported him missing when he didn't arrive home from work on 2 December 1978. It transpired that he had never arrived at work. There was no record of him having been depressed and no reason why he should disappear. Was the mother still alive? wondered Horton. How had she coped with the mystery of her missing son? Had it eaten her up over the years? He guessed so.

He stood up and stretched, again considering what Adrian Stanley had been trying to tell him. Mentally he replayed the meeting in that small hospital room and Stanley's struggle to speak. But he still couldn't make sense of it. Perhaps if he visited a second time Stanley might be better. That would have to wait until tomorrow. It was time to go home to the boat. There was nothing more he could do here. If the enquiries into the dress and those into the archive file led nowhere, and if Lisle didn't turn up and there were no reported sightings of him or Yately, where did that leave them? What other avenues could they explore?

Horton stared out of the window as he considered this. There were still the missing notes. He recalled the book in Lisle's house on the history of the Island. Had their research led them to discovering something valuable or something that someone was prepared to kill for?

He grabbed his jacket and helmet. Tomorrow he'd get the name of the author of that book on local history he'd seen on Lisle's table and arrange to see him while he was on the Island. He had no idea where it would lead, probably nowhere, but when there was sod all else to go with it was worth a try. And tomorrow he'd hear what Oliver Vernon had to say, not only about Hazleton's antiques and paintings but about Russell Glenn. He'd also have Glenn's guest list, if PC Johns didn't forget. Not that he thought any of the names would leap out at him as villains; in fact he was sure they wouldn't. He didn't know what he expected from seeing the list and neither was he sure what he'd gain from seeing what had been written about the little boy abandoned by his mother on a foggy and chilly November day in 1978, but in just over twelve hours he'd find out.

EIGHTEEN

Friday

'Is this all there is?' Horton asked, incredulous, looking up from the few pieces of paper in front of him at the stout, sullen-faced woman standing the other side of the scratched wooden desk. The room reminded him of an interview room at the station, except at the station the paint wasn't peeling from the walls. She looked like a prison warder standing there in her black skirt and jacket and crisp white shirt.

'It's all that's in the file,' she snapped.

Horton recognized an evasive answer when he heard it. He hadn't expected much but he had certainly hoped for more than just three pages stating his movements from the council flat where he'd lived with his mother to the three children's homes and two foster homes before ending up with police constable Bernard and his wife Eileen Lichfield, who had changed the course of his troubled youth for ever and for good. Where were the notes on his behaviour, his schooling, his health? Why was nothing recorded about the times he'd run away in an attempt to find his mother, only to be brought back by the police? And why was there no record of what had happened to his mother's belongings?

'Then there must be another file,' he said sharply, rising. He saw no need to put himself at a disadvantage by continuing to sit while she stood.

'Not according to this.' She stabbed a fat finger at the paper in her hand. '249/615/1 Horton Andrew.'

He stretched out a hand. She seemed reluctant to pass the paper over, but he held her hostile gaze until, with a loud exhalation, she thrust it across. She was correct, but Horton had too many years' experience of officialdom not to know that something that ended with the number one indicated there must be other numbers after it.

'I want a copy of this, and everything that's in the file, and before you say that's not possible, I know it is. I'll wait.'

She looked about to protest before turning and flouncing out with as much indignation as she could muster. He wondered why she was so hostile. Was it just her natural demeanour or had she heard he was a copper and for some reason disliked all coppers. Perhaps she'd got a speeding ticket that morning or had had a row with her husband. Perhaps she didn't like the look of him. Or maybe she was simply in the wrong job because he would have thought that an abandoned child, now an adult, would have drawn some sympathy.

He crossed to the grimy salt-spattered window and stared across the busy road at the modern flats to his left and then at the small boats and the iron-clad warship HMS *Warrior* in the mud of Portsmouth Harbour to his right. His eyes ached and his head felt as though it was stuffed with cotton wool after another fitful night, tossing and turning over the murders of Yately and Hazleton, and when he wasn't thinking about that and how he might have averted Hazleton's death his thoughts had turned to contemplating what might be in his file. His early morning run along the seafront had done nothing to banish his anxiety over the latter and now that he was here it hardly seemed worth it. Curiosity, both a curse and a necessity for a police officer, had driven him. That and the fear of what he might find had made him determined to keep the appointment. It would have been easy to cancel it, to make excuses that he was too busy, particularly in light of the murder investigation, but he hated feeling afraid. He'd experienced fear too many times in his childhood and youth and knew its debilitating and humiliating effect. Because of that he'd vowed years ago to use fear as a servant not as a master. One thing was clear to him now: someone didn't want him to see the files held on him. Why?

His mobile rang but he ignored it as he considered the question, and there was another. Not only *why*, but *who* didn't want him having access to all the information that must have been written about him and, more crucially, written about his mother.

He gazed across the busy harbour, his mind racing. He knew that files on children in care had in the past been kept for a minimum period, which had usually been until the child reached adulthood. So why hadn't the sullen-faced woman simply said that his files had been destroyed when he'd reached adult age? Why hadn't the social services department told him the same, instead of granting him access? The answer came quickly: because there was nothing on record about them having been destroyed, and, if that was the case, did that mean it was just a clerical slip-up or that records about him existed somewhere? Did someone have them, but had overlooked the sheet of paper pertaining to 249/615/1 Horton Andrew? And could that someone be Detective Chief Superintendent Sawyer of the Intelligence Directorate?

The door opened and he spun round to see the stout woman holding the photocopies with a frown of disapproval on her face, but this time he saw it without the prejudice of his past and it intrigued him. Again he considered her manner and wondered what she had been told about him. He hadn't shown his ID or announced his profession, only given his name, but someone had prejudiced her against him, why? And what the devil had she been told? Sawyer had to be behind this. But if he was, then even more important and curious was how had Sawyer known that he'd request his files? Someone had alerted them, which meant his file must be flagged, either that or his mail was being intercepted, but he thought the latter unlikely. A cold shiver crept up his spine while his heart skipped a beat. Someone had left what meagre record there was on him deliberately, just to see if one day he'd come asking for it.

Tersely, he said, 'I'll contact you on Monday. Meanwhile, I suggest you search your archives.'

He swept out not waiting for her reply, knowing it would only be negative. She wasn't going to search because there was nothing to find, but his visit here, and his command, or rather the threat that he'd be back, would trigger action from someone. All he had to do was wait and see what kind of action and by whom.

He checked his messages and found one from WPC Claire Skinner who was at Arthur Lisle's house. Horton had rung DC Marsden early that morning and asked him to find out the title and author of the book he'd seen in Lisle's dining room. She had both and was contacting the publisher to get the author's address. She'd call him back with it.

Horton headed for the hospital where he found Adrian Stanley asleep and alone. He sat for a while with the elderly man, willing him to wake up. His mind wandered back to their conversation in the apartment overlooking the Solent on Monday morning. There didn't seem any hint then of what Stanley might now be trying to tell him. Puzzled, Horton let his gaze travel around the small hospital room, his eyes alighting again on the photograph beside Stanley's bed of him receiving his gallantry medal from the Queen alongside his wife. Horton frowned. Something had nagged at him the last time he'd been here but he couldn't pinpoint what. Now, it suddenly came to him. He hadn't seen that picture on Monday. He would have remembered it and commented on it. So why hadn't it been on display in Stanley's apartment? It

must have been a proud moment for Stanley. Perhaps he'd kept
it in his bedroom. Horton slipped out of the room and into the
corridor, where he called Robin Stanley.

'Has your father said anything more?' he asked when Robin
came on the line.

'I'm afraid not, Inspector.'

It was what Horton had been expecting. He said, 'The photograph of your father receiving his gallantry medal, where did he
usually keep that?'

'It's strange you should mention it,' Robin replied, causing
Horton's heart to quicken. 'It's always kept on the mantelpiece.
Dad was very proud of it but when I collected some things for
Dad for the hospital I found it buried underneath some tea towels
in a drawer in the kitchen.'

Horton's mind raced as he tried to grapple with the significance
of this. 'Perhaps it was broken and your father meant to fix it?'
he suggested, knowing that the picture beside Stanley's hospital
bed didn't look damaged to him.

'No. It was fine.'

So why would Stanley hide it? Surely there was only one
answer: because he didn't want Horton to see it. The breath
caught in his throat. He thanked Robin Stanley and quickly
returned to Adrian Stanley's hospital room. Stanley was still
asleep. Horton lifted the photograph and studied it carefully. It
was just an ordinary picture of a proud man and woman and yet
. . . Horton recalled Adrian Stanley's struggle to speak, surely
he remembered Stanley's eyes travelling to this picture, or was
that just his overactive imagination?

With his heart thumping against his ribcage, Horton turned
the frame over and lifted off the back, but with searing disappointment found nothing; no hidden notes, no comments on the
rear of the photograph, not even a date. Then why had Stanley
hidden it? Did it have anything to do with the armed robbery
that Stanley had helped to thwart? Had one of the criminals in
that robbery been involved with Jennifer or known something
about her disappearance? Horton knew he'd have to check.
Although eager to do so, it would have to wait because his phone
rang. Seeing it was WPC Skinner he stepped out of the hospital
room and answered it as he headed from the ward. She'd not

only got the author's address but had spoken to him, and Ian Williams said he'd be very pleased to talk to Inspector Horton or any member of the police if it would help with their investigation.

'He said that Colin Yately had visited him,' Skinner relayed excitedly.

'When?'

'In October, February and three weeks ago. Yately wanted some help with some research he was doing for a book.'

It was as Horton had suspected but it could still mean nothing. He told Skinner that he'd be over to talk to Mr Williams in a few hours. He hurried back to the station to find Walters and Cantelli in CID. Cantelli he could trust, and after calling him into his office he told him what had happened at the social services office and at the hospital. Cantelli looked increasingly concerned but made no comment. Horton asked him to research the armed robbery that Adrian Stanley had thwarted, which had earned him his gallantry medal, and to find out everything he could about it and the whereabouts of the perpetrators.

Cantelli nodded solemnly. He didn't ask if what he was doing was wise because it wouldn't make any difference, he'd still do it. Instead, the sergeant said, 'Why wouldn't Stanley tell you this?'

'Perhaps he thought it would reflect badly on her or badly on him because he hadn't done his job properly.' Horton ran a hand over his head. 'I've got no idea, Barney, and it's probably a waste of time, but that photograph means something and it has to be linked with that armed robbery.'

'I'll see what I can get. PC Johns has brought in the guest list for the charity reception on Glenn's yacht tonight. It sounds a posh do. There are a lot of nobs on the list and one or two actors and footballers.' Cantelli handed across the sheet of paper. Horton quickly scanned it finding his name at the bottom. There were no villains he knew. He asked Cantelli if he recognized any.

'No, but I'll get Walters to run a check on them. And you should know that Walters is moonlighting for Danby tonight. He's just told me that he's on security duty on Glenn's yacht.'

'Then God help us. Knowing Walters' luck something's bound to go wrong.' And that reminded Horton about the blue van. He asked Cantelli to check with the Scientific Services department to see if the video unit had managed to enhance the registration number or anything else on the van to help give them some clue as to its owner. 'Did Johns have any luck finding out if the RIB from Glenn's yacht has been launched?'

'It has. It was launched on Monday morning when Russell Glenn and Lloyd took it out for a trial. One of the engines wasn't working properly so the mechanic was called in and it was given another test run on Tuesday.'

'It wasn't taken out at night?'

'Not according to Johns, but he said he couldn't push his luck by asking too many questions because Lloyd is as sharp as they come. As well as having muscles he's also got brains, and he carries a lot of clout with the crew. Johns reckons it's Lloyd and not Glenn who gives the orders to the skipper and second mate who then dole it out to the crew. Glenn spends a lot of time in his study.'

'And Avril Glenn? What does Johns say about her?'

'A real looker and lovely figure but then you know that already. She seems pleasant enough and friendly but not overly friendly. Johns says she seems to spend more of her time with "the bearded Vernon and that smooth bastard Keats than her husband", I quote. And Danby deals direct with Lloyd.' Cantelli hauled himself up. 'I'll see if Elkins has managed to pick up anything from Customs and the Border Agency.'

Horton headed for the major incident suite, making an effort to focus his thoughts on the investigation instead of mentally running through all the possible connections between Stanley's armed robbery and his mother. Uckfield was in his office. First, Horton got an update from Trueman.

'There's not much, Andy. The fingerprints found on the telescope in Yately's flat are too smeared and vague to match anyone's, including Arthur Lisle's. We've got a couple of smudged prints from Yately's apartment, which don't match his daughter or any of the residents. And there are some prints from Lisle's house that don't match with the personal items taken from there or his family and they don't match with Hazleton's or Yately's. There have been a few reported sightings of Arthur Lisle on the Island, which Sergeant Norris and his team are checking out.'

Horton glanced across at Uckfield who was scowling at his computer. With a backward glance at a tired-looking Trueman, Horton swiftly crossed to the big man's office, knocked briefly and entered.

'I hope you've got something worthwhile to say, otherwise you can bugger off.'

The bags under Uckfield's bloodshot eyes looked as though they should have been put out weeks ago and his craggy face was grey with fatigue. He waved Horton into the chair opposite.

'That bastard Dean's just waiting for me to cock up so that he can go running to head teacher to tell him what a useless prat I am. For Christ's sake, why didn't you seal off that flat and take the old man seriously?'

And I bet you've told Dean that it's all down to me, thought Horton angrily. Well, Dean hadn't come bellyaching around his door yet, and so far Bliss had failed to rub salt into his wounds; she was too preoccupied with her pet project and, Horton guessed, too wary to come down on him too hard in case DCS Sawyer was his new-found friend.

Ignoring Uckfield's remark, Horton said, 'I want to interview the author of a book on the history of the Isle of Wight coast that was in Lisle's dining room.'

Uckfield rolled his eyes. 'Can't see where that's going to get us.'

'Neither can I at the moment,' Horton retorted, 'but Yately visited this author in October, February and three weeks ago, and as those notes have gone missing, along with Lisle and his laptop computer, and as Lisle apparently took the notes, it's worth talking to the author . . .' Horton stalled. There was something on the edge of his mind, something he'd just said that was significant, but try as he might he couldn't grasp what it was. Irritatingly it refused to come.

Uckfield exhaled noisily and threw himself back in his seat. 'Might as well waste more time,' he said airily. 'Like checking out that archive file.'

'Cheer up. Oliver Vernon, the antiques expert, might have something significant to say about Hazleton's valuables which could give us a lead.'

Uckfield snorted. Horton beat a hasty retreat before the Super could voice his opinions about that, and before he could ask what Cantelli was working on.

An hour and a half later Horton was pulling up outside Hazleton's house, where a patrol car was sitting on the driveway. He nodded at the officer outside and found the other officer with Oliver Vernon in the lounge.

'I think I've died and gone to heaven,' Vernon said brightly, shaking Horton's hand.

'That good, eh?'

'I'd say,' he enthused, crossing to the mantelpiece. 'Take this.' He pointed to a black wooden glass-fronted box on the mantelpiece that contained a thermometer and had a gold clock with roman numerals mounted above it. 'It's an antique French Empire clock, and is absolutely beautiful, not to mention in pristine condition.' He touched it almost sensuously. 'It was made around 1820 and its seconds dial and thermometer make it unique. For a collector it could fetch up to five thousand pounds, maybe more. And look at this pair of Famille Rose vases either side of it. Exquisite. May I?'

Horton nodded. Vernon lifted one of the small vases and handled it delicately while inspecting it. It was just over a foot high. Horton saw that it was decorated with Chinese characters in a fenced garden amidst rocks, blossoming trees and floral sprays.

'This is amazing,' Vernon breathed. 'I can hardly believe it. Early twentieth century, Chinese. Could fetch anything up to forty thousand pounds at auction.'

Horton was surprised, though he shouldn't have been, recalling what Trueman had said about Hazleton's accounts.

With a flushed face, Vernon continued, 'Can these antiques be traced back to previous owners?'

'We haven't found any paperwork for them.'

Vernon raised his eyebrows. 'Unusual, but not unknown. Do you suspect them to be stolen?'

'Do you?'

Vernon gave a knowing smile. 'I can't remember seeing any of them listed as stolen, or hearing about it. In my business it pays to keep a track of these things.'

'And what precisely is your business?' asked Horton lightly, before quickly adding, 'Oh, I know you're an auctioneer but . . .'

'I'm not actually. I'm an art historian.'

Horton contrived to look baffled, and as if this was new information to him, when Avril had already told him this and Walters had discovered that Vernon worked as a freelance valuer, researcher, lecturer and consultant. He wanted it to lead to them discussing Russell Glenn.

Vernon smiled and gently replaced the Chinese vase. 'I research rare and valuable antiques, art treasures like this vase, jewellery and paintings for clients. When I find something, often after years of research, I offer to buy it on behalf of the client, if it's available for sale, and even if it's not I will try and persuade the owner to part with it, or rather my client gives me authorization to bid to a certain level, depending on how desperate he is to acquire it. Other times I will trace a lost antiquity without necessarily having a client and then I will match it with a client who will appreciate it.'

'And is that what you do for Russell Glenn?'

'Yes.' Vernon's eyes scanned the room. They fell on the painting of a sailing scene that looked like it had been executed at Cowes Week, which Horton had noted on his earlier visit. 'I know what Russell wants and if I'm not mistaken . . .' Vernon swiftly crossed the room and peered closely at the painting. Horton exchanged a glance with the uniformed officer, who knew better than to interject. Vernon gave a low whistle and spun back, his face flushed with excitement. 'Russell would love to own this, *if* it's genuine,' he quickly added. 'And I think it might be. He loves beautiful things, paintings in particular, but he also buys rare pieces of jewellery for Avril. This painting appears to be a Raoul Dufy, which is remarkable because it looks like "Regatta at Cowes", and it can't be because "Regatta at Cowes" is hanging in the National Gallery of Art in Washington DC.' Vernon ran a hand through his hair.

'Who's Raoul Dufy?' asked Horton as a thought struck him. Could tonight's reception on board the superyacht have been designed for the purpose of Oliver Vernon buying, or rather overseeing the purchase, of an item of jewellery for Glenn? It couldn't be a painting because that would be too conspicuous to bring on board; all the items were being viewed on screen in the on board cinema so whatever it was had to be small enough to be brought on to the yacht by one of the guests without being noticed, especially if that item had been obtained illegally to begin with. With growing excitement Horton thought that at last he might be getting to grips with the real purpose of Glenn's stay in Portsmouth. The charity auction was just a smokescreen. Did that mean Avril was party to this exchange? Before he could reason that one out, Vernon was speaking.

'Dufy was a French Fauvist painter. They were renowned for emphasizing bright colours and bold contours in their work, as you can see in this painting. Dufy died in 1953. He is very noted for scenes of open-air social events, like this one. It's either a very good forgery or Dufy painted more than one picture of the "Regatta at Cowes" in 1934. And if it's genuine it will fetch a fortune at auction. You are looking at a very fine collection here, and the glassware and porcelain I've already seen in the dining room is in incredibly good condition and valuable. This man clearly had an eye for beautiful things.'

Too fine an eye. How could an office manager have afforded to buy these kinds of things, wondered Horton? The simple answer was he couldn't. These either had to have been stolen or they were Hazleton's pay-off for smuggling. 'Did you know Mr Hazleton?'

'No. I only wish I had. Is there a next of kin?' Vernon asked keenly.

Horton knew the way Vernon's mind was running, get in early and offer to handle the sale.

'We're still trying to establish that. For the time being I'd appreciate it if you would handle this matter confidentially.'

'Of course.'

'Could you make an inventory of what's in the house, giving an estimated value of each item?'

'It will be my pleasure. I'll begin right away.'

'An officer will accompany you.'

'To make sure I don't steal anything?' Vernon grinned. 'It's all right, I understand and I'd welcome an extra pair of hands and eyes.' He consulted his watch. 'Depending on what else I find in the house I might have to return tomorrow.'

'That's fine and I appreciate your help, Mr Vernon.'

'Oliver, please. I hear you're attending our little shindig tonight.'

'Yes, but I don't think I'll be bidding for any of the items on a police inspector's pay.'

'You might get carried away in the excitement of the moment.'

'If I do then I'll have to ask you to re-auction it. Does that happen?'

'Not in the circles I operate in.'

'The rich and famous. And they have deep pockets, like Russell Glenn.'

'Very deep. And, as I said, they like special pieces and they're not too fussy about their provenance.'

'How long have you acted for Glenn?' Horton asked casually.

'Five years.'

'How did you get to build up this select band of clients? I'm curious that's all,' Horton quickly added, smiling; he didn't want to make it sound like an interrogation.

'Recommendation. And a reputation for being discreet. I do a good job for one client and the word soon gets around. I started off by discovering a very beautiful lost piece of . . . well, let's just say something very valuable and treasured.' Vernon fingered his short fair beard with his slender fingers. 'I successfully nego-tiated its sale, no questions asked, nothing made public and just built my reputation from there. There's nothing illegal about what I do, Inspector. I don't steal anything and I don't sell on stolen goods, not unless they were stolen three or more centuries ago and no one knows or can trace their rightful owner.'

'And it's all tax free.'

Vernon pulled a face. 'That's not my business.'

No, thought Horton. Tax evasion wasn't Detective Chief Superintendent Sawyer's usual remit either, but he could be working alongside other agencies to crack Russell Glenn for it. But Horton suspected that either Glenn was about to purchase some art or antique treasure and Sawyer was keen to get hold of it and those involved in the transaction, or Glenn had something to sell. And perhaps *he'd* been invited on board to verify that everything, as far as he could see, was above board. He thought of the guest list that Cantelli had shown him earlier and wondered what Walters would discover from checking the names on it. Who was the secret buyer or seller?

Vernon's voice broke through his thoughts. 'I recommend that you either move these valuables or make this house rock-solid secure. I won't say anything but word has a habit of getting out.'

It hadn't so far but Horton took the point. He said, 'An officer will drop you back to the Hover terminal when you're ready, and in time to make sure you're not late for the auction tonight.'

He nodded at the officer to stay with Vernon and gave him instructions to take written notes. He didn't want Vernon using a mobile device to record the items for fear it would get out on the Internet. Outside, Horton detailed the other officer to remain there and to be vigilant. Then he called Uckfield, who answered immediately. Horton relayed what Vernon had told him. 'Better ask the National Gallery in Washington DC if their Raoul Dufy is still hanging there,' Horton added jokingly. 'Apart from that it looks as though Hazleton came across these items illegally, either having stolen them or they could have been his rewards for helping in a high-level smuggling operation.'

'You're not going to give up on that, are you?' Uckfield cried in exasperation.

'Like you're not going to give up on the theory that Lisle killed Hazleton and Yately because his wife had an affair with them.'

'At least it explains the dress. Hazleton couldn't have stolen from the Jenkins estate, because Dennings says Jenkins left everything to two charities and they've confirmed they received it. His team's still checking the rest of the names in that file.'

Horton rang off but Uckfield's words nudged what had been chewing at the corner of his mind. *Checking the rest of the names in that file.* Files. His mind flashed to the files he'd seen that morning in the social services office, or rather hadn't seen. And now he knew what Arthur Lisle had been checking for in that archive file. Of course the names on the front of the archive box tallied with the contents and the office manager's database, because the file that Lisle had sought had never been put in the box to begin with. Horton smiled. It was so simple. Victor Hazleton had been the office manager in 1980. He had complete control over the archive files. If he had robbed someone's estate what simpler way to cover it up than to keep the paperwork himself or destroy it so that nobody could check it? Only someone had finally discovered Hazleton's little secret: Arthur Lisle.

But that didn't explain *how* Hazleton had done it, or why he was dead instead of Arthur Lisle. Horton's excitement subsided. He had felt that he was getting somewhere but he was still up that blind alley. He just hoped and prayed the local historian, Williams, might throw some light on to it.

NINETEEN

Horton was shown into a small study crammed with books and papers in a modern house in the middle of undulating countryside not far from the coastal resort of Sandown.

Ian Williams, a lean man in his early fifties, with short light-brown hair, bright intelligent eyes and a cheerful small face, gestured Horton into a seat with a friendly smile. He'd made coffee, over which they talked about a shared interest in a love of the sea and sailing.

'I heard about Colin Yately's death on the radio. Terrible. He first contacted me in October last year, again in February, and three weeks ago,' Williams said, getting down to business.

Horton sat forward, not bothering to disguise his keen interest. 'Why did he contact you?'

'He was researching the Island's history, or more specifically Island families and the people who had shaped it in some way. William Arnold was one such person. He was appointed Collector of Customs at Cowes in 1777; a very hard-working, honest and determined man. He pressed for a faster cutter based at Cowes to stop the smugglers but when he didn't get one he bought and fitted one out of his own pocket. Through his determination smuggling decreased. Then there was Hans Stanley who bought the Steephill estate to the west of Ventnor in 1770. Stanley was MP for Southampton from 1754 to 1780 and was made Governor of the Isle of Wight for life in 1774.'

'You told Mr Yately about these people.'

'Yes, and others, including John Morgan Richards, the tobacco magnate, who bought Steephill Castle in 1903 and continued the tradition of entertaining the rich and famous there.'

Horton felt the stirrings of disappointment. As he bit into a digestive biscuit, he was beginning to think this was a dead end, just as Cantelli's enquiries into the armed robberies had been. His mind spun back to the call he'd received from Cantelli just before he'd knocked on Williams' door. Both of the armed robbers that Adrian Stanley had arrested were now dead. So there was no point in pursuing that line and, as Cantelli had said, Adrian Stanley must have been trying to tell him something else. Horton had asked how Walters was getting on with Glenn's guest list. No one suspicious so far was the result, which was what Horton had expected. He wondered if he should tell Sawyer what he suspected. Not until he'd finished with Ian Williams, and despite liking the man and enjoying his company, he thought he should make that sooner rather than later.

Williams was saying, 'Mr Yately was also very interested in Dr Arthur Hill Hassall who was sent to Ventnor to convalesce from tuberculosis, which was a killer in the nineteenth century, as you probably know. He was so impressed by the beneficial effect of the mild climate of the Undercliff that he wrote to *The Lancet* in 1867 advocating the building of a hospital for tuberculosis patients. It was the beginning of a revolutionary and highly effective treatment, but even more effective was the coming of antibiotics in the 1950s which put an end to the hospital.'

Williams sipped his coffee. He looked as though he was getting into his stride and could wax lyrically for hours on the subject, but Horton didn't have hours. He wanted to get back to the mainland long before the reception to see if DCI Harriet Lee or anyone else from the Intelligence Directorate was lurking on the boardwalk, watching Glenn's yacht. And he wanted to corner Mike Danby to establish exactly how much he knew about any attempt to buy or sell whatever precious item was going to exchange hands tonight.

'Mr Yately was also very interested in another prominent family of Ventnor, one which had a considerable influence in transforming it from a small fishing village to a town.'

Horton's head snapped up, his interest suddenly aroused. They were almost the same words Yately had used in those notes. He sat forward. 'And they were?'

'The Walpens, as in the Chine,' Williams smiled.

The chines, caves and coves of the Isle of Wight. That meant little on its own but Horton felt a pricking sensation between his shoulder blades that told him this had to be relevant, a feeling which deepened when Williams added, 'In fact, when Mr Yately came to see me for the third time, three weeks ago, it was the Walpens he was particularly interested in.'

And two weeks ago Arthur Lisle had requested an archive file from the storage company. Horton couldn't recall the Walpen name on the list of contents for the simple reason that it had never been entered. He'd been correct. God, he was close. He could feel it, smell it. He could almost touch the answer, it lay tantalizingly close, just outside his grasp. But he felt certain that soon the pieces would come together. Not caring if he betrayed his excitement, he said, 'Tell me what you told Colin Yately.'

'First we discussed the name Walpen, for a reason. Walpen Chine is on the south-west coast of the Island. It's a sandy ravine, one of many such chines on the Island created by erosion of soft Cretaceous rocks. It leads from the cliff top to approximately halfway down the cliff face above Chale Bay. It's now dry and the river bed can be seen heading back uphill to the cliff edge. It's believed that William Walpen took his name from the Chine because he appeared out of nowhere and nobody can trace his lineage or history prior to 1835.'

Horton couldn't see how this was relevant to the case, but it had to be. 'Go on,' he urged.

'Walpen was a rough sort of man, blustery, big, tough, but extremely wealthy and generous. No one knew where his wealth came from and there were several stories surrounding it. One was that he'd been a fisherman and had made a huge fortune from smuggling, the other that he'd come from a wreck off Walpen Chine, looting from it gold and jewellery. But if he'd been a local fisherman someone would have known him and there is no wreck of that period that ties in with Walpen's appearance. So the other theory is that Walpen broke away from a ship off Chale Bay, escaping with stolen jewels and gold, and there is a possibility that the ship was one of a fleet of packet steamers provided by Louis Philippe for Charles X on his flight from France for England in August 1830. It's known that Charles X brought valuables with him to pay for his new life in England.'

Several ideas were swimming around Horton's head but he shelved them for the moment to concentrate on what more Williams had to tell him.

'Walpen began to invest his money in building projects and most specifically in the boom in building in Ventnor as it became a health resort. In 1844 he married the wealthy daughter of a landowner. She inherited when her father died, only to die a year later in 1856, childless, making William Walpen even wealthier. He then married a woman thirty years younger than him, in 1862, Mary, who after many miscarriages and stillbirths finally produced a son, Elliott, in 1872, dying herself in childbirth. William didn't remarry but put his energies into his business which now included shipping, hotels and land. He died in 1893 leaving it all to Elliott, then aged twenty-one. But Elliott, with a good education and a quick brain, was an even better businessman than his father. He also got heavily involved in Cowes Week and indulged his passion for yacht racing and the America's Cup and was a keen astronomer. He married Julia in 1905, but she died in 1914, so, like his father before him, Elliot remarried a young woman, Lisa, in 1920, who produced Sarah Walpen in 1921. Elliot died in 1935 and his wife in 1955. Sarah took herself off to America in 1957 and that was the last anyone heard of her.'

Thoughts hurtled through Horton's mind. So much added up: sailing . . . Cowes Week . . . the Raoul Dufy painting . . . astronomy . . . Hazleton's telescope . . . the Thea Porter dress that Yately had been wearing when his body had been found, possibly purchased in America, and in 1976 Sarah Walpen would have been fifty-five and within the age range Dr Adams had said the buyer of the dress might have been. But none of these were evidence of why Yately was killed.

Williams said, 'Sarah Walpen must have died in the States and I'm not aware that she ever married. The line died out with her and I told Mr Yately this.'

'How did he seem when you told him?' asked Horton eagerly.

Williams considered this for several moments. 'Satisfied. Yes, that's how I'd describe it. And possibly even triumphant.'

At last Horton was beginning to feel a little triumphant himself. His visit here hadn't been a waste of time, on the contrary it had given him the key to the case and that key was Sarah Walpen. Colin Yately had discovered, or had had an idea about what had happened to her. Horton did too.

When he ascertained that Ian Williams could contribute no more to the case, Horton quickly and warmly thanked him and hurried outside, where he drove a short distance away before calling Uckfield. Quickly, he gave the Super a potted summary of what Williams had told him, ending with, 'We need to find out if Sarah Walpen died in the States, but it's my belief she didn't. I think she returned to the Isle of Wight and Hazleton killed her and stole her possessions to fund his lifestyle. I think Sarah Walpen arranged to buy a house here, the place of her birth. She asked Wallingford and Chandler to act for her in the purchase of the property. They did, or rather Arthur Lisle did. On her return Hazleton struck up a friendship with her, before killing her and stealing from her so he could buy that big house on the cliff top and retire from Wallingford and Chandler to live the life of a gentleman. When Yately began his passion for local history he discovered the Walpens and was curious to trace the last of the line, Sarah. He mentioned it to his new friend who shared the same interest, Arthur Lisle, and Lisle recalled acting on the property purchase for Sarah. He couldn't remember what property she'd purchased, hence his request to see the archives files.'

'But there's no Sarah Walpen named in that file,' protested Uckfield.

'Exactly, because Hazleton, as office manager, never filed the papers. And he erased all trace of her from the office records, so it was never entered on the computer.'

'And when Lisle discovered this he called on Hazleton,' interjected Uckfield excitedly.

'Yes, but initially without mentioning Sarah Walpen. Remember Lisle checked the files two weeks ago, a week after Yately had consulted Ian Williams for the third time. I think Lisle bided his time, doing further research with Yately, until he was certain about Sarah Walpen. Then last week Lisle must have told Hazleton that he and Yately knew the truth. Hazleton must have fobbed them both off, saying he'd confess, and then lured Yately to meet him in the bay beneath his house where he killed him.'

'Could he have the strength for that?'

'Dr Clayton says that Hazleton was very fit and strong for his age and he could have surprised Yately. He knocked him out and then bound and gagged him.' But there were still things that didn't add up. He thought back to Dr Clayton's report on Colin Yately's death. He'd been tied up and almost drowned until the poor man had given his tormentor the information he wanted. Horton suspected that the information was what was contained in his historical notes about the Walpens. Could Hazleton have been physically capable of that? There were other anomalies too.

Frowning, he added, 'I know that doesn't account for Yately wearing what I think must have been one of Sarah Walpen's dresses. Hazleton would hardly have wanted to draw attention to that, unless it was some kind of sick joke. And it doesn't explain how Yately ended up in the Solent when Hazleton didn't have a boat.'

'Lisle had one though,' said Uckfield. 'Perhaps Hazleton persuaded or bribed Lisle to keep quiet about it. But Lisle then realizes he'll be at Hazleton's mercy, he collects all the evidence from Yately's flat, i.e. the notes, visits Hazleton and kills him. Then he kills himself, unable to live with what he's done.'

It made some kind of sense, but Horton still wasn't sure.

Uckfield added, 'I'll get Trueman working on this Sarah Walpen. We've no sightings of Lisle for the weekend between Yately's death and his showing up at Yately's apartment, so perhaps he was hiding out at Hazleton's house and that was when the guilt set in.'

Horton thought of those blows that had killed Hazleton. Could Arthur Lisle have inflicted them? People were capable of all sorts of terrible things when desperate, angry or provoked.

Uckfield continued, 'We've got a sighting of Yately, but it's for the wrong time. It's the Monday before he was killed. He travelled to Southampton on the hi-speed Red Jet. Bought his ticket by cash, but one of the staff there recognized him. She's been interviewed and it seems genuine but I can't see how that helps us.'

And neither could Horton.

Uckfield said, 'He probably went to do some sightseeing. Apparently he was carrying a briefcase and camera.'

'I didn't see either in Yately's apartment, not on my first visit or our second one.'

There was a minute pause before Uckfield said curtly, 'I'll check with Taylor.'

Horton knew Taylor would confirm that neither had been in the flat, and Horton didn't recall the witness mentioning Lisle carrying them. Lisle might already have put them in his car before returning to Yately's flat when the witness had seen him. Or he could have put both in the briefcase, unless Yately had taken them with him when he'd met his killer. And why would he do that? *Because the briefcase and camera contained something that would incriminate the killer in the death of Sarah Walpen.* Horton's pulse quickened. And if that were so, then had Yately gone to Southampton on the Monday before his death to collect and photograph the final piece of evidence? What was it? Horton needed to think and there was one place to do it: Victor Hazleton's house.

When he reached it, there was no sign of the patrol car or Oliver Vernon. He must have finished his cataloguing and been taken to the Hovercraft terminal. Perhaps the sight of the bank of fog Horton could see out to sea beyond a RIB had persuaded Vernon to call it a day, and time was getting on. Horton checked the house; it was securely locked but he recalled Vernon's advice about removing the valuable items. They'd have to see to that tonight.

As he crossed Hazleton's garden, Horton's thoughts returned to Colin Yately and his trip to Southampton. If Yately had been on the Sarah Walpen trail then what had taken him to Southampton? The city might not have been his final destination. He could have caught the train to London.

Horton stood at the top of the cliff path as his mind raced with possibilities. If he was correct in thinking that Sarah Walpen was returning to the Isle of Wight where she'd purchased a property through Wallingford and Chandler, then how would she have been travelling? By aeroplane? The city of Southampton had an airport but it didn't take transatlantic flights, not even now when it was a bloody sight bigger than it had been when she must have returned. And they didn't know exactly when that was, but it had to be before Victor Hazleton had retired prematurely early in 1986, when he'd suddenly had enough money to live like a gentleman, and most probably after October 1980, when Arthur Lisle thought he'd handled the property conveyance. But Southampton, like Portsmouth, did have a port and the Southampton port, then as now, took the big cruise liners. With excitement Horton recalled the book he'd seen on the table in Arthur Lisle's dining room on British passenger ships. Now, Horton knew exactly where Colin Yately had been visiting on the Monday before his death: the headquarters of the company owning the cruise ships which sailed from Southampton.

He reached for his phone. Uckfield was engaged. Horton called Cantelli. After bringing him up to speed, he said, 'Contact the shipping company headquarters in Southampton and find out if Sarah Walpen was a passenger on any of their liners sailing into Southampton in the period from October 1980 to December 1985. If so, which one? Find out when it docked and if Sarah Walpen disembarked.'

'Surely she must have done, otherwise she'd have been reported missing.'

Horton knew she hadn't been. Rapidly thinking, he said, 'Then Hazleton must have met her at her house and killed her there.'

He turned and stared at Hazleton's house. Into his mind drifted a fragment of the interview with the Walkers. *He was always coming back with something he'd picked up at some market or antique shop.* Or rather, Horton thought, picked up from Sarah Walpen's house, which meant it had to be close by, because it was the reason why Hazleton had fed those false stories to the police all these years about smugglers and illegal immigrants. It was a bluff. Hazleton didn't want the police to investigate. On the contrary he wanted everyone to think he was a crank, because that way he could come and go as he pleased and he could steal from Sarah Walpen's house without anyone knowing about it. That was until Colin Yately had turned up. And Horton thought he knew exactly where Sarah Walpen's house had to be.

TWENTY

I t took him forty minutes to find it. It would have taken less but for the fog, which had rapidly rolled in and was now so thick he could barely see a yard in front of him. The air was still and deathly silent, except for the occasional boom of the foghorns filling him with a chill foreboding that seemed to reach inside and squeeze the breath from him. He knew that Sarah's house had to be well screened from both the sea and any road or track that had once led to it because no one had discovered it for over thirty years, and that meant it had become overgrown with shrubs and trees. He remembered seeing a dense copse of trees when he'd explored this area on Wednesday and headed towards it. With relief and excitement he soon found himself on a well trodden narrow path that Victor Hazleton had frequently used. From out of the fog suddenly loomed a sprawling derelict Victorian house which must once have been a splendid building. How fortunate for Hazleton to have bought his house on the cliff top so close to it. Or was it? Perhaps he had made the owners an offer they couldn't refuse.

Horton thought about returning to Hazleton's house where he could pick up a mobile phone signal and call in with the location, but he decided that he should wait for the fog to clear. From his years spent sailing he was acutely aware that fog was very disorientating and he might think he was heading for Hazleton's house when in reality he could be going in the opposite direction, or worse, end up falling over the cliff and into the sea.

His thoughts flicked to Russell Glenn and the reception on board the superyacht. Glancing at his watch he saw it was only just after four o'clock. It felt much later than that because of the fog and the fact that so much had happened. But it meant he had time to explore here, return to Hazleton's house, and get back to Portsmouth in time for the charity reception at eight thirty. He didn't want to miss that and his chance to talk to Glenn.

He found a rough path cut through the undergrowth and

followed it to the rear of the house. The ivy, brambles and weeds had been cleared from the door, so it was clearly Hazleton's way inside. Horton pushed at it and it gave easily to his touch. The fog seemed thicker now and Horton reached for his pencil torch. Its thin beam of light barely pierced the gloomy interior as he stepped inside and on to a filthy flagstone floor. It was dark and dank, and perhaps it was the fog stretching its cold tentacles inside, along with the groaning bindweed, that made it feel evil and caused him to shiver. But there was no mistaking the rancid smell that permeated the air. It was death.

He tensed and edged forward. The fog soaked up the meagre light his small torch emitted, but he could make out a few items that told him he was in what had once been the kitchen. Moving into a passageway he was relieved to find sturdy flagstones underneath him instead of gaping rotten floorboards. To his left was what remained of a staircase torn apart by ivy and weeds. The smell was worse here and a cold sweat gripped him as his heart raced with the inevitability of what he would ultimately find. Crossing the hall he stepped inside another room. The darkness was too deep to penetrate, however the stench told him what was there, but not who. The breath caught in his throat. One thing for certain, it wasn't Sarah Walpen. She'd be bones by now.

Beneath him now were floorboards and a glance down warned that a step forward could result in injury. And it would take a long time for anyone to find him, *if* they ever did. He didn't want to end up like Arthur Lisle, because he was convinced that was who he would find in the next room. And he wasn't about to verify that, not now, not alone, and not in the dark and the fog. It was definitely time to leave. He turned to go.

It was all wrong, though. If Hazleton had agreed to meet Lisle here and had then killed him, how did he end up in the boot of Lisle's car? Simple, Hazleton hadn't killed Lisle, but had stumbled on someone doing just that and so had to be killed himself. And who the blazes could that be? Was it the same person who had killed Yately? It had to be. And that person had put that dress on Yately's body, hoping that it would be identified. But that was a very long shot, and the killer hadn't done it as revenge for Sarah's death, because why kill Yately when he had nothing to do with it? Sarah didn't have any relatives, and if she'd had a lover, he'd be a very old man by now, much older than Hazleton, and incapable of carrying out three killings. So why had Yately's killer wanted the body in that dress? And why had Yately's killer wanted him silenced and the trail covered up with the further killings of Lisle and Hazleton?

The house creaked and groaned as the fog reached inside. It felt as though the place was giving itself up to the dead. *Time to leave.* He could reason all this out in the safety of Hazleton's driveway or on the ferry back to Portsmouth, not here. He stepped forward. The floor creaked behind him. Spinning round, he could see nothing and no one. He turned and his foot caught on something. Experience and instinct told him what it was. Surely he couldn't have been so disorientated as to have stumbled into the room and found Arthur Lisle. But no, there was the rotting staircase to his right. He'd gone further into the passageway instead of the kitchen. His breathing laboured as he played the thin beam of his torch on the floor. Steadily, with his heart pounding, he took in the bloody mess of the head, the sightless staring eyes. But there was no mistaking who it was. With a shock he saw that it was Russell Glenn. Shit! He'd killed himself.

That was Horton's first thought; his second was anger that the chance of interrogating Glenn to find out if he'd had a connection with Jennifer had been snatched from him. His third was disappointment, followed by the realization that Glenn hadn't killed himself. For a start there was no gun and Glenn had been shot in the head. And from what he could see, Glenn hadn't been dead for very long. Horton hadn't heard a shot but the fog could have muffled the sound, and neither had he heard any vehicle approaching. He stiffened. He had seen a boat though before the fog had come in. A RIB. Russell Glenn's RIB. He must have been coming here to meet his killer. And who the hell could that be? More to the point, was the killer still here?

Horton spun round, sensing rather than hearing someone behind him, but he was too late. The blow struck him across the back of his head, and as his legs buckled beneath him and his face hit the dirt and dust of the rotten floorboards Dr Clayton's words flashed before him: *a single blow to the back of the head is rarely enough to kill someone unless the victim is unfortunate enough to have a thin skull, but several blows can.* The last thing

Horton wondered as the darkness swallowed him up was what type of skull he had.

TWENTY-ONE

T he thick type was the answer, thankfully, because a short time later, maybe only minutes, Horton opened his eyes to find his head pounding and his mouth full of dust. Gingerly, he rose, trying to focus his vision in the dark, wondering why the killer hadn't finished him off, but immensely grateful that he hadn't.

He staggered up, swaying a little. His head was hurting but he was alive, and that was the main thing, not like Glenn beside him. Horton couldn't immediately see his torch and he wasn't going to waste time searching for it. He only hoped he could find his way out of the house without it and not stumble over Lisle's body deeper in the dark interior.

His eyes were growing accustomed to the gloom and within a couple of minutes he found himself staggering through the kitchen and, with relief, outside into the damp clinging fog. Hastily, he followed the path to the front of the house. He recalled there was a turn and then it was straight ahead to the low cliff top. Clearly, Glenn had come on the RIB into the bay either alone or with his killer. If he'd come unknowingly with his killer, then the RIB would be the murderer's means of escape. And if Glenn had come alone for his rendezvous, then either there was another boat down in the bay or the killer had already been on the Island. Horton knew that no one could have got close enough to the house by road, but it was always a possibility that the killer had a car parked further away.

But no, Horton heard the spluttering of a boat engine and hurried in its direction towards the bay. The killer was a fool to try and get away in the fog. He could be dashed to pieces on the rocks, and Horton very much wanted this killer alive. His mind was racing with thoughts at Glenn's unexpected death. Who could have wanted him dead and why? How was it connected with

Sarah Walpen – because it had to be, why else would Russell Glenn have come to her house? Had Glenn killed Colin Yately, Arthur Lisle and Victor Hazleton to prevent a secret from being exposed?

Horton recalled the expression on Glenn's face when he'd come on deck and stared at him on Monday evening. He thought he'd witnessed recognition and thought it had been directed at him, but perhaps it hadn't been. Perhaps there had been someone nearby or behind Horton who had caught Glenn's attention. And Horton swiftly recalled what Cantelli had told him: Glenn had joined the Merchant Navy in 1968, working on cargo ships and tankers, joining Carnival Cruises in 1978 until 1981. Then he'd re-emerged in the UK in 1985 with enough money to buy up a chain of hotels. Where had that money come from? Not from a merchant seaman's pay.

Horton put the strands together as he rushed towards the shore. Was it possible that *Glenn* had met Sarah Walpen, killed her and stolen from her? And he'd come here because someone had threatened to expose his secret, a secret that Colin Yately and Arthur Lisle had discovered from their research and been killed because of it. Glenn could have killed them, and he could also have killed Victor Hazleton because Victor Hazleton could identify him, but who had killed Glenn? Clearly someone else who knew the secret, and that person could have been who Glenn had seen behind Horton on the boardwalk.

The sound of the engine trying to start again ripped through the air, slicing into Horton's thoughts. He had only minutes to reach the RIB before the murderer disappeared into the fog. Sprinting towards where he hoped the cliff was, his mind teemed with thoughts. Glenn would never have come here alone. Lloyd went everywhere with Glenn, so PC Johns had said, which meant that Lloyd must be the killer and Horton's assailant. But *if* Glenn *had* come here alone then there was only one person it could be trying to start the boat's engine.

With relief he hit the cliff top and scrambled down to the shore. Glenn's killer froze.

'Give it up, Vernon,' Horton said, stepping forward.

Oliver Vernon brought the gun up and levelled it at Horton.

Horton stiffened but made every attempt to keep his voice

even as he said, 'Perhaps you didn't mean to kill Russell Glenn. Perhaps it was an accident. The gun went off in the darkness of the house. Perhaps it was self-defence.' Horton eased another two steps forward, the fog muffling his voice and making it sound taut and strangled even to his ears. How convenient for Vernon to have been on the Island, brought here at Horton's request. No patrol car had dropped him back to the Hover terminal; Oliver Vernon had seized the chance of the fog and being here, working for the police, to make his move. He must have called Glenn and asked him to meet him at the old Walpen house, bringing with him payment for his silence, and Horton was beginning to see what that payment might be.

Vernon's fair bearded face was deathly pale. The hand holding the gun trembled slightly.

Horton continued, while slowly easing forward. The cold sea lapped at his shoes. 'Glenn came here at your request but he intended to kill you. You didn't expect that. You struggled, got the gun from him and it went off. Was that how it was?'

There was a moment's fragile silence. The sound of a distant foghorn seeped through the mist. Then Vernon spoke. 'I didn't know he'd have a gun. That wasn't part of the plan.'

No. Horton saw it all clearly. Incredulous, he said, 'You didn't think a man like Glenn would let you steal from him?' But clearly Vernon had. Horton recollected from the few photographs of Glenn that Walters had printed off, and from what he'd seen of Glenn on the deck of the superyacht, his dishevelled appearance, gold-rimmed spectacles and distracted bewildered air, but there had been that one photograph capturing Glenn unaware which had shown a different man. The shambolic Glenn was an act, designed, Horton reckoned, to disguise a razor-sharp brain and a ruthless mind. Glenn must have fooled a great many people in his time. Had he fooled Avril? Somehow Horton doubted it.

'What was it Glenn had that you wanted? A piece of jewellery?' Horton stalled; again something tugged at the back of his mind, but now was not the time to examine it. He recalled what Ian Williams had told him, that William Walpen had emerged on the scene out of nowhere, and wealthy. 'Was it a ring? A brooch? A necklace? Ah, a necklace,' Horton added at Vernon's startled look. 'And it belonged to Sarah Walpen.'

'You know about it?' Vernon answered, surprised.

'Let me see if I've got this right.' Horton stepped a little closer, while he considered how to get the gun away from Vernon without either of them getting injured or killed. 'Glenn met wealthy Sarah Walpen on a Carnival cruise liner where he was working as a deckhand and discovered she had no living relatives and a great deal of money. He killed her and stole her money, forging her signature and taking her jewellery, including this valuable neck- lace, and other items, to kick start his business and his fortune. He discovered that the necklace was different from the rest of the jewellery he'd stolen from Sarah and he couldn't sell it for fear of it being traced, but as you told me, Oliver, there are people who will buy things no questions asked, and who don't care how they've been obtained.'

Horton moved a half step nearer. His feet were frozen but that was the least of his concerns. He tried to see the make of the weapon pointed at him. How many rounds were left in the barrel? How could he get it off Vernon before getting a bullet in the head like Glenn?

He continued. 'Victor Hazleton worked for the legal firm who had handled Sarah Walpen's affairs. When Hazleton realized she was not returning he began to plunder her estate, selling off her valuable items to fund his lifestyle. But he couldn't do it all at once or through one auction house on the Island because it would look too suspicious, so he took trips to the mainland to dispose of the antiques and valuables through various auction houses, claiming he'd lost the original paperwork or found the item in his grandmother's attic or some such story. Then he showed up at Landrams where you were working, and with a piece of jewel- lery that Glenn hadn't stolen from Sarah Walpen, perhaps because she'd been wearing it at the time of her death.' And if she had been then her body must be in that derelict house, thought Horton. He didn't know yet how Glenn had killed Sarah, or disposed of her body, but that would hopefully come later *if* he could get the gun away from Vernon without it going off.

Vernon said, 'It was a ring. When I examined it I could hardly believe what I was seeing. It was part of a reputed missing collection of jewels, which had been brought to England by Charles X when he fled into exile from France in 1830.'

And that fitted exactly with what Ian Williams had told Horton. He kept his eyes fixed on Vernon's face. The gun was still pointing at him but it was as if Vernon was no longer aware it was in his hand.

Excitedly, Vernon continued. 'The Esmeraude Collection belonged to a former lover of Charles X given to her by him. Its diamonds were set in silver, and the emeralds set in gold, and it was designed and executed by the French Royal Jewellers Jacques-Evrard and Christophe-Frédéric Bapst in 1819, the same time as a tiara worn by the daughter-in-law of Charles X, Marie-Thérèse.'

Vernon's voice was growing more excited, and although the gun was still levelled at Horton he hoped in Vernon's agitation it might waver for a moment and let him take his chance. The fog oozed around them. Horton listened intently to Vernon while edging his way minutely forward and looking for his chance.

'Because the tiara was made with materials provided by the state, Marie-Thérèse returned it to the treasury when she came to England with her husband, and her uncle and father-in-law, Charles X. Charles though was rumoured to have brought with him the Esmeraude Collection, said to comprise a necklace, a comb, a pair of drop earrings, a ring, a pair of bracelets, a brooch and a belt clasp.'

The cold sea lapped gently at Horton's ankles. He kept his steady gaze fixed on Vernon standing in the rear of the RIB above him.

'Charles claimed the jewellery had been stolen but many believed he had hidden it to prevent it being used to pay off his debtors in England. I had a private client who would jump at the chance to add the ring to his collection, so I bought it on the client's behalf from Hazleton privately. He had no idea of its true worth and I got it for a song, although Hazleton was pleased with the amount he got. I wondered if he had the rest of the missing collection but I didn't want to alert him of its value. I told him that I would help him sell any other items, no questions asked, and that it would save him having to travel to the mainland and all the hassle of having the things valued and authenticated. At first he didn't like giving me a small commission, but I convinced him I could get him more money selling privately and he was soon on board. I used to visit him at night. I didn't want anyone to see me and sometimes I'd come by boat into the bay. I'd hire a RIB. It wasn't often, twice a year, three times maximum. I knew he lived alone. But although I tried to pump him he wouldn't say how he had got hold of the ring or the other items. I did some research on the old man and discovered that he'd worked for a legal firm on the Island. He'd never been abroad so he must have come across the ring here and that fitted with the collection possibly having been lost at sea when Charles X was sailing past these waters, although nothing in the archive showed a shipwreck, which made me think someone had stolen the collection and swum ashore.'

And Horton knew that must have been William Walpen, or whatever his real name had been, and they'd probably never know that. He said, 'And then you discovered that Russell Glenn had the Esmeraude Necklace.'

'Yes.'

'How?'

'At first I thought Hazleton must have sold the necklace to Glenn or to someone who had sold it on to him, but when I gently pumped Hazleton it was clear he didn't know anything about a necklace. I told him that if he had a necklace or any other jewellery in the same style as the ring I could make his fortune. I knew he would have to look. He was a greedy little man and a thief, that much was clear from the items he gave me to sell, which had no provenance, so the night I told him about the jewellery being worth a fortune I followed him to the derelict house, up there.' Vernon jerked his head but his eyes didn't leave Horton.

He continued. 'Hazleton rummaged around inside the house for a while and after he'd left I stayed on. I found three steamer trunks with the name Sarah Walpen on them and the cruise ship label. Inside one of the trunks I found what was left of Sarah Walpen. The rest was easy. Sarah Walpen had been on SS *Agora* in 1981 and I discovered two rather odd things about that cruise ship and that year.'

'Russell Glenn was a deckhand on board it.'

'Yes,' Vernon said, surprised that Horton knew this. 'It was also due to dock in Southampton, but because of a dockers' strike all the passengers and some of the crew were transferred on to a ferry in the Solent and taken into Portsmouth instead. The cruise ship couldn't get into Portsmouth Harbour because it was too big.'

And Horton saw how easy it must have been in the ensuing chaos for Glenn to tick off Sarah Walpen as having disembarked. Sarah's belongings were sent on, as already arranged, to the empty house waiting for her, along with her body. Her furniture had probably been shipped there earlier. After a while Victor Hazleton had wondered why there was outstanding paperwork for her at the lawyer's office and, on investigating, had found a ready fortune, easily accessible, with no questions asked.

Horton said, 'So you thought that as Glenn had the necklace, and had never said a word about it, he must have killed Sarah Walpen and stolen it from her.'

'Yes. He must have forged her name on her accounts, and stolen other valuable items from her, which started him on the road to wealth.'

'And you decided to blackmail Glenn into handing over the necklace.'

Vernon sniffed but didn't answer.

Horton said, 'And is that why you killed Colin Yately: because he was getting too close to the truth and would ruin your scheme? You tortured him into telling you about Arthur Lisle and the research they'd done on Sarah Walpen. So after tricking Lisle into collecting the evidence from Yately's flat you then killed him. Did Victor Hazleton see you? Is that why he had to die? Or had you already decided his usefulness was at an end, and you saw an opportunity to get rid of him and frame Arthur Lisle for it?'

'No! I've no idea who killed them and I've never heard of Arthur Lisle or Colin Yately,' Vernon said, surprised.

Did Horton believe him? It sounded like the truth, but Horton wasn't going to let that influence him. The gun was still pointing at him, but Vernon seemed almost to have forgotten it was in his hand. Horton eased a step forward, feeling the icy waters reach up his calves. He was within reach of the RIB now, looking up at Vernon at the rear of it, close to the engine. But Vernon, in his excitement and increasing agitation, didn't seem to notice how close he was.

Vernon insisted. 'I found a man's body in a small inlet in the cliff, just in the next bay, on Monday morning. I'd come here to collect more evidence from Sarah Walpen in case I needed it to persuade Glenn to part with the necklace. I thought Hazleton must have killed that man because he'd discovered his secret. It was a perfect opportunity. I dressed the body in one of Sarah's dresses, which I fetched from one of the trunks in the house. I thought the media would pick up on it, you know, "mystery of man's body found wearing old-fashioned dress in the Solent", that kind of thing, and then I could send a message to Glenn telling him they might discover it was a dress belonging to Sarah Walpen, and that if he didn't do what he was told, the police would get a hint of who the dress belonged to. Not that Glenn knew it was me.'

You wanna bet, thought Horton.

'I put that man, Yately, in a RIB I'd hired and took him into the Solent.'

'Tying the dress around his ankles to act as a buoyancy aid and dropping him off somewhere by the Nab Tower, letting the tidal flow take him into harbour,' Horton said stiffly. 'And you killed Arthur Lisle and Victor Hazleton. You put Hazleton's body in Lisle's car and drove to Chale Bay, where you dumped the car.'

But Vernon was looking confused. 'No.'

'You expect me to believe that!' scoffed Horton, thinking he didn't have long. The cold sea was numbing his legs. He had to avoid getting cramp at all costs. Desperately he flexed his toes inside his sodden shoes and shifted forward as much as he dared. Now his hand could touch the RIB and he was looking up at Vernon.

'Give me the gun, Oliver, it's over,' he said evenly, his heart thumping. He reached up his hand and held it there. But clearly Vernon was not ready to give it up. Horton pressed, 'A good lawyer will convince a jury it was self-defence or accidental.'

'I don't need a lawyer. I've got this.' Vernon reached into

the pocket of his jacket. As he did so Horton took his chance. Swiftly, he reached out with both hands, grasped Vernon's ankles and heaved with all his might. The necklace flew from Vernon's hand as his body was wrenched backwards. Vernon let go of the gun, screeched and twisted over to reach for the necklace in the sea, giving Horton the chance to jump on board the RIB and plonk himself squarely on Oliver Vernon's back.

'The necklace, I must get it,' Vernon squealed.

Horton reached into his pocket for his handcuffs, pulled Vernon's hands behind him roughly and clasped the cuffs on his wrists.

'Let me go. I have to get the necklace,' Vernon squealed, almost crying in desperation.

Horton picked up the gun and released the bullets. He put both in his pocket.

Then he reached for the lines on the side of the RIB and swiftly bound Vernon's ankles.

'Please, you must get the necklace,' Vernon pleaded.

Horton jumped off the RIB and walked around to where the necklace had been flung. He peered down into the shallow water and as he did the picture beside Adrian Stanley's hospital bed sprang into his mind. And with complete clarity he saw exactly what it was Stanley had been trying to tell him.

TWENTY-TWO

They found what was left of Sarah Walpen and Arthur Lisle two hours later. The fog had lifted leaving a clear early evening. Horton stood in the bay beneath Sarah Walpen's house and took several deep breaths, trying to rid his lungs of the stench of human decay and his mind of Lisle's decomposing body. Taylor and his crew were already inside Sarah's house and arc lights had been erected, making it look even more pathetic than it had in the fog. Oliver Vernon had been escorted away to be interviewed by Dennings. Horton had no taste to hear his tale again, or his bleating about the necklace. It was a stunning piece of jewellery of glittering diamonds and emeralds, as Vernon had described, and it had already cost too many lives. Horton doubted Vernon would give them the name of the collector he'd had lined up for it.

While he'd waited for SOCO and Uckfield to arrive, Horton had returned to Hazleton's house by way of the fields, leaving Vernon secured. There he'd picked up a mobile signal and called first the incident suite in Ventnor, then Uckfield, before ringing Cantelli.

'I've been trying to get you for hours,' Cantelli said, with relief in his voice. Then Cantelli had told him that he'd found Sarah Walpen listed as a passenger on the SS *Agora*, and had discovered Russell Glenn's name on the list of crew.

Horton had quickly relayed what had happened and what Vernon had said. Horton asked Cantelli to get him the names of boat owners at Ventnor Haven. If neither Russell Glenn nor Oliver Vernon had killed Yately, Lisle and Hazleton, then only one person could have done. Horton had then ridden the Harley along the top road until he'd found the track off it that led down to Sarah's house and he'd relayed instructions to the patrol cars on how to find it. Someone had brought him a pair of socks and shoes to replace his sodden ones.

Uckfield joined him at the water's edge 'Vernon's still insisting he didn't kill the others.'

'He didn't.'

'Then who the hell did?' Uckfield cried, surprised.

Horton checked his watch. It was almost six thirty but if they were lucky there was still time. He turned and headed back up the cliff top. Uckfield had no choice but to follow him. 'Where are you going?' he said breathlessly.

'Newport.'

Uckfield frowned. Then he raised his eyebrows. 'You don't mean Yately's former wife killed her husband and the others?'

'No, but Yately's divorce was how Arthur Lisle and Colin Yately became friends. They discovered a mutual interest in local history, which unfortunately led to their deaths.'

Horton gave Uckfield the address and directions, and half an hour later he watched Uckfield pull up beside him outside the offices of Wallingford and Chandler. Horton pushed open the door and was once again staring up at the photographs on the wall behind reception.

'I was just leaving,' Chandler's secretary Linda said nervously. Horton showed his ID in case she had forgotten who he was, though clearly she hadn't. 'We need a word with Mr Chandler. Would you tell him we're here?' But Chandler must have seen them pull up because he entered reception.

'No need. You can close up, Linda.'

Before she could do so two uniformed officers stepped inside. Linda scuttled away wide-eyed. Chandler frowned, but said pleasantly enough, 'Shall we go up to my office.' It wasn't a question.

As he led the way up the sweeping staircase to the first floor Uckfield threw Horton an irritated glance. Horton knew Uckfield would have liked the facts before they'd entered the premises but Horton didn't know them all for certain yet, though he suspected that most of what he'd managed to put together would be close to the truth. No one spoke until they were seated in Chandler's tastefully decorated and spacious office, when Horton introduced Uckfield.

Chandler's eyebrow rose in surprise and a solemn expression crossed his face. 'I take it this is about poor Victor's death and Arthur being missing. You obviously have some news and by your demeanour I deduce that it isn't good.'

'We've found Arthur Lisle. He's dead,' Horton said bluntly.

The eyebrow went up and down. 'This is rather a shock, Inspector.'

'I don't think so.'

'I . . . maybe not.' Chandler frowned. 'I wasn't completely honest with you on your first visit, and I apologize for that, but I felt some loyalty towards Arthur. When you said that Victor was dead, I couldn't believe that Arthur could have killed him, but Arthur must have discovered that Victor had an affair with Abigail. That, and being distraught over her death, must have unbalanced him.'

Good try, thought Horton, and it's what they had once thought, but not now. Although only Dr Clayton, at her post-mortem, would be able to confirm exactly how Arthur Lisle had died, not even a suicide could rise up and drive his car into the sea with a body in the boot. Evenly, Horton said, 'That's not why Victor Hazleton died. He, Colin Yately and Arthur Lisle died because you couldn't bear the thought that Hazleton's greed and his systematic theft of a client's estate, plus the fact he could have killed that client, would expose your firm and ruin your reputation.'

Both eyebrows shot up this time and Chandler's face flushed. 'Are you implying that *I* killed them? That is a ludicrous accusation. I resent it and your tone and—'

'You can resent it all you like,' Uckfield growled, leaning forward, quickly picking up on Horton's meaning. 'But it's the truth and you know it.'

Horton would have preferred to play it more slowly and carefully but that was not Uckfield's way.

'I refuse to say any more, not without a lawyer present,' Chandler bristled.

Horton picked up Chandler's phone. 'You'll need one.'

Chandler glared at Horton. He snatched the phone from him but didn't make the call. 'First, tell me exactly how I am supposed to have killed them,' he sneered.

Uckfield stood up. 'That's what you're going to tell us.'

But Horton ignored Uckfield's impatient tone, and said, 'Prompted by their research into influential people on the Island, Yately and Lisle discovered the Walpens, and that their lineage ended with Sarah Walpen who had gone to live in the States in 1957. But Arthur Lisle remembered the name and was convinced he'd handled a property matter for her in the 1980s. He could find no record of her death or any record of her living on the Island since 1957, which he found rather puzzling. He couldn't remember the exact date he'd acted for her so he went to see Hazleton to ask if he remembered, and was amazed he was living so well. Hazleton must have fobbed him off with some feeble answer but Lisle was suspicious. Gradually, as Yately uncovered more history of the Walpens and relayed it to Lisle, he began to see what must have happened. His memory jogged, he finally remembered when he had acted for her, in October 1980. But when he requested the archive files there was no record of the transaction and none on the computer. So why wasn't it on the system? One person could easily have erased the computer file and never archived the documentation:

Victor Hazleton. But Lisle said nothing to Hazleton about it then. He wanted proof.'

Uckfield sniffed and crossed to the window, where he turned and steadily eyed Chandler. Dashing a glance at Uckfield and then back at Horton, Chandler said coolly, 'Go on, Inspector.' He replaced the phone.

'Hazleton retired in 1986 and bought that house in 1990. We know that Sarah Walpen took a cruise before deciding to settle on the Island but she never reached her new home.' Or at least she didn't alive. 'The property transaction was conducted by post and fax and all the paperwork and the deeds to the house were held here at your offices. I'm not sure when Victor Hazleton became curious, a year, maybe two years later, perhaps when he was about to archive the files, but he realized the deeds had never been collected. He called at the house, found it empty and clearly neglected. Sarah Walpen's belongings had been shipped over and were in the house but they'd never been unpacked, and the furniture had just been placed in the rooms without being arranged. He saw the trunks with the labels on them and discovered that the SS *Agora* had disembarked on to a ferry in the Solent because of a dockers' strike at Southampton. Inside one of the trunks he found the body of Sarah Walpen.'

'This really is an incredible story,' Chandler said in a supercilious manner.

'Extraordinary but true. Hazleton waited to see if her killer returned or her body was discovered, but no one came and the house slowly fell into disrepair. He kept the deeds, extracted all the paperwork pertaining to the property transaction, and wiped the files clean. He could never take over the house because that might have been too risky. Instead he began to unpack her belongings and found many valuable antiques and jewellery, which her family had amassed over the generations and which she'd built on. Much of the furniture was also valuable, and while he was still fairly young, he could access the house before it became too overgrown. He transported a lot of the furniture, which he pretended was his, to his new house when he bought it in 1990. He began to sell the smaller items, slowly, piece by piece, in different auction houses in the south of England. No one cottoned on and he amassed enough money to live a life of luxury until he was killed on Tuesday night.'

'This is a fascinating tale, Inspector.'

Horton ignored him. 'Arthur Lisle couldn't find any record of Sarah's property transaction, and now that his memory had been stirred he remembered that she'd mentioned something about a cruise before settling down.' Horton didn't know that for certain but he thought it probably a good guess. 'So Yately set off for Southampton on the Monday before his death to view the records of the passenger lists of the liners coming in to the port from 1980 to 1986, when Hazleton retired. Yately, a thorough, patient man, found Sarah Walpen. He took a photograph of the entry and returned excited. Arthur Lisle came to you and told you about the fraud, and said that you had to call in the police, which was the last thing you wanted.'

Chandler sucked in his breath. He held Horton's eye contact and frowned. Horton could see his mind racing, looking for a way out.

Horton continued. 'You told Lisle that you needed to speak to Colin Yately first and make absolutely sure. Lisle said he'd call Yately and ask him to meet you, at your suggestion, at Sarah Walpen's house on Wednesday evening, but Lisle couldn't make it. Lisle must have worked out or finally remembered where Sarah's house was, or perhaps he checked with the Land Registry. He'd already visited Hazleton and seen his antiques paraded around the house, so knew it had to be nearby. But Lisle had arranged to go away until Monday, we're not sure where yet, but we'll find out. I suspect it was a walking break, visiting the places he and his wife had walked when they'd first met.' Horton recalled the photographs of Abigail and Arthur Lisle in walking clothes at the Brecon Beacons, which he'd seen on the mantelpiece in Lisle's house.

'You met Colin Yately. Knocked him unconscious and tied him up. You left him in that house until you could decide how to dispose of him. You had a little time on your hands because Lisle wasn't due back until Monday.'

'This really is incredible.'

Uckfield snorted and made to interject, but Horton got there first. 'On Saturday night you took your fishing boat, which I think we'll find is moored at Ventnor Haven, around to the bay on the high tide.' Cantelli had yet to confirm that but Horton could see he had guessed correctly, and the office manager had told them that the day Arthur Lisle had asked to view the archived files Chandler had been out fishing, with a client.

'You returned to Sarah Walpen's house and forced Yately down to the shore, where you tortured him into telling you that he'd written notes about Sarah Walpen and what had happened to her. You took his keys off his key fob, leaving him with the picture of his daughter, because you had to give the keys to Arthur Lisle and say that Colin had given them to you. Lisle would have been suspicious if you'd given him the key fob as well because he knew that Yately would never part with the picture of his daughter. You then left him to drown, callously waiting until he had, before hauling him out using the winch on your fishing boat. Then you untied him and left him in an inlet in the small bay while you decided how to dispose of him. You weren't sure yet whether you needed the body to frame Lisle or Hazleton. Only the body showed up in the Solent, not far from Portsmouth Harbour, and you assumed it had been washed out to sea, but then you didn't know about the dress.'

Chandler couldn't hide his surprise quickly enough for Horton not to notice, but said nothing.

Despising the calculating killer in front of him, Horton pressed on. 'On Monday evening you called on Arthur Lisle, or asked him to come here after hours. You gave him Yately's keys and asked him to collect Yately's notes, the camera and briefcase. If anyone saw him it would throw suspicion on him as the killer. You told Lisle to bring them to Sarah's house, where you said you'd arranged to meet Yately, and the three of you would decide what action to take.'

Horton wished they could shove the gruesome pictures of Lisle's decomposing body under the solicitor's nose; maybe they would if Chandler decided to continue with his denials. It might shock him into telling the truth.

Grimly, Horton continued, 'You killed Lisle, but Hazleton was on one of his little nocturnal jaunts and saw you. That suited you fine. You killed him, stuffed him in the boot of Lisle's car and drove it to Chale Bay where you ditched it, hoping that we would believe Lisle had done so and then killed himself. You live not far from there.' He recalled what Cantelli had said: *Chandler lives in a large country manor house at Kingston*, and that wasn't far from Chale Bay. 'You walked home that night. We'll check with your family, of course.'

Uckfield stepped forward. Brusquely he said, 'You'd better make that call.'

Chandler took a deep breath. 'There's been some mistake.'

Horton saw that he'd finally shaken him. Good. He hoped the smug bastard would be shaken a great deal more by the time they'd finished.

'Tell that to your lawyer,' Horton snapped, rising.

Uckfield went out into the corridor and called in the uniformed officers waiting there.

Slowly Chandler rose. 'Victor Hazleton was a snob and a horrible little man. He'd take every chance to rub my nose in the fact he had more money than me. Him, a mere clerk!'

'That was no reason to kill him,' snarled Uckfield, as one of the officers took Chandler's arm.

'Wasn't it?' snapped Chandler. 'I wasn't going to have everything I've worked for, and my father worked for, brought down by him and his filthy dishonesty. I wasn't going to let him ruin my practice and my son's future, not to mention my family's name.'

'No, you've done that yourself,' Horton said tightly, as Chandler was led away.

'Pompous prat,' Uckfield pronounced after him.

And a ruthless killer; a man who thought he could destroy lives and get away with it, thought Horton.

'Good result,' Uckfield rubbed his hands. 'And we've beaten Wonder Boy's deadline.' He reached for his phone.

'There's Avril Glenn.'

'Shit. No one's told her about her husband.'

'I'll do that. I know her.'

'You never said,' Uckfield said, startled.

'I'd like to do it before the charity reception tonight.'

'Christ, I'd forgotten about that. I heard the Chief's going to it. I'd better come with you.'

'He won't be there until later. Might be better though if you called him and briefed him.'

Uckfield brightened at that. A malicious gleam spread across his face. Horton knew what he was thinking. It would be one in the eye for Dean. 'I'll do it on the ferry.'

The cold evening air helped to clear Horton's thumping head. It had been a long day and it wasn't over yet. 'What about interviewing Chandler?' he asked.

'Tomorrow will do when his brief shows up. Let him stew in a cell overnight. I'll get him shipped back to the mainland for the questioning and a confession.'

If he'll make one, thought Horton, heading for the ferry. And even if he didn't Trueman and the team would dig up the evidence and check Chandler's movements. And they would show him photographs of Lisle's body. Horton spared a sorrowful thought for Rachel Salter and for Hannah Yately, before his mind switched to his forthcoming meeting with Avril and the unpleasant task that lay ahead.

TWENTY-THREE

Horton waved his ID at the security guards at the marina office at the top of the pontoon. There were three more than usual and two of them were coppers who tried to avoid his gaze. He headed down to Russell Glenn's superyacht. Lights blazed from every porthole but there were no guests on board yet. The reception wasn't due to start for another hour. He'd just managed to catch a ferry, leaving a no doubt fuming Uckfield at the terminal, kicking his heels, or rather cursing vehemently, while waiting for the next sailing. He was glad. He wanted to be alone with Avril when he broke the news.

Climbing on board he didn't need to show his ID to Walters. 'Where's Lloyd?' he asked.

'Not sure, haven't seen him for hours. Mr Danby's with the skipper, up there?' Walters jerked his head towards the flybridge. Good. Horton hoped he'd stay there. 'Not come to fetch me, Guv, have you?' Walters asked warily.

'Why would I want you?'

'Dunno. Good bit of extra money this, wouldn't want to lose it.'

'I think you might have to.' Walters' face fell, but before he could comment Horton pushed open the glass doors and stepped into the gleaming luxurious lounge where the smell of new leather, mahogany furniture and deep-pile wool carpets greeted him. Beyond it he could catch the faint aroma of food that was no doubt being prepared for the reception. The steward was behind a bar in the far right-hand corner setting out bottles of champagne in ice buckets. He asked Horton to wait while he fetched Mrs Glenn. Horton crossed to the seaward windows and gazed across the harbour at Gosport beyond. It had grown dark. The lights of the harbour and the tower blocks behind it glinted down on them. It made him think about his own childhood gazing across a brightly lit city from the eighteenth floor of their council flat to the dark sea beyond, watching the lights of the boats slowly cross a black horizon with a panicky feeling that he'd be encased in the tower for ever. The memory startled him. The thought that he was alone, afraid and imprisoned caught at his breath and tightened his chest, but before he could explore his feelings the door behind him opened and he spun round to see Avril smiling. She was exquisitely dressed in an expensive, figure-hugging aquamarine-blue evening dress, and immaculately made-up. Her blonde hair shone and her pale-blue eyes greeted him with a friendly smile. It made his heart lurch but this time with disappointment, not excitement or lust.

'Andy, what a surprise,' she said, moving forward to greet him when his solemn expression stalled her.

'Can you leave us, please.' Horton addressed the steward.

Avril frowned and nodded.

In the silence that followed Horton heard the engines of a boat heading into the harbour. Part of him wished he were on it.

'What is it? What's wrong?' Before he could speak, she added, 'It's Russell. Something's happened to him. He's had an accident.' Her complexion paled. 'That's what you've come to tell me.' Her worried blue eyes scoured his face. 'He went out ages ago on the RIB. He should have been back by now but then the fog came in. I assumed he'd moored up somewhere.'

'He's dead, Avril,' he announced bluntly.

'Dead! But how—'

'Oliver Vernon killed him.'

'Oliver! No. I don't understand . . .' she stammered, sinking down on one of the leather seats.

'He claims it was an accident and that Glenn had a gun and intended killing him, rather than letting him have the necklace.'

'Necklace? What necklace?' Her eyes widened.

Was her surprise genuine? He didn't think so. 'The one you told him Glenn had. Sarah Walpen's necklace.'

'Who's Sarah Walpen?' she asked him, bewildered.

Horton steeled himself to continue. 'Perhaps you don't know about its origins, and perhaps Oliver tricked you, but you knew Russell had the necklace and Oliver told you he had found a buyer for it, one who would pay a considerable amount of money, enough for you to leave Glenn.'

She opened her mouth to speak then decided not to. Instead she shook her head.

Horton continued. 'This buyer or his representative was to come here tonight and collect it while everyone's attention was focused on the auction.' And that was who the Intelligence Directorate were after. 'What was the plan, Avril? That the necklace would be passed to this buyer but that Glenn would be found dead in his study the next morning? And with lots of police officers around as security, including me at the auction, to say it couldn't possibly have been you or Oliver Vernon. But then I unwittingly gave you and Oliver a better plan by calling Oliver in as valuer. Oliver seized his chance to demand that Glenn meet him with the necklace, otherwise he'd tell everyone at the auction how Glenn had made his millions. The fog made it perfect. Oliver could kill Glenn, take the necklace and everyone would think that Glenn had got lost in the fog, had an accident and had been killed. His body would have rotted in that old house just as Sarah Walpen's has.'

She stared at him, her forehead creased in a deep frown, but he wasn't fooled.

'But your husband was never going to submit to blackmail. Surely you must have known that?' And he saw that she did. Oh, clever Avril. He'd forgotten how clever.

Whether something in his expression betrayed his thoughts or she sensed them, he didn't know, but she rose and crossed to the bar. 'I have no idea what you're talking about. This is such a terrible shock.' She poured a drink, but with a steady hand.

Horton continued. 'You used the necklace, and probably expressions of undying love to Oliver, to trick him into black-mailing Glenn, knowing that Glenn would go armed and that Oliver would have to kill him, or at least that's how you planned it. You didn't care about Oliver, the necklace or your husband but you do care about wealth. Russell Glenn would never have divorced you because he loved you or rather, I should say, he saw you as a beautiful thing he wanted to possess, and, as Vernon told me, Glenn loved owning beautiful things.' Horton knew he was correct by the tiny flicker in her eyes. 'And Glenn does not give up his assets easily. He had you trapped, Avril, and, as you said in the bar on Monday night, you hate traps. But once you were in this one you found it difficult to escape. Not only because you'd grown so accustomed to wealth, but because you were afraid. Glenn might have fooled many by that dishevelled appear-ance and absentminded act but behind it was a ruthless man, and one who had killed at least once that we know of, and he prob-ably used Lloyd to kill for him when and if it was demanded. Lloyd was also to make sure that Glenn knew exactly where you were and what you were doing every minute of the day and night when Glenn couldn't be there. Your husband was possessive and extremely jealous.' Horton saw he'd got that right.

'You wanted Glenn's wealth and you wanted him dead. Well, you've got it, Avril. Congratulations. It was convenient that Colin Yately and Arthur Lisle stumbled on Sarah Walpen at the right time, adding weight to the blackmail. Convenient for you but unfortunate for them.'

'I've never heard of those men.'

'But you know Oliver dressed the corpse of one of them in one of Sarah's dresses to make your husband believe the black-mailer meant business.'

She shook her head, looking bewildered, and sipped her drink. Horton hadn't expected her to play the full grieving widow bit, not yet and not in front of him; that performance would come later.

He said, 'You told Russell the same story you told me, that

you wanted to stop over in Portsmouth and see it for the last time, and make amends for deserting your mother with a fund-raising reception. Russell agreed because he knew that you were planning something, but he didn't know what. Oliver Vernon had discovered the background to the missing necklace and Sarah Walpen's house on the Isle of Wight, and for your plan to work you needed to be close by, because when Glenn would be found dead in his cabin, you could reveal that he was being blackmailed but you didn't know why, leaving the police to think his black-mailer had inadvertently killed him in a struggle.'

She swallowed her drink and nursed the empty glass, taking it with her as she returned to her seat, looking confused and bereft, but Horton knew it was an act. Equally, he knew it would fool everyone except him. And if Vernon kept quiet about their collusion, as Horton was inclined to believe he would, then Avril would be OK. And even if Vernon didn't, Avril would deny that she knew her husband had left to meet him, and she'd certainly deny that she knew Glenn would take a gun. With the best lawyers, which she would certainly have, Avril would be in the clear. She might have plotted to steal her husband's necklace and break away from him, but that was all. And even then she could prob-ably bring evidence to say he was a hard, ruthless man.

After a moment, she said, 'I know nothing about Oliver killing Russell. Russell was often moody but I loved him, and Oliver was rather infatuated with me. But I'd never have left Russell and I certainly didn't want my husband dead.'

And that was the story she would stick to. There was nothing more to be said except for one thing.

'Where's Lloyd?'

She blinked. 'Around somewhere, seeing to the security arrangements, I guess.'

'I don't think so. In fact, I think you'll find he's gone.'

She frowned. 'Gone? Didn't he leave with Russell?'

'You know he didn't. Why didn't Glenn take Lloyd with him to meet Oliver?' A point that had gnawed at Horton ever since he'd discovered Glenn's body and found Oliver Vernon trying to start the RIB.

'I don't know.'

Horton studied her closely. Maybe she didn't. Or maybe she

didn't know the *real* reason, just that Oliver Vernon had told Russell Glenn that he had to be alone when handing over the necklace. Normally Glenn would have ignored that advice and taken Lloyd with him anyway, but this time he didn't. Why? Because Glenn couldn't find Lloyd. Lloyd had already cleared out.

'Goodbye, Avril.'

She made no attempt to stop him. He felt both disappointed and relieved. A weaker woman would have begged him to stay, pleaded that he must understand how much she had hated or loved or feared her husband, made up all sorts of stories as to why she couldn't have wanted him dead or the reverse, but Avril held her nerve to the last. It was nothing more than he had anticipated. The Avrils of the world, like him, had been brought up the hard way. You quickly learnt that silence was often your only weapon.

His heart was heavy at the thought of Avril's deceit and even heavier at the idea she had colluded in the murder of her husband. What would she have done if Russell Glenn had killed Oliver Vernon? Tried again in some other way to rid herself of her rich husband, most probably.

Climbing on his Harley, he saw the Wightlink ferry easing its way into its narrow berth. Uckfield would be on it. He, along with Uniform, would no doubt meet the new Chief Constable at Oyster Quays and head for Russell Glenn's yacht, where they would find a distraught widow.

Horton's mobile rang. Seeing it was Uckfield he ignored the call for the third time and headed out of the city for the large building straddling the hill that overlooked Portsmouth. Once there he cleared his mind of the case, not without difficulty, and made for Adrian Stanley's hospital room, where he drew up startled. It was empty. Or rather there was a man inside it, but he wasn't lying on the bed and he wasn't Adrian Stanley.

He spun round. 'Oh, Inspector, I was just going to call you,' Robin Stanley said. His face was drawn and his eyes sorrowful. Horton's heart sank; he knew it was bad news. 'My father died this afternoon at three fifteen. He had another massive stroke.'

'I'm sorry.' So that was it as far as Stanley was concerned. Horton's hope of discovering some news about his mother's disappearance from either Glenn or Stanley had come to nothing. After a short pause in which Horton bit back his disappointment, he said, 'Did your father say anything more?'

'No.'

Horton let out a long slow breath as he surveyed the hospital room. Robin Stanley had stripped it of his father's belongings but Horton hoped there was one thing he would allow him to have a copy of. 'The photograph that was beside your father's bed. I'd like to see it again, if I may.'

'You could if I knew where it was.'

Horton started with surprise.

'When the hospital called me this afternoon it wasn't there.' Robin Stanley pointed to the bedside cabinet. 'I asked the staff if they'd seen it and I've looked everywhere but it's gone.' He frowned. His eyes filled with tears. 'Dad was so proud of that moment and so was Mum, why would anyone take that? It doesn't mean anything to anyone else.'

But Robin was wrong. It meant a great deal to someone and Adrian Stanley had known that.

'Do you have a copy of the photograph?' he asked. Robin Stanley must have – it was his father's proudest moment.

'There's not one in Dad's flat. I can look at home but the house is in a terrible state. We were burgled last night and every-thing's still all over the place.'

Horton's gut twisted tighter. Then the photograph would be missing, Horton had no doubt about that. And he didn't think Robin Stanley's burglary had anything to do with the others that had been happening in the north of the city. There would be no sighting of a white transit van outside Stanley's house, but Horton wondered if there might be one of a muddy blue van.

Robin Stanley dashed a hand over his eyes. 'It's all so . . .'

Horton wanted to reach out a comforting hand but couldn't. All he could repeat were the words, 'I'm sorry,' and he was; genuinely sorry. More sorry than Robin Stanley could ever know.

He left. There was nothing more he could do and he doubted that whoever had ransacked Robin Stanley's house had left any fingerprints. He had reached the Harley when a car door opened and a tall man in an immaculate suit stepped out, leaving in the passenger seat a dark-haired Chinese woman: DCI Harriet Lee.

Horton held Detective Chief Superintendent Sawyer's steady gaze, as he said, 'Adrian Stanley's dead and the photograph is missing, but then you know that. Did you take it?'

'No.'

'Do you know who did?'

'No.'

'Or the reason why it was taken?' Horton could see that Sawyer knew something. But what that was, Horton didn't know. He said, 'Russell Glenn's dead.' No doubt Sawyer already knew this, even though his expression gave nothing away. 'Was it him that you and DCI Lee were interested in, or was it Oliver Vernon or Lloyd? Or perhaps it was someone who was going to attend the reception tonight?'

There was a fraction of a pause before Sawyer answered. 'We believe that Glenn had been financing high-level criminal activity.'

'Involving Zeus.'

Sawyer made no comment and showed no reaction.

Horton said, 'You thought Glenn, or this other person coming tonight, might help lead you to Zeus.'

'Might have done,' Sawyer answered.

Horton wanted to ask him about his missing social services file, and about his mother's personal belongings, but to do so would mean bargaining for some answers and Horton wasn't sure he wanted to do that yet. He put on his helmet. Sawyer let him go. Horton needed space. And he needed to think.

Fifteen minutes later he pulled up on the seafront and switched off the Harley. He stared across the black sea to the lights on the Isle of Wight in the distance. In 1981, because of a dock strike at Southampton, a liner had disembarked its passengers here in the Solent. One woman had not alighted alive. Had Russell Glenn killed her or had she died naturally and he'd seized the opportunity to steal from her and begin a new life? They'd probably never know, unless Dr Clayton could penetrate the secret from Sarah's bones. But what he did know was the necklace Oliver Vernon had taken from Russell Glenn's dead body had been a fake. A superb one, but a fake, and Vernon would see that the moment they asked him to examine it closely in a good light, not in the dank, derelict interior of a rotting house or in the fog when Vernon had been more preoccupied by the gun in his hand. The real necklace was with Lloyd, wherever he was; ready to be passed on to the next private collector, his real paymaster. How long had Lloyd and his real boss planned this job? Years, Horton thought; long enough for Lloyd to prove himself a loyal and trusted employee of Glenn's, and to wait for the right opportunity to present itself, which was Avril and Oliver's plan to blackmail Glenn into handing it over. Lloyd switched necklaces, leaving Glenn to go alone to meet his blackmailer with the fake one. Horton knew they could look for Lloyd, but they wouldn't find him. There was no longer any point in Sawyer's surveillance of Glenn's superyacht because the purchaser wasn't going to show. Maybe he never intended being there because Lloyd would have switched necklaces anyway.

And the necklace brought Horton back to Adrian Stanley. He knew now what Stanley had been trying to tell him. It had been something to do with the brooch that his wife had been wearing in the photograph taken when Stanley had gone to the Palace to collect his Queen's Gallantry Medal. Had PC Adrian Stanley stolen it from Jennifer's flat when following up the missing person's report, or had someone given it to him as payment for his part in stifling what he had discovered?

Had Stanley's first stroke been deliberately provoked by shock, or fear? Had someone entered Stanley's apartment after his visit there on Monday morning, terrorized the man or threatened him into keeping silent about what he knew about Jennifer's disappearance?

Horton recalled that blue van. But that could have been a decoy, and perhaps the girl with the dog, the man with the canoe or the jogger with his iPod plugged into his ears had been watching Stanley and waiting. And why now? Simple: Horton had made contact with him and with the social services, and if Sawyer knew that, then so too did the person who wanted the real reason behind Jennifer's disappearance kept secret.

Well, on Monday Horton would return to the social services offices to see if they'd managed to find any more files about his childhood, but he knew they wouldn't have. Just as in 1978 someone had wiped the trail clean, so they had now. Only this time they'd left a small trace: a missing photograph. The fact that the photograph *was* missing was his first big break, and it was their first mistake. With a grim smile, Horton swung the Harley eastwards and headed for his yacht and home.

AUTHORS NOTE

That Charles X fled to England from France in 1830 and there was a dockers' strike at Southampton in 1981, forcing passengers to disembark from the SS *Canberra* off Spithead instead of Southampton, is fact. The existence of the Esmeraude Collection and the SS *Agora* are entirely the result of the author's imagination.

Susan Elizabeth Hague is a real person whose husband bid at a charity auction for her name to be used in this DI Andy Horton novel, thereby helping to raise £1,500 for the Sarah Duffen Centre, Down Syndrome Educational Trust, in Southsea.